Gary Bryson is a broadcaster and writer. He began his career at the age of 12, devising radio dramas on an ancient tape recorder and broadcasting them out the window of his Glasgow home. His mother wanted him to be a plumber. His neighbours wanted him dead. He survived both, and after many adventures, washed up on the shores of Sydney clutching a degree in journalism and a packet of fig newtons, both of which he bartered shortly afterwards for a job at ABC Radio National, where he currently contributes to the long-standing documentary series, 'Encounter'.

He lives in Sydney with his wife and two children. *Turtle* is his first novel.

turtle

gary bryson

ALLEN&UNWIN

Allen & Unwin
83 Alexander Street
Crows Nest NSW 2065
Australia
Phone: (61 2) 8425 0100
Fax: (61 2) 9906 2218
Email: info@allenandunwin.com
Web: www.allenandunwin.com

National Library of Australia
Cataloguing-in-Publication entry:

Bryson, Gary, 1955–
Turtle/Gary Bryson

978 1 74175 366 0 (pbk.)

A823.4

Set in 13/16 pt Adobe Garamond Pro by Midland Typesetters, Australia
Printed and bound in Australia by Griffin Press

10 9 8 7 6 5 4 3 2 1

For Jenny

ON A WARM, SUNNY MORNING in the summer of 1976, I took a last big breath and slipped gently under the folding waters of the Firth of Clyde, one arm waving goodbye to my family who were watching from the shore, my mother's cries flat and distant and then lost forever in the gurgling darkness. Over and over, down and down, no turning back. It was my eighteenth birthday.

That was my curse, and that's how it was, though I don't expect you to believe it, not a word. Nor do I expect you to believe that I swam like a turtle through all the oceans of the earth, or that I held my breath forever, just as I'd been taught to do, or that it was thirty-two years before I broke the surface, and when I did the blinding foam and the clear, clean air was like a mother's kiss to a lost child found.

I drowned that sunny summer's day, just as the curse predicted. I drowned and I didn't drown, lost to one life and tumbling, turning, gasping for breath in the next. That's how it was, I swear to God.

Aye, that's how it wis, right enough.
Straight doon tae the bottom an
goodbye reality,
don't bother wi the postcard.
But Christ on a bike, wee man,
ah never meant ye tae stay there furever.

1

THAT LOOK ON HER FACE, like the world was melting.

Mum had told me to keep an eye on my baby sister while she was in the butcher's. But I took the brake off the pram, just playing with it, and it rolled off the edge of the pavement and tipped onto the road, showering the baby with the morning's shopping, the screams bringing Mum running from the shop. She didn't say a word, just gave me that look before she picked the baby up and righted the pram. By the time we arrived home I'd forgotten all about it, but as soon as we were in the door, she turned and skelped me hard across the back of my bare leg. Then again. Hard skelps, with the palm of her hand. She was shouting, too, her face squeezed with the effort, her dark hair coming loose around it. That's what I remember, the wild hair and the hate in her face, like she didn't know how to stop. The rest of the day is lost to me now, just a feeling of being pushed away, maybe something worse. I suppose I deserved it.

I could say that it was all different. That my mother loved me anyway, that she found in me some qualities that made her proud. But the truth is—as the truth always is—sleek and jagged-mouthed, turning and squirming and ripping at your fingers as you try to grasp it. Why was Mum sick in bed all the time and why was Dad never there, and why was I, alone among my siblings, cursed to die by drowning? And why would you be interested anyway? Maybe you should just mind your own bloody business and leave me to struggle with this on my own. No, don't go away. Not yet. There are other questions. Like why did my brother have all his fingers broken, one by one, so that he was never quite the same again? And why is Joe Kelso dead and his killer never found? And why did Anna McColl smile at me at 4.18 on the afternoon of Tuesday, the ninth of October, 1975?

Anna McColl was in my class at school and I thought for a long time that she thought I was a wanker, like I thought everyone else thought. She spent a lot of time not looking. Not looking at the teacher, not looking at the blackboard and not looking at me. Especially not looking at me. Despite that, it has to be said, she was a looker. Dark hair and big brown eyes are what I remember now but I'm sure I could make up more; the way she wore her clothes, the creases around her eyes when she laughed, her kiss, the smell of her skin.

And I remember this: She had a habit of eating her hair while she sat, abstracted, at her desk. She would chew on the ends and then blow on the wet bits. I watched her do it, hoping to catch her eye. But she wouldn't look.

Where exactly are they, these two kids, so close together and so far apart? I can tell you that. Glasgow, a run-down school in the suburbs. It's raining. It's always raining. At least that's how I remember it. Bleak, and cold, and always raining, though maybe I'd think differently if I still lived there. The truth is, I'm not really Scottish anymore. Only when I want to be. Sometimes I'm Italian and sometimes Australian. It's confusing, but I've made what I can of it. In 1975 I was Scottish, though known as 'the wop' because of my Tally surname. Being called 'the wop' was not a term of endearment on the part of my schoolmates. It was vicious, persecutory; a territory fought over with fists and feet and which I always lost to the plook-faced playground imperialists.

A quick backflipper, because the truth is too close for comfort. Anna McColl *never looked at anyone*, but she smiled at me. Can I hide behind that? Yes I can, and I will. The exact time and date is noted in my diary for the year 1975, under the heading *Tuesday October 9*. In scrawled handwriting it says: *4.18 pm. Anna McColl smiled at me.*

The diary is a cheap blue one from school. It's battered and faded and some of the pages have fallen out. It's the first time I've laid eyes on that diary for over thirty years and, let me tell you, I'm in shock. I'm dizzy and my stomach is in knots and I have to lie on the floor and curl up into a ball. *Anna McColl smiled at me.* As I read the words I can feel my eyes heavy with the tears that, until this minute, have failed to come. I can hear the clamour of schoolkids at the bus stop, sense their slow-motion movement around me; I can see her smile and I can remember my answering, too-big grin.

Some background . . .

My name is Donald Lachlan Pinelli, as a boy known variously as Smelly Pinelli, Pin-head, or, as already mentioned, the wop. My brother—my *half*-brother, let's get this right—his name is Kenny Drummond. Killer Kenny, football forward, lover boy, rock star, though I called him Mr Disco, because he could never sit still for a minute, and because he was a right doolie. He loved to dance and show off and tell everyone how good he was at everything. The galling thing is, he *was* good, the bastard, and I hated him for it. I hated my sister too, but more about her later.

Let me tell you about Mum. She was a Glasgow girl from the Maryhill tenements. She lost her father to the drink when she was only three years old, and her two brothers eleven years later in the war. My granny scraped by, taking in other people's washing, but after her brothers went off to the fighting Mum had to leave school and go out to work too. She found work as a fishmonger, which was a skill you had to learn, not just some bide-your-time-until-you're-married job in a factory or behind a counter at Lewis'. She was determined to better herself. But though she would never admit it, she nursed a bitterness inside towards the father who had abandoned her and the brothers who had left home so easily, laughing in the face of death. Maybe that was the root of all her later problems. Or maybe not. There were other things besides abandonment. Worse things.

At the age of nineteen she married William Drummond, a riveter, who took her to live in Govan. He worked on the big ships that they used to build on the Clyde in the days when the city was black with old soot. The war had been over for four years, but people were poor and tired and miserable, waiting and grieving for the men who weren't coming back. The grey streets and the rain and the bitter winters and the price of coal and the shortages. Rationing was still on and there was so much you needed that you couldn't get and so much yearning for something better. Yet Mum insisted that she and Drummond were blissfully happy for nearly three years.

We were that happy, son. Blissfully happy. Bill wis sich a good man. Wid ye like a wee biscuit?

And maybe they were happy. But just before their third wedding anniversary she was abandoned once again when Drummond the riveter died in a fishing accident near Millport, where the family was on holiday for the Glasgow Fair. He and his brother Josie had gone off that morning in a rented dinghy. The day had been mild enough with a slight swell and a haze out to sea that hurt your eyes to look at, but which held the promise of a glimpse of sun. None of the many passing boats—fishing trawlers bringing home their catch, coal luggers, tugs, pleasure craft—had spotted a dinghy in trouble, but the two men were never seen again. It happens sometimes. I can see Bill Drummond standing at the pointy end, taking a pish over the side of the boat. A sudden movement, a man overboard, an attempted rescue. Then, when the ripples have passed, nothing. The sea's big enough to keep a secret. It's a place of shadows fluttering and flitting, stinging and biting, eyes that never close, feelers and tentacles waiting under rocks and bits of old shipwrecks, cold mouths feeding on dead sailors and tasty morsels from the sewers of the city. The sea hides, and the sea reveals. Believe me, I know all about it. The best way to survive is to have your own big, comfy shell to curl up in, hard enough to resist whatever the next tide brings in.

The dinghy was found washed up on the beach near Fairlie, on the Ayreshire coast. Drummond's cap was in it and though it was wet and the blue ink had run, you could still read the inscription *Love from Trixie* on the label. That was Mum's name: Trixie. Her maiden name was McDuff. She clung to the cap and waited for her husband, but though she grieved and pined and yearned and felt her life empty out like an old bucket of slops, even all this wasn't enough to make her who she was. There was more still: while Drummond was newly missing but not yet pronounced dead, Trixie discovered she was pregnant. And, even before her first husband buggered off to the ocean deep, never to be seen again, there was the Tragedy of Auld Smith the Fishmonger, and a curse that couldn't be lifted; Trixie's transition from happy, carefree, gorgeous girl—*ye could be a model, so ye could*—to nervous-breakdown-prone housewife, clairvoyant, and prime candidate for Worst Mother of the Century, really began, as she tells it, with a box of rotten fish. But we'll get to that in a bit. First things first.

Drummond the riveter was off swimming with the fishes and Trixie clung to his old cloth cap and she waited while her belly swelled and she felt the future Mr Disco taking shape inside her. Twisting and jiving and doing the hokey-pokey. And probably the mashed potato, too. Every now and then he gave her a kick, demonstrating his future prowess on the soccer field and his special knack for never letting anyone forget he was around. Mum moved back to Granny McDuff's and that's where the dancing fiend was born, minus the midwife because she was late, and the doctor because he was drunk. Granny McDuff put on her best scowl, rolled up her sleeves and got handy with hot water and towels. When it was over, she took one look at my brother and fell in love with the wee bugger and it was her, in the end, that brought him up.

By that time Drummond had been all but forgotten. 'Death by misadventure' was pronounced while Trixie was still pregnant, and as soon as my brother was out of her belly, she set about tidying up that part of her life. She put away Drummond's old cloth cap, left the baby with Granny Mac, and headed for the dancin'. In the dim light filled with hope and strangers, and to the music of the Ed Farrow Dance Band playing 'Mean to Me', she met my dad. *He danced like an angel.*

His name was—is—Carlo Pinelli. At the time they met he still lived with his parents and worked in his father's cafe, dreaming up ways to make big-time money, not all of them legal. But Trixie didn't know that then. To her, he was dark and handsome and exotic, with an air of mystery, and he danced like a man smiled on by the gods. As they danced he held her in his gaze and she melted, she said, like chocolate, into his strong arms. Something like that. *Ah went aw runny inside, son, and ah thought, this is the wan. This is the man fur me. How aboot a wee sandwich?*

The deal was clinched when Trixie discovered that Carlo had his own car. They got married a year later. Carlo's dad, whom everyone called Pa, wasn't at the wedding, though Nonna was, and there's a picture still of the three of them and Granny McDuff. They're all looking stiffly at the camera, the older women flaunting feathery things over dark coats and round hats, Trixie in a white wedding dress (Nonna was not happy about *that*), and my dad in a dark suit, smiling and frowning at the same time.

What can we say about this old photo? Well, first and foremost, it's what you might call prescient. And if that sounds like a wanky thing to say, here's more. It reflects the essentially unbalanced nature of Carlo's character—his uneven smile, one side of his mouth up, one side down, so that you don't know whether he's happy or sad. Crooked, you might say. That mix of amusement and exasperation I came to know so well. There's a bulge in his jacket that may well be a gun.

And Trixie. You can already see what will become, in time, a recurring theme of her personality—namely, the deep depression which will again and again descend upon her, locust-like, eating away at her vitality, poisoning her dreams. She's smiling her model smile, her forties-style glamour girl, wide-mouthed, big toothy smile; the one you put on when you're in trouble, when you're drowning in a sea far deadlier than the one that took Bill Drummond. Her hands clutch a posy of flowers which have already begun to wilt.

And the oldies? Granny McDuff is scowling. True to form, she wanted nothing to do with the wop family that Trixie had foisted on her. *The best thing aboot Carlo,* she would say, *is that he isny German, though no far aff it. And didny they Tallies fight on the same side durin the war? Ah'm tellin ye, girl, they wir aw fearties, so they wir. They've nae fight in them. When times get bad he'll be nae bloody use tae ye at all. You mark ma words, ye'll be sorry so ye will. And that wee yin'll be sorry too.*

She wasn't referring to me, of course, but to Mr Disco, just over two years old by then, and present in the photo as an unseen lock of hair that Trixie hid in her bodice for luck.

And Nonna? For her part, Nonna kept silent. You can see the silence in her eyes in the photo. And that's all we need to say about her for the moment.

A fractured family; a curse that missed its due date but that made itself felt in other ways for thirty years and more; a turtle that swam through oceans real and imagined, and that held its breath for an eternity. That's about it. And Anna McColl, let's not forget her, because while all these ingredients were being stewed together slowly, but just before the lid blew off the cooking pot for good, she smiled at me.

How did a confused and hapless Italo-Scot cope with being smiled at that autumn day by the girl of his dreams? Sometimes, despite yourself, you take a chance. We were standing at the bus stop, kids milling about, cries and yelps as someone's schoolbag sailed onto the road and into the traffic. It wasn't mine this time. I turned to see who the victim was and Anna was standing there, just behind me. She looked at me and she smiled and the sun came out and sparks went off in my head—then I started to worry that my fly was undone and I wanted to check but I couldn't because I wanted those eyes to drink me in forever. So I smiled back. Not the kind of tight-mouthed pretend smile that would have said what I was really thinking—You're taking the pish, aren't you?—but a real shiny-toothed oh-my-gosh smile that said, Hi, I'm so glad you noticed me, let's go and get married right away and live in a room and kitchen and have ten kids. She looked away. I stood there thinking up opening lines which remained unsaid until the bus came and she got on it but I didn't because it was full.

That's pretty near the truth, for me. As for Joe Kelso being dead and my brother having his fingers broken, I just made that up to get you reading this far, but now that you're here I can tell you that there's more to the story of Anna McColl than a stupid grin and a receding bus. I can tell you that I didn't see her again for another thirty-two years. I can also tell you that when I stood bereft at the bus stop under that bleak Scottish sky I noticed that my fly *was* actually open. And that seems to me to be the problem with life: that your greatest fears are probably going to be realised and that you have to be so, so brave just to do the most ordinary things, like smile at someone without looking like an eejit.

Hello? Is there embdy in there?
Knock wance fur yes an twice
fur naw.
An three bloody times
if ye came up the Clyde in a wheelbarra.

2

THE PROBLEM WITH THE PAST is that there's no getting away from it. Sometimes it feels like something sharp and solid, a material thing, a vital cog in the mechanism of the here and now. Sometimes it defies the laws of motion, as though life can't move forward without also moving back. And sometimes, when it takes on the texture of hardened steel and you're crouching there with all that wild machinery whirling around your head, you see and feel things that you were never meant to see or feel.

Or maybe not. It's all there, but you have to want to see it, and I haven't wanted to see it for a long, long time.

It's ten to one on a Thursday afternoon. I'm lying on the floor of what used to be my bedroom. The diary lies beside me, open at the page with the message about Anna. I've got a lot to think about: Anna, the diary, my whole fucked-up childhood. And Trixie, former fishmonger, housewife, clairvoyant and madwoman. My mum. It's been nearly three hours since the taxi from the airport dropped me off at the gate of her house and I walked up the driveway through the drizzle to the front door. The key was where I thought it would be, in the recess under the doorstep. It was always there, in case we locked ourselves out, but also in case Trixie took one of her turns and wouldn't get out of bed to let us in. The door fell open into the gloom of the hallway and then, after I had crossed the threshold, it shut behind me with a familiar faint rattle that had me suddenly anxious. I had forgotten to knock three times before I came in. In my mind I could hear Trixie's voice, rough with admonishment and nicotine: *Ye'll be the bloody ruin a me so ye will! Get oot an mind the door! How many times dae ah huv tae tell ye!*

For a moment I wanted to go back outside and knock on the door three times to drive away the bad luck lurking there on the doorstep waiting for its chance to get into the house. I stood there, trying to resist it, my back to the closed door for support. I stood there for ages in the cloying, musty closed-up smell of the house, finding it hard to breathe until I calmed down enough to convince myself that it didn't matter anymore, the madness—it was as dead as Trixie herself. Because she is dead, my mother. She's been dead these last four days.

Her funeral's tomorrow. I'm supposed to be at the undertaker's where she lies, face made up and hair resplendent, waiting for me to come and kiss her cold forehead and tell her how sorry I am. But I'm finding it hard to leave the house because it's thirty-two years I've been away and there's too much pressing on me. Too many memories. The whole house is a badly-healed scar.

And even though Trixie's dead she's still here the way she always was; in the rumple of her unmade bed, the ticking of her wristwatch on the dresser, the lingering smell of lavender. She's there in the folds and bulges of her old worn armchair, the dirty dishes in the kitchen sink, the stinking fag ends spilling from ashtrays. The frozen blooms of plastic flowers on the sideboard.

And she's watching me, I know she is. With that look on her face that would curdle cream. I've got here too late.

When the call came I was at home in Sydney. I've settled there, if settled is the right word for it. An uneasy kind of accommodation with life in which I eat, I sleep, I work. I have an ex-wife and two kids. Two boys. They live in America now, too far away for me to see them, though maybe one day I'll visit. Maybe not. Sometimes I think it's best I don't.

I live alone. Mostly I can distract myself from the nagging disconnection and the sense of worthlessness that's dogged me all my life, the legacy of a broken childhood, of a family that didn't work as families should, of a mother who didn't know how to love. Or maybe it's all my own fault. My own pathetic, self-pitying, blame-everyone-else-but-me excuse for failure. Whatever it is, I can mostly cope with it, though sometimes I go under, locking myself in the flat with the curtains closed night and day, the lights off. I pace the floor, my mind turning, until I collapse exhausted on the bed and the world spins on, an endless round of dreams and illusions.

This is how it was when the phone rang that autumn night and I picked it up and a female voice with a Scottish accent asked for Mr Pinelli. I assumed it was a cold caller, trying to sell me something I didn't want.

He's not here. And even if he was, he doesn't buy anything over the phone.

I hung up.

A few minutes later the phone rang again. Persistent bugger. I picked the phone up and dropped it back on the cradle.

It rang again. This time I let the answering machine handle it. I walked into the bathroom and locked the door and splashed cold water on my face while whoever it was recorded her bloody sales pitch.

When I listened to it later it wasn't a sales pitch at all. I didn't recognise the woman's voice, and she didn't give her name, but she said she was an old friend of my mother's. And then she said that my mother was dead, that she'd been unwell for some time, and that she'd taken a heart attack the night before and had passed away a few hours later. The funeral was on Thursday. My mother had asked for me, in her dying moments. Maybe there was time for me to get to the funeral, if I wanted to come?

And that was all.

I knew I should be feeling something other than what I felt at that moment; a sudden lightness, a sick ripple in my belly, a sense of relief. My mother. Dead. Where was the funeral to be held? What kind of service could it possibly be? I imagined her grave, fenced off in the unconsecrated bit of the graveyard, sharing eternity with suicides and atheists and what they used to call 'fallen women'. I had no idea if she'd still lived in the same house in Glasgow. But it was a fair bet. She and that house were one and the same. And suddenly then I could hear every sound, smell every smell, see every speck of dust suspended in the low light. I could hear the patter of rain on the old slate roof, the drip, drip, drip from the blocked gutters and the rattling of windowpanes in a storm. And I saw Trixie, too, sitting in her armchair, lit by lightning flashes like a B-grade horror flick, an evil smile splitting her green witch's face.

I couldn't decide if I should go back. I was up all that night, wrestling with myself. Fuck the lot of you, that's what I really wanted to say—it had always worked in the past. But something nagged at me now and I couldn't figure it out. My mother had asked for me on her deathbed. That's not something you can easily say *fuck you* to. Yet what did it mean, this asking for me, as if after all this time I still existed for her and she for me? As if we were any normal mother and son, visiting each other, interfering in each other's lives, me fixing her rusting gutters, she worrying about whether I'm eating properly? As if we had any kind of connection that death would sever? It didn't make any sense, but I couldn't stop myself trying to make sense of it.

And then, late into the night hours, I was lying in bed, my head bursting despite the painkillers I'd taken, half awake despite the sleeping pills, and I heard it: an old, familiar voice in my head. An unmistakeable voice that I hadn't heard for more than thirty years. A voice that made me sit up suddenly and reach out for it, yearning, but thinking I must be mistaken. But there was no mistaking it; scaly, like it was soaked in nicotine and whisky, cantankerous and mocking, a black and white voice from a black and white world. A voice from my childhood. Hearing it again that night was like hearing the voice of God, hearing it and wondering if you'd actually heard it or if you were finally falling into the madness that you'd always expected was waiting for you. I was wide awake now. I got up out of bed and I could feel my legs shaking under me, my heart pounding too fast. I felt my way to the bathroom, where I filled the sink with water and did something else for the first time in thirty-odd years; I stuck my face in the water and I held my breath for as long as I could.

When I surfaced, gasping, my hair dripping and the blood pounding in my head, I knew for sure that the voice was real, and that it was telling me something I needed to listen to. It was telling me to go home, though not quite in those words. Never in those words. Go home, it said to me, it's your last chance to sort things out. You'd be a fool not to take it.

That's what it told me. My last chance. I'd be a fool.

As the sun tugged slowly at the windows and the birds in the garden started up their tuneless cackle, I realised it was right, the voice, just as it always had been. My mother was dead, and her death changed everything, a completion and a new beginning. Despite our long years apart, her imprint on the world, her life, her death, her deeds both right and wrong, were part of who I was and who I am and who I might become. I had to go and stake my claim. That's why she'd asked for me, I decided, and that's why in the morning

I booked the next flight to Glasgow, a city I no longer knew. To a family I never really knew.

And here I am.

Voices in my head? Hearing things in the night? You must think I'm mad, schizophrenic or something, condemned to living in a shadow world beyond the reach of normal folk. I'm not schizophrenic, although I have my share of problems, believe me. The voice I heard that night is the least of them, and in the past has even been the solution. That's all I want to say about it for now. I'm embarrassed to have to admit that I've travelled halfway across the world because a voice in my head told me to, and *that* voice in particular. And now I'm here, I find he's travelled with me. Yes, it is a he, this voice—a he of sorts, anyway. He wants me to tell you all about him, how he saved me once before and how he's come back to save me again. Save me from myself, this time. Shite. The truth is the old bugger can't bear to be left out, carping and badgering, pushing and bullying, forcing himself into the story. But I won't let him. I won't.

I've spent the past three hours walking slowly through my mother's house. I've seen no one else and don't expect to until the funeral. On the kitchen table I found a note telling me that the service starts at eleven-thirty tomorrow and that my mother is being looked after by McMurtrie's Funeral Directors in Shettleston. If I want I can view the body between one and three pm today. I don't recognise the handwriting, and the note isn't signed. Presumably it was left there by the same friend of my mother's who phoned me in Sydney.

All this time I've picked at things. Books, ornaments, photographs. Pulling down vaguely familiar boxes from cupboards and shelves and spilling their contents onto the worn carpets. Everything is bathed in the light and shade of childhood, and though you'd expect it to look smaller and pokier than my memory of it, instead it's me that seems to shrink as the house reabsorbs me into itself, weaving back into its texture the troublesome loose thread that I am and have always been. I don't resist.

I found the diary in what used to be my bedroom, rummaging through a cardboard box filled with old books and comics, yellowing school jotters with scrawled essays and history notes. I wasn't particularly drawn towards it, just pulled the box down from the high shelf to see what was behind it. The blue diary caught my eye, something familiar, a dragon's head drawn in felt-tip on the cover, names and slogans which no longer held any meaning. I dimly remembered getting into trouble at school for losing this diary and not being able to note down my homework. I leafed through the mostly empty pages of 1975, until I came upon October the ninth and the faded entry in scrawled handwriting, and a memory that left me doubled up and sobbing on the floor. I cried that morning not for my poor mother dead and gone, but for things lost that should have long been found, and for things found that should have stayed lost. That's how it was.

But now I have to go to the undertaker's. I pull on my shoes and find my jacket in the hallway. Then, checking that I have the key, I open the front door, step out into the daylight and close it behind me. I don't knock on it three times before I leave, and I don't give a tinker's curse about the bad fortune. It can come in and make itself right at home. As far as I'm concerned, it had done that a long time ago, and no stupid trickery of Trixie's could make it otherwise.

The undertaker's is one of a number of shops along Shettleston Road. Part of a long, sandstone terrace, with three floors of flats above. The facade is dark, the windows opaque. Only the sign above tells you what's here: MCMURTRIE'S FUNERALS AND MEMORIALS. DIGNITY IS OUR WATCHWORD. The door gives a discreet chime as I enter, and the noise of the traffic dulls when it shuts behind me. The reception area is suitably low lit. There's no one here, just a desk to one side and, directly ahead, a door with a small window. The Door of Death, I'm thinking. Beside the desk a fish tank glows. A soft, innocuous music is being piped into the room and the whole ambience is obviously designed to calm. But I'm not calm. Not in the slightest. Now that I've actually set foot inside the undertaker's I'm afraid of what lies ahead.

For a moment I don't know what to do. Maybe I could just leave. I don't need to see her body, do I? But the truth is that I do need to see her, I *want* to see her, because it's my last chance ever to say the things that I should have said to her long ago. And then, I have to admit, I want to see her because for a long time I only wanted to see her dead.

As I stand there dithering I find myself drawn to the fish tank. I peer into it. The movement of the fish is mesmerising. I imagine myself in there with them, coursing through the warm water, the fish swimming with me and against me, sudden schools of them wheeling around and away, clearing to reveal their world, its rocks and ledges and sand and seaweed and all the hiding places I crave.

Can I help you, sir?

My head is practically in the fish tank, and just before I look up I notice, in the gravel at the bottom, the ceramic wreck of a pirate ship, fish swimming through the holes in its hull. I'm surprised to see a miniature skeleton with a wooden leg and a pirate hat standing at the wheel. Intimations of mortality. I look up at the young woman who's just come in. She's smartly dressed in a black suit, crisp white blouse, a name tag on her lapel. Sheena. She has one of those startlingly pretty, pale Celtic faces, dark wavy hair and blue eyes. Freckles on her nose. She looks serious, professional, concerned just so for any possible bereavement I might bring with me. I'm standing there, my hands on the fish tank, blinking at her, and for a moment I forget why I've come.

Do you wish to make a booking? She's putting on a posh accent, but I sense it's not how she speaks at home.

The fish, I say.

The fish?

Yes. They're beautiful.

Oh, aye, they are that. Mr McMurtrie's awfully fond of them. He looks after them himself, you know. If it was left up to me they'd probably turn up their fins and die.

Well, at least they're in the right place for it.

She gives a wee laugh and looks away, embarrassed at having mentioned the D word. There's a bit of a pause.

Ah, actually, my name's Pinelli. I'm here to see my mother. I think you've got her in there somewhere? I'm pointing to the door behind her.

She consults a book on the desk. Oh, yes, Mr Pinelli. Your mother is ready for you.

I'm not entirely sure I'm ready for *her*.

A look of professional sympathy before she steps from behind the desk and opens the door.

Will you follow me, please? Just through here.

When you walk through the Door of Death, it's best not to go unprotected. I knock on it three times, smile at Sheena's puzzled look. She smiles too, then walks on through. I follow her into a large dark room, set out like a chapel. Rows of seats. At the end a partition, three doors leading into three rooms, one of them lit with a soft glow. As Sheena leads me towards it I see through the open door the tastefully marbled and polished decorations. I see the table in the middle of the room. I see the coffin resting on it. I don't want to go in.

I'll leave you with her, then. Just let me know when you're ready. Sheena gives me another smile and leaves me to it, her heels tapping away on the parquet floor.

In her coffin, Trixie looks smaller than I remember her. And older. I'm shocked to see how old she looks, and how light and insubstantial she seems lying there, hands folded on her lap. Her hair's brushed, her eyes are closed, her face is made up with a bit too much rouge. She looks peaceful, which is an odd thing to see, because she never looked peaceful in life. She's hardly recognisable.

But I know it's her, not a substitute, not a clerical error, not a fantasy. It's her, she's dead, and now I can't ever tell her to her face that I think she was the worst mother who ever lived, that she should long ago have been locked up and the key melted down. And I'm angry with her for being dead, for never listening to me, for not listening to me now. I hit the coffin, but only gently, with my fist. *Stupit wee bugger, why didn't ye come hame sooner?*

We were all a nuisance to her. We, the sorry bunch who were her children. We were never the worst thing that happened to her, but we were never the best thing either, she made that very clear.

Her compulsive feeding thing. Why am I thinking of this now? If she was alive she'd be offering food. *A wee sandwich? A wee biscuit?* It was her substitute for love, as if you could avoid any other kind of closeness just as long as you stuck food in your kids' mouths. And besides, it was bad luck not to offer food. Anyone who came into the house had to have a cup of tea and a wee something. Except maybe on Trixie's worst days, the days when there was nothing to offer. Days on end when she stayed silent, lying in her bed staring at the ceiling.

I still don't fully understand it, and maybe I never will. But there are family stories to sift through, stories that harbour, within the telling and the retelling, some inkling of why things were as they were. Stories about Carlo, about me, my sister and my half-brother. About Trixie, too, and how she came to be the way she was. About *who* she was before she was my mother. I'll tell you that story now. She won't mind. She looks peaceful, she's not going to offer me something to eat, she's not going to shout, swear or otherwise object. She's not going to argue.

She's dead, right enough.

Okay pal, ignore me then.
Ah'll jist shut up fur a while, pretend
ah'm no here. Ye kin blether on
wi yer stupit wee stories, aw the shite
ye tell each other tae try an make
yer lives mean somethin.
But ah'm warnin ye, everythin's gauny get mixed up.
People miss the point,
tell fibs,
get the wrang endie the stick.
Think they know the score when they huvny goat a scooby.
Aye, ah'm lookin at you when ah say that.

3

TRIXIE WAS A FISHMONGER. She knew all about fish. Not just the flesh and bones; she knew their hearts, their souls, their secrets. All the intimate details of their fishy lives.

She knew, for example, that fish swim in the currents of their own passions. That their days are measured in the slow wearing of rocks in river valleys, and in the passage of a grain of sand across an ocean floor. She knew that deep within the darting shoal, each fish yearns to be alone, and that each solitary hunter merging with the shadows pines for the companionship of others. She knew all this, and more: that kissing a fish will cure cold sores; that rubbing your skin with mackerel oil will remove blemishes; that feeding your husband a mix of powdered saith scales and cod's roe boiled in milk will restore his lost virility. She knew all this. And she knew too that all these creatures, seemingly so remote and cold, shed silent, unseen tears. Of joy and sadness, love and hate. Of pleasure and of pain.

But she gutted them anyway. Cut off their heads and tails and filleted the flesh from their bones. She did it with love, she said, and sometimes with prayers, and always with wonder for the joy that she felt for their existence. Trixie was like that. Nothing was simple, not even fishmongering.

She loved fish, and all the creatures of the water in all their infinite variety, though to be sure, there wasn't much variety to be had in Glasgow in those days. Cod, haddock, plaice and mackerel, all from the ocean blue. Trout and salmon from highland streams. That was about it. But they made good eating—deep-fried with or without batter, pan-fried, with or without breadcrumbs, baked boiled stewed, soaked in salt and vinegar, served up with chips or mash but rarely with lemons because it was a poncy kind of middle class thing to do.

Trixie worked for Auld Tam Smith in Partick, and she'd worked there since leaving school. Tam Smith wasn't really old at all, he just seemed like he'd been around forever. Smith's Fine Fish his shop was called, and it had pretensions right enough, though it was really just your average fish shop, plus the odd delicacy and shop girls that smiled. It was hard to keep it going when people had no money, and Smith himself was not beyond a bit of black marketeering, or for that matter selling dubious produce to the punters. He was a mean old bastard, so he was, and tight as a kipper's arse. He'd have you sacked as soon as look at you. For petty things. Like being surly with some old rascal of a customer, or for dropping a fish in the sawdust, or for being late only once.

In charge of the girls was Myrtle, older than them and unmarried, which marked her out; spinster, old maid, unlucky in love. *On the shelf.* Myrtle worked with Smith on the ordering and the books, and she was strict with the girls in the shop. She was always watching, she was always there. Smith thought she was the cat's pyjamas. He would give her fish to take home for her tea and he would lean close to her when they were doing the books. Smith had a wife and four kids that no one ever met, and he and Myrtle were having an affair. They thought it was secret, but everyone knew about it, even the delivery boy. When the shop closed and everyone else had gone home, these two unlikely lovers would repair to the office above and there, it was said, they indulged in all manner of jiggery-pokery, the dirty buggers.

They were a fearsome pair, they were. But Trixie had a repu-tation for standing up for the girls when Smith was in one of his ugly moods. She was the older sister, looking after them, getting them to question their pay if it was wrong, arguing with Smith and with Myrtle if their accusations were unrea-sonable. The girls loved her, she said, and the boss put up with her because she was such a good worker. Shite. The boss put up with her because she'd once caught the bastard out the back with his hand up the skirt of a frightened wee shop girl. God knows what he might have done if Trixie hadn't threat-ened to cut his balls off with her filleting knife, holding it low with the point in his crotch while the girl escaped. From then on he kept a wary distance, and his guilt and his fear gave Trixie some power over him. That's why he put up with her.

Can you see the old bugger? He's got these flat eyes that seem empty but take in everything. His right ear is deformed, an accident on the docks when he was young. It's ragged, with the rough shape of a turtle plunging downwards. But he's handsome in his own way in his waistcoat and shirt sleeves and his big moustache, a pipe in his hand. And look, here's Myrtle, tall and dark-haired, trying too hard to be elegant in her pre-war suit and sensible shoes. They both reek of fish but no one notices because everyone reeks of something or other.

Why am I telling you all this? Because there's a story. It's not a very nice story, but it's the story Trixie tells. *It's true, so it is, hope tae die.* And it's a story that needs to be told.

Right, then. That box of rotten cod.

The fish had been in a questionable state when Smith bought them from one of his shady pals. A real bargain, but he had to sell them quick before they went off big-time. The crates were dumped one Saturday morning in the gutting room, where Myrtle told Trixie to get to work on them immediately. Trixie began to sing as she opened the first crate and pulled out a fish. She fancied herself as a singer when she was young, and was always belting out something or other while she worked. But now she stopped mid-verse and wrinkled her nose. She called Myrtle back.

These ur aff. Look.

She held up the fish and it flopped in her hand, its eyes opaque and dull. Myrtle looked.

They're alright.

Ye canny sell these, Myrtle, they're aff.

They're very slightly aged, Mrs Drummond. They're most certainly not off. Myrtle with her frosty look. But they will be off if you stand here all day arguing about it. And you'll be off with them, so just watch your lip. She swept out of the room.

Trixie picked up a fish and split it open. She pulled the guts out and washed the cavity and scraped the scales off. Then she took her filleting knife and she expertly filleted the bones, throwing the head and tail in a bucket with the other scraps. She worked quickly and in anger, for the fish were off and she knew it, and they better hope the inspector doesn't visit today but he won't anyway because it's Saturday. *Uch well, it's their ain bloody funeral.*

When she had done with the filleting, she and Smith arranged the fish on trays. Smith painted them with something that made the flesh glimmer. He whistled while he worked and cracked the odd joke. Trixie said nothing. They put the fish in the window and Smith priced them—the cheapest, freshest-looking cod fillets anywhere in Glasgow.

He sold the whole lot within three hours and was in a good mood for the rest of the day, chatting with the customers, winking at Myrtle, making the girls laugh with his stupid jokes. But Trixie wasn't laughing. Something was churning in her guts and her hands were tingling. She had a bad feeling about this business with the cod, and she was glad when it was time to go home.

That night, long after Drummond had stumbled home from the pub and collapsed into bed with his clothes still on, she dropped into an uneasy sleep.

This is what she dreamt:

She was lying flat on a rock, looking into the clear depths of an ocean pool. Something was moving. Some very large fish, larger than they ought to be. As she watched, a shape became defined, and then another. There were people down there, alive under the water, and the fish were herding them into a cave in the rocks. The people were struggling, kicking at the fish, their mouths opening and closing silently, their faces tense with dread, their bodies twisting and turning and their hair swirling in the depths. And then Trixie was in the water too, thumping the massive scaly bodies with her fists, screaming soundlessly for them to stop. She grabbed someone's arm and pulled them free and found herself looking into the distorted watery face of Smith. He winked and swam off towards the surface but suddenly Trixie was being pushed into the cave, and the light from above was fading and there was seaweed and sharp rocks, and there were eels, fat and slimy, and they brushed against her and she was suffocating, drowning, lost . . .

Later she would say that when she woke up, sweating and kicking and gasping, she knew everything that was going to happen from then on. She knew that all of life was written somewhere. That everything was planned and accounted for and that nothing could be changed no matter what you did. She also said that dreams were real. That they were like windows into all the other lives we could have lived, the possibilities missed, the opportunities lost, the tragedies averted.

She was talking shite. Trixie knew nothing about dreams, but guilt was already clawing at her because she knew about the fish.

It was no surprise to her when the news broke on Monday morning that there had been an outbreak of food poisoning. Seven people in the hospital, three of them critical. And it was also no surprise when the news came later that morning that someone had died. By then, Trixie's feeling of dread had hardened into a knot in her stomach.

The dead man was a regular in the shop and a real old bugger, harassing the staff and always complaining about this and that and the next thing. He had something to complain about now alright. His lifeless finger pointed accusingly at Smith's Fine Fish, and he was backed up unanimously by the sickly codfish eaters who had thought they were getting a bargain. It wouldn't be long before the inspectors showed up.

An afternoon of almost unbearable silence followed. The shop like a morgue, the girls whispering and wondering what was getting *his* goat. Trixie knew, but she wasn't telling. Myrtle knew too, and you could sense that things had changed between her and Smith, something had loosened that would soon come apart. In the meantime, she and Smith and Trixie did a kind of slow dance around each other, avoiding talk, as if saying more than the absolute needful would open the floodgates of guilt, recrimination and shamefulness. When Smith took Trixie aside, his face was white and ragged, and he looked shiftier than usual. He'd heard from the inspectors, he said. There would be an investigation. They would close the shop down and they would all be out on the street.

Ye huv tae dae whit ah tell ye.

Trixie looked at him. She watched him grow uncomfortable, but she said nothing.

Ye huv to say there wis nothin wrang wi the fish. Can ye dae that? He spoke too quickly, anxious to get the words out before he swallowed them whole.

How's that gauny help? They were bad whether or not ah knew they wur.

Look. Ah can get us aff.

The way he said 'us'. It was a knife pointed at her throat. It was her fault too.

If ye dae whit yer telt, someone else'll get the blame. The point is that we didny know the fish were aff. That's the point.

There's a man deed fur God's sake!

Listen, hen. There're jobs at stake. Yours. Yer mates'. Ma business.

Stick yer effin business. Trixie was angry. None of this was her fault. But she was bigger than Smith then, towering over his hunched form. Surprising herself, she said, Gie's a pay rise. Me an aw the girls. Ten bob extra, every week.

Ten bob?

Smith swallowed, shook his head, trying to follow this turn of events. He said, You can huv five. But no them.

Ah canny help ye, well. Trixie pushed past him.

Wait! Five an six. That's final.

They settled on six shillings and sixpence each for Trixie and the three girls.

The inspectors came, Smith was investigated. Everyone was questioned, but Trixie carried out her part of the bargain and she was amazed and troubled by how calm she felt about it, and how easy it was to lie. Eventually, Smith went to court, where he testified against the man who had sold him the cod. How he did it no one really knew, but he was let off with a small fine, while the guy who supplied him with the tainted fish was sent to jail. Outside the courtroom there was an argument between Smith and some hard-looking men who were not at all happy with the course that justice had taken. Smith jumped into a taxi and escaped, went back to the shop and the routine and he tried to pretend things were normal. But they were not.

Myrtle walked out that afternoon without a word. She just took her coat and her bag and disappeared into the sunset, leaving Smith to contemplate the abyss he had created for himself.

Trixie watched Myrtle go and she heard the fishmonger banging and cursing upstairs. Her resolve was crumbling. Maybe it *was* her fault?

Smith had killed a man, but she could have stopped him if she'd really made a fuss about it. And then she'd used the man's death to bargain with Smith. She argued with herself: The girls deserved a wee bit extra. But didn't that old bastard Smith deserve to be in jail? She should have told the truth. But hadn't she saved all their jobs? Was it not worth it, to trade the life of one dirty old man that nobody missed when there were families to feed and rents to pay? And maybe the punishment of having to shell out a decent wage to his workers—maybe that was punishment enough for Smith.

Or maybe not. It wouldn't add up. The casualness of her lie—it wasn't even questioned; no one in authority thought her worth more than her word.

Trixie was turning in on herself. In the weeks before the trial she had already felt the world begin to change, to be somehow less certain. At night in her dreams there were storms and dark woods, strangers' faces leering out of the fog, dead men's fingers pointing and the ground opening up beneath her while she stood, unable to run. And more and more there was the cave under the sea and the giant fish and the squirming people pushed and dragged under the rocks.

And then, terrified of sleep and exhausted, she had started to see things in the daytime. A fish she was gutting became a human hand. The slops bucket squirmed with worms. Fish heads mouthed silent curses. She heard voices from within the walls accusing her. *Liar. Murderess.*

Finally one morning, a few days after the conclusion of the trial, Trixie in the gutting room let rip a scream that would mince diamonds. They found her sitting in the sawdust on the floor, holding herself and rocking backwards and forwards. She wouldn't stop sobbing. Smith told her to go home to her husband and to come back when she was feeling better and not to think too much about what had happened or about the poor man who was dead. Don't blame yourself, he said.

And she did go home to her husband but she couldn't stop thinking about it. And the more she thought the more she began to see that she really was to blame and that she had bargained with Smith to make herself feel better and it hadn't worked and now it seemed she was no longer able to control the world around her. So she said nothing, and she did nothing, except she took to her bed and listened to the voices in her head. She stayed there night and day, the fire not lit and the dishes not done. The tea not even made. And Drummond down the pub, utterly lost. *And then somethin funny happened, son. Ah canny explain it, but it changed everythin. Every damn thing changed. C'mon, huv a wee piece uv sponge cake.*

What was it that changed everything for Trixie as she lay in her bed in the dull light of the streetlamp, ghosts playing in the corners of the room? Some kind of a fever, she said. Sweat on her pillow, restlessness eating away. An uneasy oblivion, neither sleep nor death. She found herself in Partick, she said, in her slippers and her old coat. It was late. The wind was howling, threatening snow, and she was freezing. She must have walked the long way because the ferry had stopped for the night and the nearest bridge was some distance up the river. It didn't really matter because here she was, standing outside Smith's Fine Fish, shivering from cold and from fear. The shop was dark, but in the room above a light shone behind closed curtains.

She said later that she wasn't herself, and that's just as well because the Trixie I knew was bad enough and I couldn't have handled this version, sleepwalking the streets half-dressed. She wasn't herself. The voices, the visions, the dark depression and then finding herself here like this. The wind was blowing old newspapers down the gutters, streetlamps flickered, a car drove past, but none of these things were solid. The only thing that mattered was that yellow light above the shop. She was drawn to this despite herself, and soon she was at the back of the building, staring at an open door and a faint glow in the hallway. Then she was walking up the stairs, wanting to turn back but impelled somehow to continue up towards the light which was coming from under the door of Smith's office. At the landing she paused. She could hear voices, hushed behind the door. One was the voice of fear, another the voice of anger, and a third something worse and far more cruel.

Now you and I would run for the police at this point, but Trixie didn't. She touched the door and it creaked open under its own weight. The room inside was a mess, chairs up-ended, books and files strewn about everywhere. And there on the floor, part of the general untidiness, was Smith, trussed like an oven-ready turkey. He was whimpering quietly and these two guys were standing over him. They greeted Trixie like an accomplice—Hello there, hen, see whit we've got here? Smith was in a right state. There was a knuckleduster on the table. And there was a knife. Trixie recognised it as her own filleting knife, the worn wooden handle and the blade sharp like a whisper.

As she watched from the doorway, a glow of pleasure passed through her at the sight of Auld Smith, helpless, and it was then she realised something that she'd been dimly aware of all along. She realised that the knife she knew so well was held firmly in her own hand. She felt its weight, and it seemed to be a part of her, gleaming and pulsing with her whole life force. She saw herself glide slowly and silently across the room, as though she and the ground were separated, as though the fabric of the universe lay threadbare at that point, and she had fallen through into a dimension of unbearable intimacy, where hate and love are one and the same. She knelt down beside Smith and with her free hand she slowly, tenderly, caressed his good ear and his poor, bloodied cheek. He looked at her in wonder and in hope, and she held his gaze and smiled. A sad, small smile.

At this point the story gets a wee bit violent. I've no taste for blood, let me tell you, and I'm just as likely to faint if I spell out the whole sorry mess. So I won't.

Here's what happened. A turtle-shaped ear was lopped off, a throat was cut, a fishmonger died. And as he died, he looked Trixie in the eye and mumbled out a curse of anger and revenge. The words themselves were lost in the last guttural heavings of his mortal breath, but Trixie felt it like a sliver of ice to the heart. And as he cursed her, she saw reflected in his eyes the fearsome shape of her own future, and all the dark and dreadful days to come. It was, she said, like seeing the colours fade from all your hopes. She stepped back from the writhing body, reached wildly for the door, and flung herself down the stairs and out the back of Auld Smith's shop. And she ran then, and she didn't stop running, all the way back to Govan.

And that was the end of her fishmongering days. Afterwards she cooked and cleaned and nurtured a little space in her head where her life used to be and which now was filled with poison and marked with a skull and crossbones. And every now and then the poison would seep out to corrupt everything around her, turning our world into a wasteland and a cruel deceit.

Because when Trixie woke in bed on the morning after this bloody vengeance, Auld Smith was dead right enough, just the way she said. And even though she hadn't left her bed all night, she knew that she had killed him with the power of her dream; she had dreamt the old bugger dead.

4

SO, YOU'RE ASKING, what happened after Auld Smith the
Fishmonger died in such unsavoury and unlikely circumstances? Well if you're looking for a crime story and all that
shite you can forget it. PC McPlod had plenty of clues but,
in the final analysis, no clue whatsoever. The case was quietly
dropped.

Convenient, eh? Because it means, Dr Watson, that instead
of solving crimes of mystery and suspense, you must apply
your superior mind to pondering the only murderess in
history who thought she could dream people dead. That's my
mother I'm talking about.

The facts are that the auld fishmongering bastard *was* dead,
and that for Trixie the world had become a place of shadows

flitting round the boundaries of real life; a parallel dimension that, once glimpsed, could never again be ignored. She lived in both worlds, and though she sometimes longed for the old one, she found the new one suited her better and she hugged it to herself, she did, this universe of ghosts and half-truths, of portents partly grasped, mysteries dimly perceived. Surely what had happened to her could only be supernatural?

She had found a gift, she said. She became a seer, and a teller of fortunes. Magic, she called it, though magic is supposed to give you power, make you able to control good or evil. I'm not sure Trixie knew the difference.

Magic? Superstition, more like. She believed in pixies, fairies, elves and witches. In the afterlife and all its fakery. She believed in all the fearful tenement wives' tales of her Maryhill up-bringing. The power of bones and coloured beads, Tarot cards and evil-smelling ointments. She wallowed in the communal anxieties rooted in old stories and matured within a world of drunken bigotry and sooty red sandstone. But for the moment, let's call it magic. It's as good a word as any.

Trixie's gift appeared not long after the Auld Smith incident. She started getting funny feelings. She would tingle all over when it happened. Her breathing would slow, she'd feel an ache in the tips of her fingers, and she could tell by looking at someone that they were going to win a fortune on the pools, or get divorced, or have an accident, or die. Or she thought she could. Her premonitions—at least in the beginning— were not always reliable; they let her down when she needed them most. Some came true, some didn't. Some were useful, some weren't.

What she sought in superstition was order and certainty: knock three times on the door to drive away the bad luck; wear one shoe for one hour if you let the bad fortune in; if a stranger comes in by the front door they must leave by the front door; never wear the colour green; eat the tail of the fish to avoid indigestion.

She was well and truly away with the fairies.

Gifts and curses. Curses and gifts. It's time for another wee diversion. A small side trip down the birth canal, to scary noises and flickering white lights. To that moment in your life when you learn that you're no longer wanted. *Slap!* Fend for yourself ya wee bugger. Breathe air. Pump your own blood. Make your own antibodies. Here's a breast, figure out what to do with it.

I was born on July the 7th, 1958, at the Glasgow Royal Maternity and Women's Hospital, known to Glaswegians as The Rottenrow. Other things happened that day: a loggerhead turtle, *C. caretta caretta*, was found on a beach near Girvan, on the west coast of Scotland. A young male about two feet long, it was well out of its usual haunts, the tropical and subtropical waters of the mid-Atlantic, and it would have found the temperatures off Girvan not much to its liking. Nevertheless, it was reported by its finder, a Mr Robert McIvor, fisherman retired of Girvan town, to be 'alive and kicking, and in surprisingly good spirits'. McIvor took the turtle home, where it was inspected by several authorities and left in his care. Its subsequent fate is unknown, though there were unkind rumours of a cash sale to a local restaurant, where turtle soup appeared on the menu for one night only.

What else happened? Only this. In the same hospital, and at the exact same moment that I emerged from Trixie's womb, Anna McColl was born.

I often used to think about our mothers meeting there, complimenting us on our maternal eyes, our paternal nose, our grandmotherly ears. And I'd think, too, about Anna and I being bathed together and laid next to each other naked on a change table while our mothers took instruction from the nurse on how to dry and dress. Did we touch each other then, grasp hands, entwine our chubby legs and exchange fluids? Oral or nasal? Pee-pee or poo-poo?

Apparently not. Trixie had nothing to tell me about Anna. But she told me all about the curse.

I'll tell you the story too, but first you have to imagine a dark living room, late afternoon, rain spitting on the windows. Outside, the sound of tyres on wet tarmac, people hurrying past, high school boys on their way home, quarrelling. In the distance a siren, police or ambulance. Inside, a clutter of clothes, toys, books and dirty teacups. Biscuit crumbs on the carpet. Trixie sits in her armchair. She's got her dressing-gown on, and a worn look under her eyes. She smokes, lighting each cigarette from the one before. Ash on her lap. I'm sitting on the floor in front of her, listening to her low voice as her story unfolds. It's the first time I've heard it. But it won't be the last. *Sometimes ah wonder if yer really ma son, son. Know whit ah mean?*

The wee boy that was brought to Trixie soon after a long and difficult birth was a joy to look upon. She held him and she smelt his newly breathing skin and she couldn't believe she could feel so much love. So much desperate, wanting, biting love that she cried as he suckled her breast and as she gazed at his puckered little face. Under his influence she felt calm, in touch with a joyful reality that wiped away the past. Everything from this moment on would be right. Everything about this baby said so; all the essentials were there, in the right proportions. He was quiet, content, bubblingly happy: a perfect baby—the only problem being that he wasn't me.

The mix-up was put right twenty-four hours later but by that time it was too late. Trixie refused to relinquish her little saviour. She abused the nurses. She ranted, she raved, she tore at her hair until the doctor ordered that she be restrained while they took the sweet little cherub—blessed, if you ask me, with a monumental good fortune—back to its rightful mother, never to be seen or heard from again. When Trixie finally clapped eyes on me she broke into bitter tears and refused to have anything to do with me. I lay there in my crib, wrinkled, mottled, possibly cross-eyed. Screaming my little heart out at the harshness of a world in which I was dependent on strangers and denied my mother's breast. It was three days before Trixie could be persuaded to bath me, and what she discovered then confirmed her worst fears. On the back of my neck was a birthmark. Small. In the shape of a turtle.

It was the mark of the curse. The curse of Auld Smith himself, those last gurgled mouthings that she couldn't make sense of in her dream. In his dying breath, Smith had cursed her. With what exactly? After many weeks of turning the matter over and over in her head, and consulting with certain renowned speywives who lived in her old neighbourhood, she decided this: her second son—he who bore the mark of the turtle—would die by drowning on his eighteenth birthday.

Trixie's capacity to conjure up a world beyond the limits of rationality knew no bounds. But whether she invented the curse or not made it no less real. We all suffered from its baleful impact, and no one more than me, though even then, as Trixie told me about the curse for the first time, while the rain spattered against the windows and the light dimmed in the corners of the room, I could feel something hard growing inside me, a clenching in my fists, a hunching of the shoulders, a refusal to feel dependent on Trixie or anyone else: the first thin layers of what would later become a shell, a carapace, a shield and a hiding place. It started then, formed in Trixie's story of rejection and in the realisation, as she spoke that rainy day, that I was and would forever be lost to her and she to me; that I was indeed cursed, and that it was my own mother who had cursed me.

5

A CURSE LIKE THAT puts a bit of a dampener on your childhood.

It was our big family secret, rarely discussed, in the way that we rarely discussed anything. Carlo thought it was all nonsense but he got short shrift if he tried to make light of it. And he was forbidden, as we all were, to mention it to anyone outside the family. Trixie was big on this—that you don't tell anyone your secrets, that what goes on within the family stays there. It was one of her refrains: *ye canny trust naebody, best tae keep yersel tae yersel, so it is.* The consequences of blabbing about it to anyone were never spelt out, but I knew that if we did, we would suffer a terrible fate; we'd wake in the morning with our lips fused together, or our tongues cleaved to the roofs of our mouths, maybe our speech replaced by the bark of a dog or the twitter of a bird. Even now, I feel an uneasiness about telling this story. Even though she's dead and she can no longer hurt me, her disapproval hangs in the air of the house, shroud-like and suffocating, smelling of lavender.

We blabbed. Of course we did. I told Wee Malkie about it one afternoon in the shed at the back of his garden. We worked out on our fingers the year that I would turn eighteen, and we discussed my options for the future.

Ye could rob banks, he said. Get lotsa money an buy things.

Ah don't want to go to jail, I said. Who wants to go to jail?

But ye widny drown in jail, wid ye?

Ah might, don't they huv baths an that?

Naw, they don't, they wash themselves in a basin. Cauld water, even in winter.

I thought about cold water in winter, breaking the film of ice in the basin, the sharp numbness of fingers and the shock as you splash your face. And then I thought about the freezing cell and the bars on the window and the whole world out there beyond my grasp.

Nah, ah don't want to be a robber. Maybe ah could be a spaceman.

Ma uncle's a spaceman.

Uch, yer face he is.

And that was about the extent of our conversation on the matter. Later on, Wee Malkie used the information against me during an argument about some other great porky that he wanted me to believe, and I realised that maybe Trixie was right. Keep yourself to yourself. Trust nobody.

So there I was, a young boy, doing all the things kids do—riding my bike, making fireworks, ringing doorbells and running away. But whenever anyone asked me what I wanted to be when I grew up, I'd turn silent, or pretend I didn't know. The answer I wanted to give—when I grow up I'd like to still be alive—was more trouble than it was worth.

Anyway, as you can see, I'm still alive and Trixie isn't. I'm standing in her kitchen with a glass of water while she lies in her coffin on the other side of the Door of Death, her still face betraying nothing of the woman she once was. I'd stood there a good ten minutes, looking at her. Then, I don't know why, I kissed her. On the forehead. And I cried, biting my lip, trying to keep it to myself. After a bit I stifled my sobs and made my way back to the reception. There were further instructions from Sheena about the funeral, then I left the undertaker's and caught the bus back here.

Now, in Trixie's kitchen there's something about the light coming through the window that makes me stand lost in thought.

My first memory of Trixie is lying on my back on the kitchen floor, looking up her skirt. I was four, and she was busy at the sink and didn't notice me at first. I don't know what I was looking for exactly but I was fascinated by the mechanics of suspenders. *Whit ur ye up tae ya dirty wee scunner? Go an play ben the room. Git oota ma sight!*

That's how my memories are: fragmented, shattered into bits and pieces that never quite fit together. A broken vase, the bits swept up into a pile and hidden guiltily in the back of a cupboard. I pick up the pieces and examine them, one by one. Some I can stick together, with gaps and chips and glue seeping through the cracks. Others seem to be parts of a different vessel, the colours wrong, the designs mismatched.

So let me try to glue another piece into place. Let me tell you about my family.

We were two families really. There was Granny Mac and Mr Disco, who lived in Maryhill, on the third floor of the council tenement where Trixie had spent her girlhood. The sooty old building was prone to damp, its porous sandstone soft and weather-beaten, but it and the dank apartment they occupied suited Granny Mac, who had lived in the neighbourhood all her life. She and Mr Disco were a strange pair, right enough, but the arrangement was a cosy one, feeding off a mutual admiration that expressed itself in nothing less than pure devotion. Touching really, though you'd swear so you would that Mr Disco was just taking his old granny for a sucker. He could do no wrong, but then, when it came to the crunch, neither could she. After himself, Mr Disco loved no one else but her.

The second family was Trixie's own special creation—her own witch's laboratory of experimental creatures inhabiting an ordinary detached house in a middle-class suburb on the eastern outskirts of the city. All pebbledash and fancy bay windows on the outside; inside, floral wallpaper and dark woodstain, picture rails and rugs laid on lino. It wasn't what you'd call modern, though in the living room Carlo had installed a huge stone fireplace which reached up to the ceiling and looked like something that belonged in California, in those movies with Cary Grant and whatsername, the famous actress with the short dark hair. But instead of Hollywood stars there was only us. Trixie, and me, and my sister Luce. There was Carlo, too, but he was more often present only as an empty armchair or an angry voice from the bedroom late at night. We noted his absence, and we mentally stored away the loss for future use.

But let's talk about Luce for a minute. Her name is Lucia, though everyone calls her Luce. She was born two years after me, at a time when Trixie and Carlo had declared a temporary truce in the long war of their marriage. At some point they must have decided that they were still in love, though what that love was—its character, its meaning—is lost to me now, if it was ever anything real in the first place. Be that as it may, my wee sister was conceived, gestated and willed into existence. From the moment she shouldered her way into life the world around me changed irrevocably, and in no time at all, it seems, our sibling forces were deployed at key strategic positions and our defences had become impenetrable. Not all of it, I have to say, was Luce's fault. In fact, if I think about it now—and I don't like to think about it very often—I might have to concede that she had good reason to hate me, the older brother who was never what an older brother should be: solid, protective, a source of secret knowledge about the world she was growing into. Instead, when she was about six months old and lying in her pram I took one of Trixie's long needles and experimented with sticking it through the hood of the pram to see how far it would go. When she was four, I encouraged her to grasp the poker that I'd heated thoroughly in the fire. I didn't mean the needle to prick her head and set her off wailing blue murder, and she surprised me more than anyone when she actually took the poker that I held out to her, but there was never any point in trying to explain it. I spat in her baby food too, once or twice, and there was no excuse for that other than wilful hatred. And as she grew older and more able, she retaliated: a dead mouse in the bottom of my bed; talcum powder poured into the pocket of my school blazer. And once, a razor blade embedded viciously into the plasticine I played with. It was total war.

Carlo named her Lucia because he said he wanted at least one of his children to have an Italian name, and it was also the name of one of his favourite aunts. She had no distinguishing marks, no curse to carry with her. She was normal, and as such she was pretty much ignored by Trixie, but Carlo, I think, liked her best of all of us, in as far as Carlo liked us at all, which is to say he liked us at a remove, as an afterthought, a more or less annoying interruption to his daily life.

At home with the Pinellis. A warming fire burning in the hearth, Dad in a cardigan smoking a pipe, Mum in an A-line skirt and high heels, kids smartly turned out, smiling in the background of their neat-as-a-pin living room. Yeah, that'd be right. Carlo never smoked a pipe, nor did I ever see him in anything resembling a cardigan. And Trixie, then, was rarely found in high heels, though she wore them later when she became a professional clairvoyant. But there were times I remember when our house was tidy. Times when Trixie sang as she went about her work, when the morning air seemed to vibrate with promise and the house was filled with light. On mornings like this, I would wake to the smell of breakfast cooking, and a feeling that the world was open-armed and smiling, ready to take me to its bosom. Luce and I would meet in the kitchen, silent and guarded. We would watch Trixie as she moved light-footedly around, rattling pans and serving up fried eggs, sausages, bacon, toast and huge steaming mugs of tea. She looked then as though she were a film-star housewife, her hair up in a scarf, an apron tied around her waist. She shone with a celluloid gleam. We watched her go through her film-star housewife routine and she seemed to me in those moments to be competent and in control. And comforting too, like a mother should be.

There was, at times like this, too much. Too much food on our plates, too much light in the kitchen, too much Trixie, playing her larger than life part in whatever film she thought she was starring in that morning. She would fuss over us. *Huv ye done aw yer homework? Pit yer warm jumpers on, an yer gloves, the weather might turn the day. Here's some money fur yer school dinner.*

Sometimes Trixie the film star would last the whole day, and we'd come home to find the house transformed, smelling of Windowlene and Ajax. The radio would be playing soft afternoon music. If it was winter, the fire would be lit and the lights on, the welcome smell of something warming on the stove. It was like walking into a stranger's house.

Trixie, then, might be found in the living room, immaculately dressed. She would have had her hair done up at Mrs Reid's the hairdresser, and she would have been shopping.

Sitting on the sofa with her legs crossed and a magazine open on her lap, she would smile and gently tell us to take our things to our rooms, not to leave our shoes on the floor, to get changed and then do our homework while she made us a cup of tea.

This is something like it was one winter's afternoon when I got home late from school. I was still in primary, and I came home with my fingers numb and my knees blue. They made you wear shorts and a blazer then, even in the depths of winter; a boy wasn't allowed long trousers until he went to secondary school. It was snowing and I was late home because Wee Malkie and I and some others had stopped to play in the park. Someone had found an old piece of cardboard and we used it to sledge down the hill until it fell to pieces. The park was full of kids all doing much the same thing, everyone too excited to feel the cold. It was nearly dark by the time I turned into our street. My shoes and socks were sopping wet, and I had torn the arm of my duffle coat, a sizeable rip in one of the sleeves. I said goodbye to Malkie at the gate by kicking him in the arse and then dodging his kick in return and closing the gate on him. He spat at me but missed and I ran down the driveway laughing until I got to the back door and then stopped because of the usual anxiety about coming home, and because this time Trixie had reason to be angry with me. I knocked on the door three times softly, and hid the torn bit of sleeve with my hand as I opened it.

The back door led straight into the kitchen and the warmth of the house made me aware of how cold I was. There was something cooking on the stove and I picked up the lid of the pot to have a look. Trixie's vegetable soup, with a big ham bone simmering in the middle. There was some fresh fish, too, newly filleted and washed, on a plate by the sink. I was hungry. In the living room the fire was blazing away, and Luce was sitting on the floor in front of it, playing with some dolls. Trixie was nowhere to be seen. I took my coat off and hung it in the cupboard under the stairs. Maybe no one would notice the rip, at least not for a while yet.

Where's Mum?

Luce ignored me. She was then around seven years old, a skinny wee thing with an untidy mop of black hair and dark eyes that could burn holes in your soul. She was the quiet type, remote and often withdrawn or preoccupied. She was also touchy, quick to take offence, quick to anger. In a family of door slammers, Luce's door-slamming performance was legendary. Even at that time, the door from the living room into the hall was chipped and warped, unsteady on its hinges from the impact of too many dramatic exits.

Finally, she looked up. She's upstairs.

I sat down on one of the armchairs and watched Luce playing. She was absorbed in pulling a tiny jumper over the arms of one of her dolls. Then she stopped and looked up at me again with a look of admonishment that was far too old for her years. Ye've ripped yer coat.

How do you know?

Ah saw ye at the gate.

Ye shouldny be lookin.

Ah'm gauny tell Mum.

Go an tell her then. Ah don't care.

You don't care about anythin.

Ah care about you bein a rat!

I kicked one of her dolls under the sideboard and watched as her face warped into something resembling a ball of flame and I thought for a moment that she was going to throw herself at me, kicking and screaming and gouging. But she got up, ran into the kitchen, and slammed the door.

I stayed where I was and tried to pretend to myself that it didn't matter. It seemed that this was how things were supposed to be, and it was kind of comfortable in its familiarity. But that afternoon was different, and if I'd known what was going to happen I wouldn't have sat there like a big stooky, just waiting for it. I switched on the telly and settled down to watch *Blue Peter*. After a while Luce came back into the room. She retrieved the doll from under the sideboard and quietly resumed her game.

When Trixie came down the stairs, she tut-tutted because it was dark and the only light came from the fire and the flickering of the TV. *Ye'll ruin yer eyesights so ye will!* She switched on the overhead light and closed the curtains, and then she came over and poked about with the fire for a bit. Luce had to move her stuff out of the way, and she huffed and puffed about it the way she always did. Trixie threw a few more coals on the fire. She stood between me and the TV so I watched her instead while she did it. There was an intensity about her movements, her dark eyes frowning in seeming concentration, though probably she was wrestling with something in her mind. Her bottom lip had that bitten look, and the lines on her forehead looked that little bit deeper than usual. She turned and caught me looking at her, and then surprised me with a half-smile, shy, in that funny way she had of smiling, though it didn't happen very often.

Whit? she said.

Nothin.

She stood up. Yer granny an Kenny ur comin over, she said.

Tonight?

Aye, ah'm makin tea fur us. They'll be here soon.

Is Dad comin?

The frown came back over her face and she looked away. How wid ah know?

She walked off into the kitchen and started clattering about with pots and pans. I knew I should have been happy that she was even talking to me, let alone that she was cooking dinner for everyone, but I can't say I was ecstatic about Mr Disco coming over. Truth be told, I tried to avoid him in the same way I tried to avoid my wee sister, though with him it was easier because he didn't live in the same house. Mr Disco was a pain in the arse, self-centred and big-headed, displaying all the signs of the monster ego to come. In a year or two he'd be attracting flocks of girls with his prowess on the dance floor, and not long after that he'd find fame as the posing and pouting leader of seventies glam rock phenomenon, Powerstrike (remember them?). Even at this point in the story, all that future success—the girls, the money, the notoriety—seemed inevitable. But for now, Mr Disco was in the middle of his soccer genius phase. He was in secondary school and was already captain of his school team, the hero of the junior championship. It was rumoured that a scout from

Glasgow Rangers had attended one of his recent matches. At least that's what he told us. It irritated me no end. I'd even put Wee Malkie on notice that if he so much as mentioned Mr Disco and his brilliance I'd knock his bloody teeth out.

The living room had become oppressive. The overhead light was too harsh and bright, chasing all the dark things from their corners, reflecting off the paintwork and making me squint. I closed my eyes, but I still couldn't rid myself of the glare, red and shot through with flickering lines behind my eyelids. When I opened them again, everything was blurred. Luce wavered on the floor before me like a mirage in the desert and then swam into focus and as she did so a ripple of something like anger swept through me, though it was more than that; it was a vague inkling, a niggling glimpse of something vast and hidden, something that wouldn't yet reveal itself fully. I got up and went upstairs to my bedroom.

There, in the cold darkness, I lay on the bed and listened to the distant shouts of kids still playing snow games in the park, the swish of cars in the slush, the muffled rumble of the city. It was about six o'clock, I supposed, but I wanted nothing more at that moment than to fall into a deep sleep, so deep that nothing or no one would be able to find me. I closed my eyes.

Was it the cold that woke me? Or the squeak of the bedroom door? Whatever it was, my eyes opened with a snap, and I found myself shivering on top of the bed as the world came flooding back. Downstairs I could hear voices: Trixie's, and the deeper tones of Granny Mac. It was dark in the room, and the air felt heavy and thick, like a winter fog. I reached over to switch on the light but it flickered on before I touched it, leaving me confused for a moment, blinking and bewildered. Then I jumped when I realised there was someone in the room with me.

Hello there, Donny boy, how's it gaun?

Mr Disco was standing next to my bed, grinning widely. How long had he been there, watching me? I wanted to crawl under the covers, to hide myself. It was as though he'd caught me in some kind of shameful act, like I'd been lying there with no clothes on or something. The cold didn't seem to bother him. He wasn't wearing a jumper, just a shirt and a pair of blue jeans. Even then, he seemed to be part of some remote, much older world of clothes and music and attitude. His brown hair was long and thick, worn with a fringe, and with the swirly pattern on his shirt he looked like someone on the telly. He was only fourteen then, but he carried with him the authority of an adult. I admit it, I was scared of him, and at that moment I was even more scared than usual. He seemed capable of anything.

And then: Ye've ripped yer coat, he said.

I stared at him, trying to make sense of this. And then I remembered the coat, and the tear in the sleeve. Why did everyone know about the stupid coat?

What ur ye goin on about, Kenny?

Ye better come downstairs, young Donald. You're in big trouble.

He was still grinning and I thought then that this was just one of his idiot jokes. I heaved myself off the bed and turned the electric heater on, even though it would take ages to heat up the room. I stood in front of it, shivering as it began to give off a feeble glow. I was still in my school uniform.

Go away, Kenny, ah want to get changed.

Maw says ah've tae fetch ye doon. She wants tae talk to ye. Now.

He headed out the door with a little theatrical flourish in his step, confident that I would follow him. And like the eejit zombie that I was, I did; out the door and down the cold stairway, step by step, creaking on the seventh and fourth as though everything was just as it should be, an ordinary walk down the stairs towards the heat of the fire and the muted voices in the living room.

Granny Mac was sitting on the sofa, with Trixie standing beside her. Luce was lying in her spot in front of the fire. Mr Disco walked over and stood next to her. His grin was really starting to annoy me, and it contrasted badly with the grim faces of the adults, who'd stopped talking, and were now looking at me like I was something the dog had thrown up. Trixie took my arm and led me into the centre of the room. Spread on the floor was the remains of my duffle coat. I say remains because that's what they were. Both arms had been hacked off, the pockets were torn and hanging, there was a huge rip up the back. The toggles were together in a little pile next to the hood, which looked like it had been put through a shredder.

For a moment we all stood around the ragged pile in a strained silence, broken only by Mr Disco's restless fidgeting. Luce was still playing with her dolls, or at least pretending to, because I caught her looking at me with something like exultation in those sharp little eyes. So that was it! Luce had taken her revenge. While I sat watching telly she'd taken a pair of scissors or a knife and I could imagine how she'd smiled to herself as she methodically snipped away at my coat, chopping away quietly at it in the cupboard under the stairs and leaving the bits on the floor. She knew fine that Trixie would find the mess when Granny Mac and Mr Disco arrived and she hung their coats up for them. And she knew fine what would follow; precisely the scene that was unfolding now.

Trixie bent and picked up a bit of the coat. Well, whit huv ye tae say aboot this?

It wisny me.

My answer sounded too pat, the kind of thing every kid says when confronted with the evidence of his bad behaviour.

Ah've jist aboot hud enough of you, Donald Pinelli. Last week ye cut up wan uv ma best scarves, and before that ye took the clock tae bits and we still canny pit it te gether. And that wis a weddin present, too.

She was quite right. I'd thought her silk scarf was a bit of rag and I'd cut it up to make a parachute for my GI Joe. And the clock? The second hand was stuck and I wanted to fix it. I was just trying to help.

As if ah don't dae enough runnin efter ye aw the time, cookin and bloody cleanin and tryin tae keep ye lookin nice. Yer faither paid a lotta money fur that coat. D'ye think we're made a money? Ye ungrateful wee scunner!

She cuffed me over the ear and pushed me roughly onto the pile of rags.

Mum, don't.

I could feel her anger like a blunt instrument on my back as she stood over me. Worse, I could sense Mr Disco grinning as he settled in for the show, and Luce revelling in the success of her plan and in my humiliation. Trixie hit me again, hard, across the back of my bare leg. And then again, and once more before Granny Mac said, That's enough. Ye'll hurt the boy, so ye will.

Ah'll bloody hurt him awright!

Trixie was shaking, strands of hair hanging over her eyes, her mouth set in a thin line. She gathered herself in, visibly tightening with the act of restraint, calling back the forces of her anger, regrouping for the next stage of the battle.

She turned to Granny Mac. Whit am ah gauny dae wi him?

Granny Mac shook her head and said, I've no seen nothin like it. Ma ain faither wid huv belted me fur somethin like this.

Trixie looked at her. I'll get one of Carlo's belts . . .

Don't be stupit, girl! Granny Mac spoke sharply. Maybe she was shocked that her daughter could seriously consider belting one of her kids. Maybe she was just trying to buy me some time, I don't know. I'd never heard her speak like this before. The room fell silent, everyone was looking at her.

Granny Mac came from some ancient world where action was the reluctant outcome of long and slow deliberation. She was then maybe in her early sixties, round and bow-legged, and she walked with a roll that gave her a vaguely drunken air. She was hard though, and heavy, like old cast iron. Her husband had been a drunk and she'd lost her two sons on the Normandy beaches and she was as bitter as a midwinter wind. And yet somewhere within her was a woman who was not cruel; who might even, for a few moments now and then, allow a tiny glimpse of compassion to sneak out into the poisoned air. Believe you me, in my family this was a rare and wondrous thing.

She spoke now, into the silence. Send the boy tae his room wi no tea.

Trixie scowled. That's no a punishment! Ah know exactly where tae send him. He kin go an sit in the coal shed till his faither comes hame.

Ya daft girl, it's freezin oot there! Granny Mac stood up and tried to push Trixie out of the way.

Mind yer ain business, maw. Ah'll deal wi this ma way.

He willny last five minutes! Ye'll be the death o him, so ye will!

Trixie and Granny Mac were each holding the other's arms. I thought maybe they would come to blows, but Trixie pushed the old woman back onto the sofa and held her there. When she spoke, her voice had that edge to it that I dreaded; quiet, determined, certain.

It's no me that'll be the death o him, maw. Don't you worry yersel aboot that. His fate's already settled. He'll die when he's eighteen, but until then he's mine tae dae whitever ah bloody well like with.

Case closed. She turned to me. Come on, ya wee bugger. Ah'll teach ye tae look efter yer things!

I kicked and screamed then. I tried to lash out at Luce and at the stupid, excited grin on Mr Disco's face. But Trixie had already grabbed me and I couldn't get at them. The whole world swirled around me and I could hear myself cursing them all in a language I didn't know I could speak. Trixie hauled me through the kitchen and out of the house. The snow was falling in huge windblown flakes that crunched beneath us as I struggled in her grip. I screamed, believe me; I wailed and squealed and ranted like there was no tomorrow—and let's face it, for all I knew there wasn't. Trixie held me with one arm while she wrenched open the door of the coal shed. She threw me into the darkness, slammed the door shut and locked it.

For a long time I kicked and hammered on the door, my screams and shouts gradually becoming sobs, before I stopped, exhausted, and sat down on the dusty floor. It was draughty, and bitter cold. I was still dressed in the short trousers and jumper of my school uniform. I hugged myself for what warmth I could find, my teeth chattering uncontrollably.

The coal shed was little more than a cupboard at the side of the house. The floor was divided by a wooden stile, behind which the coal was piled up. There were a couple of high shelves, where we kept some tools and things like spare fuse wire and the garden shears. On the floor I found an old sack, like the kind I'd seen Jock the coalman lugging on his shoulder. I first pulled it over myself like a blanket, and then I somehow found myself inside it, the smell of hessian, oily and acrid, mingling with the sharp taste of coal dust. I could feel the roughness of the sack against my bare legs, and the grittiness of the coal dust on my hands and face, and it seemed like I was rolling in great swathes of it, sooty and smoky. But I was so cold that I pulled the sack right over my head and I lay there like that for God knows how long, every now and then thinking I was going to suffocate, pushing my head out for a gulp of freezing air, pulling the sack over me again with my ears numb from the cold. I fell asleep eventually, or maybe passed out.

What happened after that? Was it really Carlo who opened the door, reached down and lifted me gently out, sack and all? Was it really Carlo who carried me into the warmth of the living room, heedless of the coal dust down his shirt front and trailing over the rug? And was it really Carlo who set me down before the fire and who hugged me and rubbed the life back into my frozen limbs, muttering encouragement?

The truth is, I don't remember. Or at least I remember, but it's like the memory of a dream you had when you were little. How much of it's the dream, and how much is what you add to it later? Someone ran a hot bath, took my clothes off and immersed me in the soothing water. Someone cleaned off the coal dust, dried me, dressed me in pyjamas and put me to bed. Someone sat by my bedside while I fell into a deep, warm sleep. I think that someone was Carlo. My father.

6

BUT CARLO MIGHT AS WELL have been an alien, green and googly-eyed, for all we really knew about him then. Our worlds connected only tenuously, as if through a wormhole in the vacuum between us, open just enough for Carlo to flit through and away again, leaving behind inexplicable traces: sometimes the house would be full of boxes of tinned Italian tomatoes; sometimes crates of whisky would be piled up in the hallway; sometimes in the garage you'd see mysterious shapes under tarpaulins. Once, to our delight, we woke to find the kitchen overflowing with boxes of chocolate biscuits.

He was a businessman, he said. He dealt in all sorts of things, foodstuffs and the like. At what point in my young life did the realisation come that Carlo, my father, was, let's say, involved in shady dealings? That he was a crook, a gangster, a thug? A man of less than scrupulous morals, engaged in all kinds of nefarious practices and in all manner of bent and dodgy doings?

He's in jail, you know. He's been there for a good few years now, and he won't be out for a good few years yet, if ever, given his advancing years. It was in the news at the time, something about embezzlement and high-level corruption, and the suspicious deaths of two of his acquaintances. The embezzlement charges didn't stick, but they got him for murder. I followed the trial at home in Sydney, the surreal footage of my father being walked up the steps to the court, surrounded by microphones and camera flashes. I expect he deserved what he got.

The first inkling we kids had that Carlo's business was not what it seemed was the time he came home with blood down the front of his shirt and a bruise under his eye. It was a summer's afternoon, and he pulled into the driveway in his red sports car, clutching a bunch of flowers for Trixie. We'd never seen him bring flowers home before, and we'd never seen him with blood on his shirt; in fact, we'd never seen him home this early. He walked into the kitchen, grinning stupidly, and gave us a story about helping someone who had been in an accident. But the flowers didn't add up, and within minutes he and Trixie were shouting at each other, and Carlo got back in his car and drove off with a squeal of tyres that startled the neighbourhood.

I should have realised the truth of the matter just through his appearance—I had seen enough gangster shows on TV to know: Exhibit One, the dark pinstripe suits, some of them double-breasted; Exhibit Two, the neat moustache, clipped in the Italian style; Exhibit Three, the sunglasses, even in winter. But that alone doesn't give us the whole picture of Mr Carlo Pinelli, businessman, because don't imagine for a moment that his suit, his shirts, his shoes, even his damned sunglasses, were anything less than top-quality stuff; Carlo was what you might call a careful dresser, and the contrast between him and the rest of us was pretty marked, let me tell you.

So there he stands, dark hair swept back, though never oiled, the faint scent of cologne that in those days only an Italian could get away with. A heavy gold watch hangs on his wrist, and, when dressed casually, he sports a gold chain around his neck. He was, I suppose, handsome enough, though not tall—dark-skinned bordering on swarthy, teeth white and even behind that devilishly crooked smile. The thing about Carlo though, was this: he was rich.

Now you might think that made us all rich, that a well-off father would provide generously for his family, setting us all up in Newton Mearns or somewhere like that, sending his kids to private schools, holiday houses in Tuscany, the whole jetsetting, Bentley-driving, luxury yachting kind of thing, with a bit of golf club snobbery thrown in for good measure. You'd think that, but you'd be quite wrong. Oh, we were certainly comfortable. We never lacked for food or clothes, we had enough toys and distractions and annual holidays. Our house was well maintained and there was always a fancy car parked in the driveway. But we weren't rich. Not in the way that Carlo was.

I'm not complaining, mind. Not really. We were after all, middle class, in that funny Glasgow kind of middle-class way where you pretend you're not because the kids from the housing estates will call you names and beat you up. We had what we needed, and more. Yet Carlo was rich, richer then than any of us knew, and he kept his riches for himself. Partly because the tax man didn't know how rich he was either, but mainly because he wasn't really one of us. His life was largely a mystery. The vague picture we had of him was of a hard-working man struggling to keep his small business viable, building it up through long hours and ceaseless attention to detail, but in fact he lived independently and separate to us. We were just another detail to be looked after; a necessary expense, to be written off by his dodgy accountants where possible.

Surely, you're thinking, a rich man needs a social life, a wife to host dinner parties, kids to be groomed to take over the reins of business, to ensure the family fortune remains intact? Well, I suppose a snob might say we were 'new money', and riffraff like us didn't adhere to the traditions and niceties of high society. And it has to be said that a gangster with dubious financial interests and connections to the underworld isn't quite in the same social league as your average respectable business magnate, though each might be as crooked as the other. But I would say this too: Carlo was ashamed of us. He was ashamed of Trixie, her superstitions and her late-night communions with spirits, real or imagined, the heavy fog she carried with her, the crazy ups and downs of her domestic rule. And he was ashamed of me, maybe, because I was so helplessly doomed. Because although Carlo scorned the idea of the curse, much as he scorned the idea of religion or of any belief other than the one he had in himself, it affected him, just like it affected all of us, and he didn't like that. Not one bit.

What Carlo liked was making money.

His story really begins at the end of the Second World War. It was a difficult time for the Pinelli family. Pa and Nonna had migrated to Scotland in the 1920s, and Carlo—though he liked to say he was from Italy—was in fact born in Scotland.

During the war, Pa had been interned on the Isle of Man as an enemy alien—four long years of separation from Nonna and Carlo, who was their only child. Pa had an almost pathological lack of interest in politics, Italian or otherwise, and was about as likely to become a fifth columnist as he was to take up Highland dancing. If you pressed him, he would tell you what he thought of Mussolini, Hitler and the whole sorry bunch of them, in terms that left you in no doubt that he believed all politicians were scum. His job, he said, was to make money and look after his family, and that's why he lived in this brutal country, because here there were opportunities and in Italy there was only heartbreak. That's what he'd tell you if you asked why he left. Heartbreak.

Exactly why Italy broke Pa's heart was never spelt out by him or anyone else. A woman? A betrayal, perhaps? Or maybe that he felt the country could never repay him for those cold, dark years he spent fighting the Austrians on the Isonzo Front during the Great War. In his later years he would talk to us about the things he saw up there in the mountains. Men freezing to death in the night. Avalanches that buried entire companies. Never enough food. During the disaster of Caporetto, he said, the Austrians came from nowhere, appearing out of the fog like grey ghosts, blood dripping from their bayonets. They made no sound as they swept down the hillsides and over the Italian lines. In the mountains behind Tolmino, Pa found himself at the bottom of a trench, buried under earth and dead bodies, unable to pull himself free as the waves of grim, grey men pressed over him. They were shooting and stabbing the wounded, clearing the trench of life, taking no prisoners. Pa closed his eyes and kept as still as he could until the tide of killing passed him by. He lay there all day and at nightfall, stiff and frozen, he disentangled himself from the arms of his dead comrades and started to make his way back to his own lines. The Italian army was in full retreat, falling back eventually almost as far as Venice. It took Pa four days and nights to find them, and when you asked him how he did it—where he hid, what he ate, how he avoided the enemy—he'd go quiet, and mutter something about how the purpose of life is above all to live, and when the thin veil of civilisation is ripped away, we are little better than the lowliest of beasts.

Whatever the cause of his heartache, he was betrayed for the second time when the British government sent him away from his family, and from his peaceful occupation of running a fish and chip shop in the Gallowgate. Up until then, he ran a scrupulously legitimate business, deliberately avoiding the scams and crooked connections of the local Italian hoods. He did alright for himself, and made enough money to put a deposit down on a house in the suburbs. But when he came back, after Italy surrendered, things changed. He was sick, he said, of being fucked around by the state, working his backside off to pay taxes just so they could throw him in a concentration camp whenever they felt like it. Besides, he had made some new friends in the internment camp, and they agreed with him that things would be different after the war, there would be new opportunities. They would all make money. Big money.

Pa was then in his forty-seventh year. Carlo was fourteen, and he and Nonna had been through a tough time too, keeping the shop going. They managed to hang on to the house, struggling to make the repayments. When Pa came home, though, he was thinner and somehow darker. He had the look of the fox, said Nonna, as though he'd sell you to the Arabs for sixpence. He'd lost most of his hair, but he'd found something else, a quality the Italians call *furbo*, a shrewdness and cunning, and no one was going to get the better of him again. He was going to make money, lots of it. Nothing else mattered. Nonna argued with him, but he wouldn't listen. He was cold to her in a way that he'd never been cold to her before, as though the very substance of her being had evaporated and she was no longer visible to him. She became more silent than ever, spending her days and evenings in the kitchen, while Pa turned the living room into an office. Strange men called for him late at night and Nonna would make them coffee and leave them to it.

Not long after the war, Pa built a garage in the back garden, one for two cars, even though he had no car at all at first. Strange machines began to appear, heavy, in painted cast iron, some with the motif of an Indian chief on the front, some with a bell. They come from America, Pa told Carlo, for the gambling. People like to gamble. But keep it quiet, eh? Tell nobody.

When Carlo left school he began working for Pa in the fish and chip shop. But he was fascinated by the machines in the garage with their big levers and their reels with painted symbols—fruit, bells, gold medallions. You put in a special metal token which looked like a coin but had a hole in the middle. Then you pulled the lever and the machine filled with a mysterious energy, seeming to crouch before it released itself with a loud crack. Then the reels would spin so fast that the symbols became just a blur before—chunk, chunk, chunk! They stopped, one after the other, and delivered their verdict— three cherries for your token back, three lemons for double, three medallions for the jackpot. More often than not, he was quick to notice, the barrels would stop at a losing combination and the machine would keep your token. Because he was always hanging about in the garage, Pa gave Carlo the job of feeding a certain number of tokens into each machine to see how much it gave back. Too much, and Pa would make an adjustment inside. Give them just enough back to encourage them to keep playing, he said. That's how we do it.

In the mornings, before going to work at the shop, Carlo would test the machines and watch Pa tinker with them, take them apart, put them together. He loved the smell of oil and metal, the way the bits fitted snugly together, the intricacy of springs and plates. Pa had set up a bench and he'd fashion pieces of scrap metal into replacement parts. The bench was cluttered with old flywheels and bits of clockwork. He showed Carlo how the machines worked, and before long had him cutting and filing and bending, testing coin mechanisms, adjusting them to accept the metal tokens instead of dimes. Late at night, an old van would reverse into the driveway, and men in dark clothes loaded the machines and took them away. Sometimes Pa went with them, sometimes not. Carlo watched them from the dark of his bedroom window but it would be a while yet before he knew where they went.

By morning the machines were back in the garage. Pa counted wads of cash on a bench at the back and Carlo would help with this too. The money was sorted and then locked in a cabinet under the bench. So much money. Carlo wanted to know what Pa did with it.

It goes to the bank.

All of it?

Some of it I give to Sandro, and some to Joe.

Uncle Sandro and little Joe were Pa's associates. Sandro wasn't Carlo's real uncle, just one of Pa's friends from the internment camp. Little Joe was a year or so older than Carlo, a quiet boy, tall and gangly, whose trouser legs were always too short.

And the other man, Pa. Does he get some too?

Pa paused and looked at Carlo. The other man was dark and sharply dressed, and when he smiled gold glinted in his teeth. Carlo had seen him a couple of times, though they'd never met. From his bedroom window he'd watched the man and his father gesticulate in conversation before they went into the garage where the machines were.

Pa said, Yes, he gets some too. One day you'll understand.

By the time Carlo was eighteen, Pa had opened a cafe as well as the fish and chip shop, and had bought himself an old pre-war car. It was 1948. Carlo still worked in the shops, but he spent more and more time with the machines in Pa's garage. He knew now how they worked, how to balance the coin mechanism, how to tension the kickers and how to change the symbols on the reels and adjust the slot depths on the reel shaft so that the machine stopped on fewer winning combinations. He knew all these things, but he still didn't know where the machines went at night, though he had a damned good idea. Carlo was sick of the chip shop. He wanted to work with the machines, to go with Pa and the others at night to wherever they went. But Pa wouldn't let him. He didn't want his son mixed up in this.

On Sundays Sandro and little Joe sometimes came for supper. They spoke Italian together, although Sandro spoke English with a broad Glasgow accent, thicker than Carlo's accent because Sandro was born and raised in Possilpark. He was a small man, jovial, with a round red face and a receding hairline, though he wasn't that old, his remaining hair still shiny and black. He liked a joke. On one occasion Carlo took advantage of the relaxed mood around the supper table to ask Sandro where they took the machines at night. Sandro looked embarrassed. His face creased into an apologetic smile and he shrugged his shoulders and held both his hands palm up and said, Ah canny tell ye, son. Ye'll huv tae ask yer da.

He won't tell me. Will you, Pa?

Pa put down his knife and fork. Finish your supper, Carlo. Here, have some more polpette.

He spooned some meatballs onto Carlo's plate. Then he got up. Come, Sandro, let's go next door.

Sandro reluctantly wiped his mouth with a serviette and stood up, nodding his thanks to Nonna, who was busy at the stove. As he passed Carlo he gave him a brief pat on the shoulder but said nothing and followed Pa through to the living room, closing the door behind him. Carlo was left with little Joe, who sat silently concentrating on his food. There was no point in asking Joe anything, Carlo thought, you couldn't get a useful word out of him. He doubted little Joe could talk at all.

Suddenly angry, Carlo stood up, his chair scraping on the lino and startling Nonna, who dropped a spoon into the sink. Even little Joe stopped eating, a forkful of polpette halfway to his open mouth. Nonna went to say something but she was too late, Carlo was already striding through the door to the living room. A moment later, he had closed it behind him and stood, calm now, looking at the startled faces of Pa and Sandro. They were sitting at the coffee table. Sandro had a notebook on his lap which he quickly snapped shut. Pa said, What is it, Carlo? I don't want to be disturbed.

Carlo felt his mouth go dry. He wanted to say something eloquent, to present an argument that made sense. You don't trust me, was all he could manage.

His words fell to the floor before they could reach across the room. The two older men glanced at each other. Then Pa said, We have business here. I'll talk to you later.

No, now. Talk to me now, Pa. Ah want to know about your business.

Later! Now leave us.

Carlo hesitated, but he turned and left the room.

Pa did come and talk to him later, knocking on his bedroom door and sitting on the chair by the window. Carlo was lying on the bed, still with his clothes on. In the dim light from the bedside lamp, Pa told him a few things, most of which Carlo had already guessed, and some of which were new to him. Pa talked about the machines and how they were taken each night to a different place, sometimes to the back room of a pub or a club, sometimes to a private address. Gambling machines were illegal, but Carlo already knew this, it was what drew him irresistibly to them. And they all but printed their own money. The punters paid cash for the tokens to play the machines, the owners of the venues were paid a cut of the takings, the police were 'encouraged' to turn a blind eye. There were eight machines. That was the extent of Pa's gambling operation, eight machines, three men and a van. But it made more money than Pa had ever made before. You had to trust people, Pa said, but the secret was not to trust too much, to be able to spot trouble coming and to know when to cut and run. If you're careful, you can make money. If not, you can end up in jail. Or worse, dead.

But Carlo wasn't scared. He asked Pa about the man with the gold teeth.

You mean Calabresi?

That's his name, Calabresi?

Calabresi. He's the money man, Carlo. He helped me get started.

You owe him money?

Yes, I owe him money.

And interest, eh?

Pa looked closely at Carlo, paused before he said, That too.

Ah can help you.

Pa sighed. You're too young, Carlo. Besides, I don't want you in this business. It's a dirty business.

Not too dirty for you, Pa.

That's enough now. Finished. Go to bed.

Pa got up and left the room.

And maybe that's where it would have ended, and Carlo would have spent his days dealing in potato chips rather than gambling chips, battering fish rather than battering rival gangsters. But fate, as they say, intervened.

One morning not long afterwards, Carlo was woken by the sound of the van rolling into the driveway. It rattled noisily to a stop and then there was silence. No doors opened or shut, no men talked quietly in Italian. The clock on the bedside table said it was two thirty in the morning. Much too early. Carlo jumped out of bed and went downstairs in his pyjamas. He opened the back door and switched on the outside light. The van had stopped nose-first against the garage doors. It seemed to Carlo to be sitting too high on its springs which meant that it was empty of the heavy machines. Maybe they'd just forgotten something? Maybe they'd sent Joe back to pick up whatever it was? But then, as Carlo watched, the driver's door clicked open a couple of inches, stopped, and then swung out heavily. A second later, someone fell out of the door and onto the bitumen. It was Pa. He lay there, cursing to himself in Italian, and when Carlo reached him he saw that his face was a mass of bruises and there was blood on his shirt.

Pa, what happened? Who did this?

Pa struggled to sit up. I'm alright!

He spoke sharply, and when Carlo tried to help him Pa pushed him away. Carlo saw Nonna standing at the kitchen doorway in her dressing-gown and slippers. She stood there with a look of something like disgust on her face, and then she turned away into the kitchen.

Pa pointed into the van. Sandro. Joe. Help them.

Carlo peered into the cab of the van but could see no one.

In the back, Pa said. They're in the back.

When he wrenched open the back doors, Carlo saw the dark outlines of Sandro and little Joe lying on a bit of old cardboard packing on the floor of the van. Sandro raised himself. He was obviously in pain, but Carlo helped him out onto the driveway and led him into the kitchen. He sat him down in one of the kitchen chairs. Nonna had made coffee and she put a cup on the table in front of him. Sandro looked only slightly better off than Pa, but there was a bad gash over one of his eyes and each breath he took seemed to be agony for him. When Carlo got back to the van, Pa was on his feet trying to talk to little Joe, who seemed to be unconscious. Blood glistened on little Joe's face, and there was a large stain soaking through one of his trouser legs and into the dirty cardboard. Pa said, He needs a hospital. Get dressed, Carlo. Quickly. You'll have to take us. I can't drive no more.

Carlo drove them to the casualty ward at the Royal Infirmary, where they told the doctors they'd been attacked by a gang of youths after a night on the town. Sandro had a broken rib, Joe had concussion and a knife wound in his thigh. Pa was badly bruised, but had got off lightly compared to the other two. The hospital kept Joe in for a couple of days, but Sandro came home with Pa, the two of them swathed in bandages. Nonna found them both clean clothes to change into and made some more coffee. In the front room, Sandro lay on the sofa while Pa sat heavily in his old armchair. Behind the bandages his skin had a grey pallor and his eyes looked weary and sad. Finally he said, I'm finished. No more machines. It's all gone. Then he told Carlo the full story of what had happened that night.

They had taken the machines to a new venue, he said, a place outside Glasgow, off the road to Coatbridge. It was a private house, a large dark stone building reached by a long driveway and set next to a golf course. All very grand, said Pa, and well out of the way of prying eyes. Not their usual sort of venue. They parked the van at the back of the house and were met there by a couple of guys who took them inside and showed them the room where they were to set up the machines. It was a ground-floor room, no stairs, an easy carry for them. Pa noticed there was another room with a blackjack table and a roulette wheel. A couple of waiters in uniform walked past with trays full of glasses, and there was a young man in evening dress setting up what looked like the bank, a table stacked with chips and a large metal cashbox.

The three of them lugged the machines in and set them up where they'd been told to. They tested them, made a few quick adjustments, gave them a polish. The float of tokens was locked in the van and would stay there until just before the punters arrived. After that, it was Pa's job to keep the bank, counting out tokens and taking the cash. Sandro would mingle with the punters, quick on the scene whenever anyone tipped the jackpot, all affable smiles and compliments for the women, a hand on the shoulder for the men. Joe did running repairs on the machines, clearing blocked tokens mostly, or adjusting the coin mechanism. On good nights, he also emptied the cashbox and sorted the tokens for reselling.

They finished setting up well before the first punters were due at around eleven o'clock. Pa went for a look around the house. He felt distinctly underdressed as he wandered through the spacious rooms with their high ceilings and oak-lined walls hung with old portraits. In one room there was a mounted stag's head high on one wall and a nineteenth-century blunderbuss on another. Pa stopped to look at a large display cabinet full of hunting trophies. He was reading the inscription on a brass plaque when he had the first inkling that things weren't quite right. As he stood there, he heard the sound of a fruit machine being played. The sound was coming from a door at the far side of the room. It was standing slightly ajar, and Pa quietly made his way over and peered into the room beyond. What he saw there made him gasp. A room full of fruit machines such as he'd never before seen, each one shiny and new, set in varnished wooden cabinets. Some were plugged into the wall and were lit up like Christmas trees, one even had four reels instead of three. There must have been about twenty of them altogether. Two men in tuxedos were testing the payouts. The machines were quiet, Pa noticed, sleek and modern. And even as he wondered what the hell they were doing here, he felt a sting of envy. What he could do with machines like these! The money he could make!

And then he saw Calabresi. He was standing at the far end of the room, counting a wad of notes. At that point, Pa said, he knew he was in trouble, though he didn't know exactly what kind of trouble, only that the man with the gold teeth shouldn't be there. The money men always kept their distance, that's how they operated, well away from the scene of the action. Calabresi growled something at one of the tuxedoed men who answered, Right ye are, boss, and started walking towards the door that Pa was hiding behind. Pa nipped away. His heart pounding, he raced back to the room where he'd left Sandro and Joe, but as he got there he was almost bowled over by a man wheeling a trolley out through the doorway. On the trolley was one of Pa's machines. He rushed into the room and straight into the arms of two burly men who grabbed him and forced him to the ground. One of them arm-locked his neck and clamped a hand over his mouth, the other hit him with something—a fist, a cosh, he didn't know what. The next thing he knew, he was lying in the dark. It was freezing, and something heavy was pushing into his chest. He touched it and recoiled in shock as his hand came away wet. It was a leg, and it was dripping blood. For a moment, Pa was back in that trench in the mountains, trapped under the weight of the dead. He began to panic, fighting for breath, scrabbling to get out. As he pushed the leg off him, a light flickered briefly and he heard a low rumble and the wheels of a passing car, not far off. It was a sign from God, he said, as clear to him as any heavenly angel, and he realised then that he was lying in the back of the van. Someone moaned next to him and he felt around in the darkness and found Joe, and then Sandro lying next to him. Joe was in a bad way. Pa struggled out of the back of the van and eased himself into the driver's seat. He pushed the starter a couple of times and jiggled with the choke until the engine rattled into life, and when he turned the headlights on he saw that they had been dumped in a narrow lane bordered by thick hedgerows. His head was pounding and his face was so swollen he could barely see, but he put the van into gear and drove off slowly in the direction of the passing traffic and found himself on the Edinburgh Road, about twenty minutes or so from home.

Now he sat there in the early morning light in the living room, slumped and exhausted. Carlo had felt himself growing angrier and angrier as Pa told the story, but he willed himself to stay calm. Pa, why did this happen?

He wanted more money. I paid him on time, but he wanted more or he would—

Who, Pa? Who?

Calabresi. We had an agreement, but he wanted more. Always more.

And you refused?

What else could I do, Carlo? Work for a pittance?

And now he's repossessed the machines. Who is he, Mafia?

Pa looked at Carlo and gave a small shrug. Mafia. I don't know.

Ye should know, Pa. Ye should know what you're getting yourself into.

I know that he's a bastard and he's fucked us good. That's what I know.

This Calabresi, how did you meet him?

Sandro knows him. He worked for him before the war.

But Sandro was asleep on the sofa. Carlo would have to wait to get the information he wanted. A plan was hatching inside his head. A crazy plan, a dangerous plan, a plan that would either set him up for life or see him under the river in a pair of concrete overshoes. But he was damned if he was going to let Calabresi walk all over them.

There are moments in our lives that make us or break us. That determine the kind of person we're going to be, the kind of mark we're going to leave on the world, whether we're going to lead, or whether we're going to follow. For most of us, these moments come and go without us really being aware of how crucial they are; it's only years later, faced perhaps with death, or forced to think about it through illness or breakdown or tragedy, that we finally recognise the missed opportunity, the wrong turning, the bad decision. Or maybe the opposite: that a crucial event has pushed us forward to success beyond our hopes. Carlo would reject this idea. Carlo would tell you that you're talking bullshit, that opportunities are there to be seized and exploited, twisted and bent to your own design. There are no happy accidents, only winners and losers.

So what did Carlo do when Pa was done over by Calabresi and company? How did he turn this incident into an opportunity for himself? He told me the story when I was a child, on one of the rare occasions we talked. He was on holiday with us, which in itself was rare enough, and I suppose he was relaxed. Personally, I don't believe a word he said. I wouldn't trust him to talk straight even if he was giving his last confession. But here it is anyway, for what it's worth. You can judge for yourself.

What he did took him nearly a year of plotting and planning. It was this: he worked hard in the fish and chip shop, afternoons and evenings until ten thirty, every evening except Sunday; he took a sudden interest in going out after work, with friends he said, to have fun. And to be sure, that's partly what he did. He went to the dancing, and sometimes to clubs. More often, though, he went to gambling dens, where he mingled with the punters—gaunt men in tight suits, women dressed in faded evening wear. Carlo noticed how silent they were, and how greedily they fed coins to the machines. But he spent more time talking to the guys who worked these places than he did gambling, and he quickly got the picture of how the operations were run.

His plan depended on one thing—Calabresi had no idea who he was. In fact, nobody in the gambling business knew who he was, because Pa had been so intent on keeping him out of it. So he was able to make a few things up for himself, about who he was and where he came from, and gradually he got to know a few people, to help out here and there, to be trusted by them.

Within six months, he said, he was working for Calabresi himself. He'd infiltrated the enemy. While Pa and Nonna thought he was out on the town trying to find a nice girl to marry, he was in fact to be found at one seedy pub or another, or some basement or private house, setting up Calabresi's shiny new machines, fixing coin mechanisms and faulty payouts, counting tokens and throwing out unruly customers, roughing them up in the best gangster tradition. He did all these things, and learnt how to do much more: how to dress well, how to use knuckledusters, how to charm and delude the boss. And Calabresi fell for it. Barely three months after he started working for him, Carlo was in charge of the fruit machine operation. If that sounds far-fetched, you should hear the embellishments: how Calabresi declared Carlo a genius for his skill with the machines; how Carlo saved Calabresi's life when an angry punter attacked him with a knife; how a grateful Calabresi introduced Carlo to his eldest daughter with a heavy hint that they should get to know one another.

Calabresi was a small man, stocky and dark and fleshy in the face. The gold in his teeth was his only affectation apart from his suits, which, though elegantly cut, were sober in style. There were large pouches under his eyes and a carefully clipped silver moustache under his prominent nose. Every time he saw him, Carlo had to fight the urge to knock him over and give him a good kicking. He had a better fate in store for him, one that would be more satisfying and long-lasting.

And anyway, he was learning a lot about the gambling business, and he was pulling good money too. Enough to buy a car—not a flash one because he wasn't stupid, and Pa had to believe that he'd saved up for it, but a nice car right enough. It was well worth it to bide his time, even to weather the attentions of the Calabresi daughter, and that's what he did. Until, one night in late November, he took his chance.

Picture the scene, a dimly lit room above a pub just off the Gallowgate. Half-panelled walls and yellowing wallpaper, fake beams in the ceiling. Outside it's wet and cold, and the boys are still dripping from the rain. There are three of them, including Carlo. They've just finished setting up the fruit machines and they've passed around the fags and lit up, taking a wee break after hauling the heavy machines up the steep flight of stairs. The room is big, but it's filled to the brim with machines, including a couple of the ones that used to belong to Pa.

But look closely now at the two men with Carlo and you'll maybe recognise the familiar features of Sandro and little Joe. They look good, don't they? Relaxed and confident. Better dressed, too. Carlo let them in on his plans some weeks ago, and they're happy to be working for him. Calabresi's men, the ones that Carlo was supposed to be working with that night, are bound and gagged and locked up in the back of a furniture lorry, which is parked in the lane behind the pub.

In a little while Carlo will go downstairs to make a phone call . . .

But right now there's work to be done. On the floor there stood a large wooden case, like a wartime ammunition box. Sandro opened it.

Whit d'ye think? No bad, eh?

Inside the box there were a number of mechanical objects, oiled and gleaming. Carlo reached in and pulled out a small assembly. It looked like a gear but with notches of different depths. He checked it over.

Looks good.

These bits of machinery were the genius at the heart of Carlo's plan. For weeks he and Sandro and little Joe had toiled in secret, stealing some of the parts, making others out of scrap metal, cutting and filing and polishing. Sandro said, That yin's fur the Bell o'er there. It's marked, see? They're aw marked, one fur each machine.

Carlo nodded. Let's go, we haven't much time.

He pulled a bunch of keys from his pocket. One by one the machines were opened and their inside mechanisms slid out. Working quickly, the three men dismantled the reel assemblies and replaced some of the parts with the specially prepared ones. Then they tested the machines and, satisfied, locked them up again. Now they were ready for the punters. There was a queue forming up the stairs as Carlo made his way down to the smoky bar and elbowed his way through a throng of men in flat caps. The sawdust on the floor was wet in spots, and a number of the men were already drunk. He reached the bar and asked to use the phone and the landlord let him through and led him into a small office. It was quieter there. He dialled Calabresi's private number. After a couple of rings, the phone was picked up and the heavy voice said, Pronto. Hello?

It's Carlo. Ye'd better get over here quick. There's trouble.

What kind of trouble?

But Carlo hung up the phone and rushed back upstairs. Calabresi, he knew, would be here within ten minutes. It was time to let the punters in.

Carlo took his place at the cash table and signalled Sandro to open up shop. Soon the room was full of people jostling and queuing to buy tokens for the machines. They weren't your usual crowd. Amongst the faded suits and fake pearls there were more than a few flat caps, the faces underneath them angular and hard-set. The room filled with cigarette smoke and the sound of handles cranking and reels spinning.

The first jackpot went off within minutes, followed by a squeal of surprise from a lady in a fox fur as the machine spewed out so many tokens they spilled over onto the floor. People stared in amazement at the amount of money she'd just made herself. Must be at least twenty quid, the jammy old cow! But their attention quickly shifted when another whoop was heard at the opposite end of the room. Another jackpot, another fountain of tokens. Then the big Jennings paid out, flashing and banging. Everyone who had a machine in front of them started furiously plying the things with tokens, others pressed behind them waiting for a turn. Machine after machine went jackpot until the whole room was pande-monium, people trying to push each other out of the way, cursing and swearing, desperate to get their chance to win. A fight broke out in one corner, and over at the cash table the growing band of lucky winners crowded around Carlo, holding up hatfuls of tokens and demanding their cash.

Carlo held up his arms. He had to shout over the racket. I don't have enough cash. The boss is just coming. He'll fix ye all up. Look, here he comes now!

Right on cue, Calabresi made his entrance, flanked by two of his goons. Before he could fully realise what he'd let himself in for, he found himself being pushed and shunted by the braying mob of punters. His sidekicks lashed out with their coshes, and that was the start of it. Suddenly there were coshes and knuckledusters and fists flying everywhere as the men that Carlo had hired especially for the occasion went about their business. Within a couple of minutes, Calabresi's bodyguards were lying in a heap at the bottom of the stairs and Calabresi himself was trying desperately to explain to the crowd that he had no cash to pay their winnings.

The crowd surged and seethed around Calabresi and he disappeared within it, his arms flailing as if he were being sucked into quicksand, his mouth opening and closing. They swept him out of the room, down the staircase and into the street, where his cries echoed off the black tenements and brought people to their windows to watch the spectacle. Calabresi and his henchmen were found later in a backstreet gutter, bruised and tattered, in varying states of consciousness.

While this retribution was being taken, Carlo and the boys went down to the back lane and opened the doors of the lorry. They untied the men they'd imprisoned in the back and took their gags off, and Carlo offered them jobs with a bit more money and a better future. They didn't take much persuading, and moments later they were helping lug the machines down the stairs and into the lorry. By the time Calabresi had had his nose broken and his wallet filched, they were well away, with Carlo, Sandro and little Joe laughing their heads off.

The next morning, Carlo told Pa that he was quitting the fish and chip shop.

What do you mean? Where will you go?

In answer, Carlo led Pa into the garage. It was full of fruit machines, gleaming like some genie's hidden treasure. Pa stood and stared at them for a long time, his jaw hanging loose, while Carlo told him the story of the previous night. Then he looked at Carlo and it was as if he was seeing a different person, someone he only partly recognised, a man who was *furbo* in a way that he himself could never be, dangerous and powerful with it. And as he looked, he felt that everything he'd strived for was futile and lost and had somehow become twisted by the inexorable logic of life and time. He was just a tired old man.

This is what you want, Carlo?

This is what ah want, Pa.

And how will I run the shops alone?

Carlo smiled his lopsided smile. Forget the shops, he said. It's your turn to work for me.

And that's how Carlo got started. Or so he said. When it comes down to it, we're all just the stories we tell about ourselves, true or false.

But whether you believe him or not, there's one very real thing in his story that Carlo left out. And it's this: while he was spending all those late-night hours at gambling dens and dance halls—or whatever the hell he *was* doing—he met my mother. He danced with her—like an angel, she said—and she melted like chocolate into his strong arms.

Something like that.

7

IT'S EARLY EVENING NOW, dark outside and raining. I sit
in the gloom of Trixie's kitchen and listen to the steady
drip, drip, drip of a blocked gutter, the gurgling of water
collecting around the drain. The end of my first day back in
Glasgow, and now there's the night to face and all the ghosts
that come with it. I don't have to stay, I could easily go to
a hotel, but something keeps me here, something perverse
but inescapable, as though after all these years of hiding I've
finally been caught, backed into a corner, no escape. It's time
to face up to things, and if that means going head to head
with the ghosts of my childhood, so be it. I've found a half-
full bottle of whisky in the cupboard. I pour myself another
glass and drift off into thoughts of how the funeral might

be tomorrow, who would be there. What we might say to each other.

When the phone rings, it takes me a while to realise what it is because the sound is unfamiliar and because it has to reach in and drag me out of my thoughts. It quite literally rings, the way modern phones don't. Then it stops, and after a second it starts again. The third time I get up from my chair and pick it up. I hold it to my ear but I don't say anything. After a pause, a man's voice says, Eh, hello.

Who is it? I'm surprised at the croak in my voice, the tired, timid sound of it.

Is that you, Donny?

Who's that?

It's Malkie. D'ye remember me? Ah thought ye might be home.

I knew the news of my return would spread fast enough, but Wee Malkie is the last person I expect to hear from. I had abandoned him all those years ago as much as I'd abandoned my family, and to be honest with you, I hadn't given him much thought since, except as another person who belonged in the past and who was therefore meaningless now. That's what I'd always believed. That escape was final, that it was possible to wipe the slate clean and start afresh, that nothing from the old could intrude on the new. I was wrong. More wrong than I ever wanted to admit. People are more than the flesh and blood and bustle that exists alongside you—the giving and taking and coming and going of the real world. No, people live inside your head, or at least some of them do. They live inside your head and you can never escape them.

That's what I'd come to believe, because I'd spent the last thirty years in dire battle with the family that lived inside me, and it's a shock now to realise that there's a Wee Malkie in there too, suddenly activated by his voice on the phone. When he suggests we meet for a pint, I find myself saying yes.

Bannerman's is an old pub about twenty minutes away from the house. I'd been there a couple of times before, as an underage drinker, and I remembered a warm cosy bar, oak-raftered and low-lit, packed with punters, a jukebox in the corner and the smell of beer and cigarettes. There was a ladies' bar at the back, which was much quieter, with tartan carpet.

I walk there now through the rain, which has turned to a steady drizzle, the kind you think isn't too heavy until you find yourself drenched. And that's how I arrive at the pub, my jacket dripping and my hair plastered to my skull. It's busy as usual, full of people with dripping clothes and wet hair, but when I look around for Malkie there's no one there who seems to fit the bill. I don't know what I expected, really. I can barely remember what he looked like beyond a tousle-haired kid, small and wiry with a face that crumpled when he laughed. Malkie and I had been inseparable, for so many years it seemed, part of each other in the way that only children can be, with a loyalty that only childhood friendships can have. But in the end, Wee Malkie betrayed me, so he did.

And he was always late.

I make my way through the throng to the bar, which isn't quite where I remembered it to be. The oak rafters and the tobacco-stained stucco is gone, replaced by low ceilings with recessed lighting. The bar is stainless steel and there's a pair of televisions high on one wall, one of which is showing replays of a soccer match, the other a parade of bikini-clad models. Both are silent. I get myself a beer and settle on a stool. I'll give him twenty minutes, I think, and then I'll get out of this. But I really want to just get up and go there and then, and I'm surprised how nervous I feel. I've always hated sitting in pubs on my own, and I know that I look as desperate as every other middle-aged man nursing a lonely glass in any pub you care to look in, from here to bloody Timbuktu. I should have shaved before I came out.

Wee Malkie betrayed me, though even now I'm not sure he meant to. Was that what he wanted to talk to me about? He didn't say on the phone, and I didn't ask, and I don't know if he even thinks about it, but I certainly do. And I'm not sure if I'm still angry with him or not.

So I sip on my pint and look around the bar, trying to recognise anyone. All the plastic-topped tables seem to be full of people, talking and laughing with each other. There's a game of darts going on in the corner, and I think maybe I know the guy who's steadily taking aim and throwing like a professional. It isn't Wee Malkie though. This guy is short, with a beer belly and grey stubble, and he's wearing a flat cap, which makes him look like the old drunks who'd peppered the streets of Glasgow when I was a kid. They always seemed to wear a flat cap and a particular kind of jacket, dark maybe, with a small check. In winter there would be a scarf tied like a muffler. The thing is, this guy's about the same age as me, and I wonder what process has gone on in his growing up that's led to him looking today exactly like his father and his grandfather. When he was young his hair would have been shoulder-length and the flapping of the flares on his jeans would have set off tornadoes in the antipodes. He would have listened to heavy metal and taken any kind of drug he could lay his hands on—acid, speed, dope. Whether he realised it or not, he would have wanted to change the world, to undermine all the old values and customs and ways of being. At what point in life do you say to yourself, that's enough of that, time to get a flat cap and perfect my darts game?

My thoughts are interrupted when I see Wee Malkie come through the door. I recognise him instantly, though he's taller and leaner than I remember, and a little stooped around the shoulders. His hair is grey and cropped and he wears a leather coat and denims, a stud in one ear. At least he doesn't have a flat cap. In fact he looks vaguely fashionable, like some middle-aged people manage to look, still part of the moment, despite the advancing years. He walks into the bar and looks around uncertainly, and I'm suddenly anxious he might recognise me as easily as I do him. I turn away. There's still time to get up and sneak out quietly through the ladies' lounge, to do what I always do—run away. But I tell myself that I'm not running away anymore, that I've stopped doing that. I'm facing things now, unflinching, resolute, strong. I slip off my stool and start heading for the door.

Donny?

The voice is just at my back, closer than I would have expected Malkie to be. He must have spotted me and come straight over, so I turn around and put a smile on. Closer up

I can see the lines on his face, the sagging under the eyes. But the grin is unmistakeable: the two squinty teeth, the same crumpled geniality.

Malkie? How's it going?

He laughs and looks at me, shaking his head. Fuck, Donny. Ye haven't changed a bit.

But Wee Malkie has changed. Not just in the obvious ways—older, bigger, wiser or more stupid—but in ways that are more subtle and which only become apparent as we talk together that night, first in the pub, and then in the Indian restaurant up the road. As kids it was always me who was top dog, and Malkie went along with it, easygoing and easily led. He didn't seem to mind doing what I wanted, content to play a supporting role in the drama that centred around my growing up. That's what I'd always felt, anyway. The Wee Malkie I knew was good for a laugh, up for anything, and not particularly bright.

But the man sitting across the restaurant table has a kind of authority and self-possession that I wasn't expecting. It shows in the intelligence of his questions, the way he listens as I tell him a highly edited version of my story. How do you tell a story like that, over dinner and a beer or two, to someone you haven't seen for thirty years? Yes, I'm editing, concealing, holding back, because that's my nature and because somewhere in the back of my mind I can hear Trixie telling me to *never trust naebody*. I can tell that Malkie isn't convinced, that he isn't going to play along, and I begin to feel that our talk is not equal. Whenever I ask him questions about himself, he very quickly comes back to my story, worrying away at bits of it, dragging it out of me. I discover exactly three things about Malkie that night. One, he's a lecturer in cultural studies at one of the newer universities. Two, he likes very hot curries. Three, he's married to my sister, Luce.

I nearly choke on my biryani when he tells me that. Married to Luce! How could that be? For the life of me I can't imagine those two together, not from what I know of them anyway. Christ, what's been going on since I was away? You can't turn your back for a minute. I take a long drink of beer and try to compose myself, to smile and seem cheerful.

When did you get married?

Uch, nearly twenty-five years now. He says this with some pride in his voice.

Any kids?

Naw. No kids. Malkie shrugs. Just never seemed tae happen. How about you?

No, I lie. Me neither. I can't bear to tell him anything about my life as a divorced loser, living in a dark one-bedroom flat in an unfashionable part of Sydney. Especially that I haven't seen my kids in years.

The conversation stumbles on in this way, each of us trying to deflect the other from anything too real. I can tell, though, that Wee Malkie isn't happy. I've seen enough unhappy people to know. And I also confirm that our friendship has not survived the long years of separation, not that there was much chance of that in the circumstances, even before I found out about him and Luce. The thing is, Malkie is there that night with a purpose, not for a pleasant conversation about old times.

The restaurant is starting to empty and I'm blethering on about Sydney, trying to make out I have some sort of good life going on over there that he should be envious of. Malkie leans over the table and interrupts me. They didny expect ye tae come, Donny.

His tone, the look of concern on his face. I want to lamp him one there and then. But I put my glass down and say, Is that right? Why not?

Uch, well, you know. The way ye left an that. Yer mum . . .

I heard that Trixie asked for me, Malkie. When she was dying. Did you know that?

Malkie looked shocked. Who told ye that?

What did she say, Malkie?

Nobody thought ye'd come, Donny. It was just . . .

For fuck's sake! I strike the table with my fist, making the dishes jump and turning the heads of concerned diners nearby. What the hell did she say? Did she want to see me?

Malkie looks away, and something in the gesture tells me he's lying when he says, Ah don't know, Donny. Honest ah don't. Ask Kenny.

I let out a long sigh. As if I'd ever ask Mr Disco anything.

So let me get this straight, Malkie. Trixie asked for me, on her deathbed, and not one of you bastards bothered your arses to try and find me. Is that it?

Malkie motioned me to keep my voice down. Look, she just wanted ye tae know that she was . . . ye know, near the end. She was haverin, Donny. She thought ye'd maybe come. She never got over the way ye left, know what ah mean?

I'm not sure I do know what you mean, Malkie.

She was hurt. Ye wouldn't believe how bad she was afterwards, what the family had tae put up with. Everyone blamed
you.

Aye, well, that would be right, wouldn't it? All my fault.

Donny, no one expected tae see ye again.

No one wanted to, you mean?

It was your choice tae leave the way ye did.

Was it?

Wee Malkie looks at me with his academic's eye. A look that
says, Think a wee bit harder, laddie, look beyond the obvious.
But I'm way ahead of him already and I realise that my uneasiness with him is because I had him all sussed out from the
beginning and I've been waiting for this moment to confirm
my suspicions. It's time to stop pretending we're friends.

Do they still call you Wee Malkie, Malkie?

A look of impatience crosses his face. Not for a long time.
Donny, listen . . .

D'you still wet the bed, Malkie? I remember you had that
problem.

Donny . . .

And your eczema, eh? God you were an itchy, smelly wee
bastard, so you were, Malkie. And look at you now. But underneath that sleek, sophisticated, twenty-first century man,
there lies an itchy, smelly wee bastard still. Is that not right,
Malkie? Who wet the bed and couldn't tie his own fuckin
shoelaces, eh?

I think he's going to get up and leave there and then. He
looks around and then back at me. Yer a fuckin arsehole,
Donny. Ye always were.

Is that your considered analysis, Professor?

Malkie calls the waiter for the bill. There's a look on his face which has really been there all night but which he had, I suppose, been trying hard to conceal. The kind of pinched look some squeamish people put on when they're forced to deal with something unpleasant, like cleaning dog shite off their shoe, or wiping up someone else's vomit. I get a sudden glimpse of the real Malkie and it isn't nice at all, but now, I think, we'll get to the point of the matter. I'm right.

Listen, pal. The family long ago disowned you, d'ye understand that? Ye don't belong here, and we don't want ye at the funeral. Nobody wants any trouble.

What sort of trouble are they expecting, Malkie?

Malkie sighs. Ye know what ah mean. He pulls something from his wallet. Kenny says tae give you this.

He slips a piece of paper across the table. I pick it up and see it's a cheque. For ten thousand pounds.

That's tae get ye back tae Sydney. An a wee bit extra.

A bribe, Malkie? Is that what this is?

It's a token, Donny. We understand what ye've been through.

The waiter comes and places the bill on the table in front of Malkie. I look at the cheque and think for a moment what I could do with ten thousand pounds and it doesn't take me long to conclude that I could do nothing that would help me feel any better. The problem with money is that it never keeps its promise and even a hundred thousand pounds wouldn't be enough to shut off the nagging in my head—the damned Trixie in my head who's always there, haranguing and harrying, leading me on into my own madness. *C'mon, son, it's no that bad. Other people go through much worse. Here, ah've made ye a cheese sandwich.* I look at Malkie but what I see is Trixie's dead face and what I feel is the grain of her cold forehead on my lips. I take the cheque and tear it slowly into strips and litter the tabletop with them.

Right, said Malkie, more to himself than to me. Ah've done what ah can.

He pulls some cash from his wallet and puts it with the bill. As he stands up to go I say, Tell them I'm goin to be there, Malkie. In fact, tell them I'll be at every one of their bloody funerals too. Just so's I can gloat. It's my reason for living, Malkie.

Malkie buttons up his jacket. Ah'm sorry for ye, Donny. Yer a poor, sad bastard, so ye are. It would have been better for everyone if yer bloody curse had come true.

And then he's gone, a flurry of rain blowing in through the door behind him. I look at the money on the table and see that he's only left enough to pay for his half of the meal.

Wee Malkie betrayed me once, so what? Just business as bloody usual. But Trixie, though. She'd asked for me. And nobody bothered to let me know.

As I sit there in the restaurant, looking at the rain beyond the glass door, I try to think about Trixie, and what it means, this asking for me, whatever the hell it was, and whether she knew what she was doing. But I'm too agitated, and I can't conjure up anything concrete to give shape to the feeling that I'm being slowly crushed under the weight of her memory, so I order another lager and sit there sipping on it while the last customers leave and the waiters hover by the door, glancing at me with closing time looks. And what comes into my head is this: the day Wee Malkie stole my lunch.

Why am I thinking about that? We were at Elderbank Zoo, on a school excursion, and Malkie was behaving like a wee shite, just like he was tonight, and that's partly why I remembered the stolen lunch. But the lunch isn't important now, though I could have killed the wee fucker at the time. Get to the point. There was something else that day at the zoo. Something I've not been talking about. Something I can't . . .

The Turtle.

There, I've got it out. It's on the page now and no amount of backspace, cut-and-paste, control-alt-bloody-delete is going to make it go away. Because before I can tell you about the zoo, the stolen lunch, Trixie, and everything else that's still hanging off this story like a spare prick in a brothel I've got to tell you about this bloody thing I've been struggling with for a long while now. This thing that's been struggling with me, flapping and flailing and desperate to be heard. This thing I feel embarrassed about, but which is too important to keep hidden, because without it there is no story, full stop.

I've got to tell you about the Turtle.

Ah'm no here, remember?
... Uch,
whit is it wi you anyway?
Ye've a face on ye that wid curdle
mustard.
Ye don't want tae talk aboot me,
but withoot me
ye've got fuck nothin tae say.
So get on wi it, wee man. Ye canny huv it two ways.

8

THE RAIN IS COMING DOWN in sheets as I walk back to Trixie's. It's bouncing off the pavements, flowing easily through gutters and drains that were built to handle just this kind of weather. I'm drenched through seconds after leaving the restaurant, my clothes sticking to me and cold water dripping down the back of my neck. Welcome to Scotland the brave and the soggy, where taking the high road is not much of an option. Only low roads lead here now. Low roads and low deeds.

Fuck the rain and all the dreech, dreary shite that passes for life in this godforsaken place. The Turtle would have none of it. Trapped in his dismal pit in the local zoo, he dreamt of waters blue and sparkling under a blazing sun, the warm shallows and the cool depths tumbling and gurgling past him with each easy pull of his flippers. Not only dreamt of it, he told me, but dreamt it fully into existence around him with the power of his own longing. That was one of his tricks. One of our tricks, to be precise, because we're two of a kind, the Turtle and I, two halves of the same desperation, two sides of the same cardboard cut-out. Both of us learnt at an early age the art of escaping inside ourselves, of taking reality and pulling it apart, rebuilding it to bear the weight of our pathetic dreams of freedom. The Turtle was a master. While he cavorted in his own private paradise, all the gawping daytrippers ever saw was a miserable, mould-infested shell and a set of flippers folded tight, cowering at the bottom of a blue-painted concrete tank. That's how he was when I first set eyes on him, but even before then I had an intimation of his coming, and of the part he was to play in my story.

For years I've kept the Turtle locked up in a corner of my memory, bolted behind a heavy door and a set of locks so fiendish in their mechanism that even he couldn't begin to fathom an escape. But that was before now. After everything and before Trixie died. Every minute since her death another cog has turned another notch; another hidden pin sprung open; another ratchet rattled its way towards the final and inevitable mesh of gears and the slow release of bars and bolts. He won't be stopped, so I've got no choice but to yet again go back to the beginning. Or near the beginning, back to when I was eleven years old. Old enough to live fully in the world my mother had created, to bend and warp with her moods, and old enough, too, to start asking awkward questions.

***

We were drowning in sunlight. So much light that the house seemed to float through it. The big window in the living room glowed with the weight of morning.

It was the morning of a day when Trixie had roused herself, tidied up, dressed herself properly. Her hair was brushed and she smelt nice and she talked quietly about interesting things. The sunlight scoured into fusty corners of the house, chasing out days and days of gloom. It all looked different. The furniture was polished and the windows spotless. The lino gleamed and the rug was freshly hoovered. For some reason, I wasn't at school. I was alone with Trixie and by that age I had come to be wary of being alone with her and it didn't happen often. But that morning, I remember, I was captivated by her. It was like she'd just returned from some faraway place after a long, long absence.

We were sitting on the couch, leafing through a book on sea creatures. A child's book, with garish drawings and blurry photographs. There was a section on shellfish, and we came to a particular picture of a shell, just like one that Trixie kept in her old display cabinet in the corner of the living room. Trixie took me by the hand and led me to the cabinet to compare the two. The cabinet was always locked. Luce and I would often peer through the glass doors in fevered fascination at all the things that crammed its shelves. Grown-up things. Dreaming things. Real-life things. There was a shark's tooth and a set of old brass weights, a porcelain doll dressed in silk, a small, carved wooden elephant, a kangaroo's paw. There was Uncle Charlie's medal from the war, and the bullet that killed him, shiny and buckled. There was the wedding present dinner set, the ceramic pixie-shoe ashtray from Cornwall, and, in the middle of the middle shelf, the seashell.

This was Trixie's special shell. The one she would consult for signs and portents or for the telling of fortunes, though we weren't supposed to know that. It was big. Curved and coiling. The opening had edges like teeth, and behind them a cream-coloured gullet that disappeared into mystery. On the outside it was mottled orange and black, and I knew that it was sacred, not only through its powers of divination, but by the way that Trixie never spoke of it. And she never spoke of it, even when we begged her to.

But now she took a key from her pocket. She unlocked the cabinet doors and opened them. She lifted out the shell, and for a long time she stood there looking at it.

And then she told me a story about an island in the far South Seas. A place of blue waters and burning sands. A land with a sun so bright that the people could only come out at night for fear of being blinded. They worshipped a turtle god, for they believed that the world was a giant turtle that carried them upon its back. When the sun went down the islanders would set off in canoes hung with lanterns to attract bellfish and night eels and silver stinging rays. And they'd dive for black pearls and sometimes they'd find shells just like this. She held it up.

If you put it to your ear, she told me, you can hear the roaring of the sea and the shifting of the sand. But if you know what to listen for you can hear much more: the scuttling of crabs; the swish of a shark's tail; the slow creak of coral growing on its own remains. Or, if you listen really hard, you'll hear the whisper of your name, and the shell will tell you what your future holds.

Aye, but does it get Radio Luxembourg?

The slap across my ear made me instantly regret my stupid quip. Trixie looked at me now as if she'd just noticed me for the first time, as though she was trying to puzzle out who this stranger was and what he was doing in her living room. I saw the shadow in her eyes and I willed myself, with all the power I could muster, to believe. To believe her wee fairytale, to surrender to its speywife's logic. If only she'd let me go. But she knelt down beside me. Her face filled the room and her dark eyes held me close.

In a voice that seemed no longer to be hers, she told me that the shell belonged to the Turtle God himself and was created as a present for his queen. Two men died, she said, taking it from the seabed. So angry was the Turtle God that he took them and he trapped their souls inside. Those who are pure of heart can listen to the shell and learn from the wisdom of the Turtle. Those whose hearts are black will hear only the rattling of bones and the awful wailing of torment as the dead souls beg you to release them.

Is yer heart black, Donald Pinelli? Or ur ye pure?

Jesus. Was my heart black? I'd stolen two biscuits from the cupboard that morning and could feel the sugary bits between my teeth even as she spoke. The shell gleamed in her hands, shining with the light of a far-off land. I could feel its power burning through me and I knew the answer Trixie wanted, and I knew my heart was black as Jock the coalman. She held the shell towards me.

Listen.

Ah don't want to.

Listen!

She drew me to her and put the mouth of the shell to my ear. I stopped struggling and I listened.

At first there was a sound like waves on shingle. And I could hear each and every stone as it ground against the others, slowly shaping themselves smooth. As I listened, the shingle gave way to a heavier, colder sound of water plying under rock ledges and surging through reefs and then I felt myself being pulled down into that sucking water, as though the shell itself had swallowed me. I struggled against it but was drawn in over my head, deeper and deeper. Far above, the waves were rising and the sky was turning black, and then I was tumbling in a hissing, gurgling turmoil, fighting to hold my breath, kicking out blindly.

But even as I panicked, I heard what I knew then I'd been listening for all along, and it wasn't the rattling of bones. Deep within the tumbling water, a single voice at first, and then another, and another. And gradually the voices merged to a harmony of such sheer and shameless joy that I swear I felt my own life slip away. I didn't care. I struggled towards that sound, thrashing out in short, fast strokes. All I wanted was to swim amongst those voices, now becoming clearer, which held the promise of something better than the life I had.

And as I swam, the voices and the sea became the same, and I was swimming through pure sound, moving easily across its gentle ebb and flow. And it seemed that I could hold my breath, perhaps forever, and that now I was a creature of the sea, a child of the Turtle God, with a sturdy shell and four handy flippers. I kicked out hard, and felt the singing water part before me. And then I soared and dived and turned and circled and spun to the bottom of the world, and when I got there I grubbed in the sand and settled under the shadow of a rock. For the first time ever in my young life, I felt safe.

And then it stopped. I was on the floor, wet and wallowing, my cheek against the cold lino. Trixie was crouching over me, holding an empty jug. She was gently touching the birthmark on the back of my neck, stroking it with her finger. And she had a look on her face that I'd never seen before. As if she'd lost something, or found something she didn't want. And maybe, too, there was a look of fear.

That was the first inkling I had of the existence of the Turtle, the first sweet feeling of the freedom I knew that he alone could bring. At eleven years old, caught in the net of my mother's madness, raised to a sad and early death by drowning—a fate as inevitable to her as rain on washday—I realised there might be a different future, a life beyond her world of spells and curses. I had no idea what that life would be, what shape it might take, how hard it might be to get there. That would come later. What I knew, at that moment—the only thing I knew with any certainty—was that I wanted to swim like a turtle.

Some while after the incident with the shell, Trixie took us down to Fairlie, to the same beach where they'd found Drummond's rowing boat all those years ago. It was overcast and cold. She lit a fire on the beach from some broken branches and bits of tarry driftwood, and while Luce and I poked at it and warmed ourselves beside the flames, Trixie stood there, wreathed in wood smoke, looking out towards the jagged sea and talking to herself. A kind of chanting—sometimes an almost soundless movement of her lips and sometimes a low muttering that bordered on the frantic. And as the waves tumbled and fell onto the beach, I saw too that she was crying, her soft tears mingling with the foam at the water's edge.

Aye right, the fuckin
Turtle God, that's me.
Ruler uv the wurld an master uv the universe.
Ye must think ah button up the back,
this shite
aboot gods an seashells.
The only shell here is the wan ye've been hidin under
aw these years.

9

IT WOULD BE well over a year before I met the Turtle in person.

I say in person because, absurd as it seems, he came in time to be my mentor, and I like to think also my friend, although he would laugh tears at the idea of being friends with anyone, especially me.

He was a narky old sod, to be honest. Caustic, with a bitterness to him that would have set a predatory shark's teeth on edge, had any shark ever had the opportunity to chew on one of his scrawny flippers. He had no time for sentimental attachments. At least that's what he implied, though trapped as he was in the squalor of his heated concrete tank, it seemed to me he had time enough for anything, and that despite his professed distaste for the world of human beings, he had time enough for me. That alone made him my friend, and therefore ready to forgive him his air of aggrieved innocence, his put-on misanthropy, his bragging and his hurtful wit. It didn't matter that my friendship was never reciprocated with a kind word or look, or the turtlish equivalent of a slap on the back. The fact is, we talked to each other.

I have to confess that it was me who started it. The Turtle was slow to respond at first, and was rarely anything but biting when he did. But he taught me all I know and, as he's lately been reminding me, he's the reason why I'm here today to tell this story.

Are you still there?

It's all a bit too much isn't it? Curses and deadly dreams, a mad mother and a criminal father, a childhood full of cruelty and spite, lives ruined, lost, saved, the betrayal of friends. And now a talking bloody turtle. A Scottish turtle, mind you, a creature of the tropics, condemned to live out its days under glowering Glasgow skies. It's all too much. But it gets worse, let me tell you. It gets much worse yet. The Turtle would say that it's the nature of life to start hopefully and plunge inevitably towards disaster, and from time to time I've shared that view and worse, I have to admit. So to get to the point, if it's a ripping yarn you're after you should give up now. Just put the damned book down and find something more satisfying, a love story perhaps, or a thriller. A story where the goodies win and the baddies get what they deserve. Because there are no goodies here, just me, my family, and a turtle that speaks with a Glasgow accent. In other words, complete and utter shite. Or, as I prefer to see it, the truth. Because sometimes they're both the same thing, truth and lies. And you can't have one without the other, can you?

As I said, it would be nearly two years before we met, the Turtle and I. Two years during which I became obsessed with all things turtlish; not only the creatures themselves, but the vast and empty oceans they lived in. It started slowly, this obsession, because after the incident with the shell there were consequences to be dealt with. One consequence was a growing urge inside me to get back to that bed of sand at the bottom of the sea—like the first cravings of some new addiction that could only be fed by once again and forevermore pressing that beautiful shell against my ear and following it back into the clear, singing water where I could swim freely and without fear. But another consequence was even more pressing. It was this: immediately after the events of that sunny morning, Trixie took to her bed. She was careful first to take her precious shell out of the display cabinet and hide it, because she didn't want me near it ever again, she said. Then she shut herself up in her bedroom. She locked the door and stayed in there for what seemed like weeks, with the curtains closed night and day while the house slowly crumbled into disarray around us. It felt like weeks, though I think now it was maybe only five or six days. She didn't respond to our anxious calls, our pathetic attempts to try and help her, our offers of tea and biscuits. Her bedroom door stayed closed, and the only signs that told us she was still alive were the smell of cigarette smoke and an occasional soft, mournful sound, like the weeping of a ghost.

For the first few days, Luce and I fended for ourselves, working our way through whatever we could find in the kitchen cupboards. Tins mostly, because neither of us knew what to do with the fish cutlets and the crinkle-cut chips in the freezer. We could use a tin-opener, and that was about it. Not that we cooperated, mind you, I wouldn't want you to think for even a minute that we cooked for each other, or looked after each other in any way. No, if Luce had the macaroni, I had the baked beans, and if she had the beans then I opened a tin of spaghetti hoops. And we both had secret stashes of biscuits in our bedrooms. After a day or two, we'd dirtied all the pots and we argued about who should do the washing up. Neither of us did. We took to eating the stuff cold, straight out of the tins. The kitchen overflowed with mess and the rest of the house wasn't much better, a litter of dirty clothes and toys scattered wherever we'd been playing our separate games, whiling away the time until Trixie should reappear. But she didn't.

Absent too was Carlo. Whether he knew what was going on or not I've no idea, but we never saw him during those days and, to be honest, we didn't expect to. We were too busy fending for ourselves, coping in the only way we knew how, by withdrawing further into ourselves, not discussing Trixie or the situation we found ourselves in, not admitting to the tiniest bit of worry or doubt. Survival wasn't just about opening tins of beans; it was about avoiding what was going on around us, pretending that nothing was wrong, that the situation we found ourselves in was somehow normal. And it was normal for us, in a way, because the absence of our parents—one way or another—was a fact of our childhood, as natural as a bedtime kiss might be to other children. We had always fended for ourselves amidst Trixie's distracted misery and Carlo's seeming unawareness of our existence.

So we carried on. We got ourselves dressed in the mornings, found something for our breakfast, went to school. We came home, watched television, squabbled over who would eat what and who got to sit closest to the electric heater that we'd brought down from one of the bedrooms. It was starting to turn cold, and neither of us knew how to light the fire. We knew nothing, really, and why should we? We were just two kids adrift, trying to pretend otherwise. And after those few days that seemed like weeks we were running out of options and reality was starting to slap us across the face. We were down to diced carrots, baby potatoes, and a couple of mystery tins that had lost their labels. Our clothes were dirty and neither of us had washed since the day Trixie locked herself away.

Then Carlo showed up.

He was there one afternoon when I got home from school. I came in through the gate and saw his car in the driveway. Trixie was sitting in the passenger seat, smoking, her hair wild and the dark rings under her eyes visible even from the gate. She glanced at me and looked away. Carlo was putting a suitcase in the boot. He slammed it shut and when he saw me he motioned to me to go into the house. Then he got into the car, started it with a roar, and drove off. Not a word.

I heard tyres screeching in the distance as he pulled onto the main road.

We found out later that Trixie had been admitted to Gartnavel Hospital, and that she might be there for a couple of weeks, maybe three. It was Nonna who told us this, after she'd made us have baths and then fed us the best meal we'd had in ages. Carlo took us to Nonna and Pa's when he came back from the hospital, and they looked after us while we waited for Trixie to get better. They lived not far from us, just around the corner, so in the mornings when we were dressed for school we would walk up the street for breakfast and there was hot buttered toast and the smell of coffee, and at dinner time huge helpings of risotto or spaghetti or Nonna's special soup, always followed by ripe pears and the hard, sharp cheese that Pa loved. In the evenings Pa would take an interest in our homework, help us here and there with a problem in arithmetic. Sometimes he would talk to me about the war, and one night he showed me some photographs of him and his comrades standing proudly around a machine gun, and the ledger he'd kept with the names of all the dead crossed out. Later Pa would walk us back to our house and put us to bed with a kiss and a kind word.

A couple of weeks, maybe three. Whatever it was, it wasn't long enough. No one mentioned Trixie. Carlo came and went, joining us for dinner some nights, but he said nothing, and neither Luce nor I asked any questions. It was as though we were scared to talk about Trixie. As if talking about her would bring her back home. I don't know about Luce, but that was the last thing I wanted.

When Trixie did come home we barely recognised her.

Sandro arrived with her, in one of the work vans. He helped her out of the passenger door and supported her as she walked slowly into the house, where she sat down in her armchair and stared at the space in front of her. They had put her on drugs—some newfangled something or other—and I found out later that she'd been given electric shock therapy. Her hair had turned grey.

And more. She seemed smaller, more human and more readable. For the first time the way she looked made sense to me. There was a frailty in the lines on her face, and in the shadows under her eyes, and in the unfamiliar grey hair that was so carefully brushed and combed. I remember thinking that she looked like a witch, that somehow all the things about her that were real were beginning to show in her face, that she couldn't any longer hide her true self from the world outside the family. It was there now for everyone to see and judge.

Sandro left her with us and went back to work. Trixie sat in her armchair, looking into space with a vacant expression. It was like we weren't there. As though, despite the fact we shared the same physical things—the living room, the furniture, the over-large stone fireplace—Trixie was nonetheless existing in a completely different universe. We could see her, but she couldn't see us. We tried to talk to her, to make contact with her across the divide. We made a cup of tea and we asked how she was and wasn't she glad to be home? Luce even climbed onto her lap and rested her head against her breast, but there was no response. Eventually Pa came round and told us to go to Nonna for our dinner, and that's what we did. When we came back later Trixie was already in bed, and she stayed there, more or less, for another fortnight.

It was the drugs, really. The side effects. Whatever she was taking—great red things like gobstoppers—they turned her into a kind of zombie. They may well have stopped her feeling depressed or whatever she was, but they stopped her feeling all kinds of other things, like being part of the world. She was well away, that's for sure.

I suppose you're wondering whether I was tempted during Trixie's absence to find where she'd hidden the shell? You're damned right I was. That shell was the best thing that had ever happened to me. It had sparked something inside of me that I never knew was there, and it had given me something that I never knew existed. Something exhilarating and forbidden and dangerous. It had given me hope.

Believe me, I searched high and low. All through the house and especially through Trixie's bedroom, and in the cupboards in the kitchen where she kept all her 'magic' stuff—the cards, the bones, the jars full of evil-smelling powders. How I wanted it, that bloody shell. How I wanted it to suck me deep into its watery comfort.

It took me nearly a week to find it. Each night after Pa had tucked us up in bed, I'd wait until I was sure Luce was asleep and then I'd sneak out and get on with my searching. I nearly gave up several times, defeated by the impossibility of trying to figure out all the hiding places in the house. But I was driven, you see. I couldn't let it rest, I couldn't stop myself looking, night after night, stalking the house like a ghost. By day I was so tired that I would fall asleep at my desk at school, and I was so drawn-looking and listless that Nonna thought I must be coming down with something.

But each night I was wide awake again, as though my craving had turned me into a nocturnal creature, fearful of the light but coming to life in the cool darkness, sure and stealthy. *A land with a sun so bright that the people could only come out at night for fear of being blinded.* That's how it felt, and how I imagined it to myself—that I was one of those people who worshipped the Turtle God and shunned the light, though I was cheating a bit because I had the big torch that was kept in the kitchen, and which I poked into cupboards, shelves, drawers, under beds and inside boxes full of old linen or dusty Christmas decorations. I was quite methodical, working through the house room by room, sorting through each cupboard box by box, putting everything back just as I'd found it. I'd even gone through Luce's room one afternoon when she was at Nonna's. But the shell was nowhere to be found.

I found lots of other things: Trixie's first marriage certificate; an old half-crown coin; an invitation to a kids' revue starring none other than the talented Kenny Drummond.

And then I found what I was looking for.

I was going through Trixie's room for the third time, trawling through the stuff in the big walk-in press. I'd closed the door and felt cocooned in there in the torchlight. The press was built in the recess above the stairs from the hallway, in what would otherwise be unusable space. It wasn't big; there was just enough room for hanging space and a few shelves built in front of where the wall angled back in line with the ceiling of the stairwell. I'd cleared some boxes on the bottom shelf out of the way and had made a space to sit on the floor while I riffled through them. I noticed then that some of the floorboards under the shelf seemed to be raised slightly, in a way that didn't look right. Shining the torch into the recess I could make out a hatch cut into the boards, and there was a hole in one end of it, just big enough for a finger or two. I reached in and the hatch lifted from the floor with a scrape of wood against wood, surprising me with how easily it came free. I crawled right under the shelf and in the torchlight I looked into the hole and I could see the lath and plaster of the stairway ceiling running at an angle under the floor. And there was something else, something that looked like a big cloth bag, tied with string, resting on a wooden beam. I reached in and I lifted it out carefully, my heart thumping with excitement. I undid the string and the cloth wrapper fell away. And there it was: the shell.

When I picked it up it seemed bigger than I remembered it. Heavier, too. I imagined I could feel within it the satisfying weight of all the world's oceans, all the creatures of the sea and all the shifting sands and hidden rock ledges of the deep. Standing in the confines of the cupboard in my mother's bedroom, illuminated by the dim reaches of torchlight, I put the shell to my ear and closed my eyes, prepared to be sucked in by the swirling waters and to leave behind forever the suffocating, loveless cruelty of Trixie and my family and the destiny they'd mapped out for me.

What are ye doin, Donald?

The voice, when I heard it, was not what I wanted to hear. For a brief moment I was completely lost, unable to grasp that the sound I heard was in fact someone speaking. When I did grasp it, I turned around so quickly that the shell slipped from my hands. It tumbled onto the floor and split cleanly into two.

Yer for it now, said Luce, who was standing at the open door. Just you wait till Mum hears about this.

Trixie didn't hear about it right away. She didn't hear anything in those first few weeks after she got home. She certainly didn't hear us talking to her. She stayed in bed mostly, and when she got up it was to wander aimlessly about the house, or to stand stock-still in the kitchen staring out the window, or to sit in her armchair and gently rock herself back and forth.

Life went on around her. Luce and I went to school, we still ate at Nonna's, and on the weekends we took our dirty laundry there for washing and Nonna made sure that we were clean too. Carlo had employed a nurse who visited Trixie once a day to see she took her drugs and to generally look after her a bit. Carlo himself stayed well out of the way. When I thought about him, which I have to admit wasn't often, I imagined him living in a hotel, or maybe sleeping on the couch in his office. It never occurred to me to ask him, on the few occasions when he did turn up, why he wasn't around more. Things were the just the way things were, and didn't everyone live like this?

I don't know whether Luce ever tried to tell Trixie about the shell. I'm sure she did, because I don't think she would miss such a chance to get me into trouble. I'd stashed the broken halves back in the secret compartment in Trixie's cupboard, wrapped in the cloth and tied up again with the string. Whether Luce's tittle-tattle penetrated Trixie's fogged mind, or whether Trixie finally thought to check if the shell was still there, I don't know. What I do know is this:

Early morning, dark, the first frost of winter pawing at the windows. Trixie's been home for maybe a month. Something wakes me. I don't know what, but I'm lying there in bed with my eyes wide open, listening, my stomach curling. With what? Excitement? Fear? I'm lying there under the covers, alert, feeling the cold air on my head. Then I get up, and for a moment it's like I'm someone else, watching myself doing it, though I'm shivering while I search for slippers and dressinggown. But the cold and the dark are real enough, and by the time I'm ready the feeling has passed. There's just me and the rawness of the morning, and whatever it is that's woken me. I creep down the stairs, slowly, avoiding the seventh and the fourth, the ones that creak. From under the door to the kitchen there shines a faint light which draws me towards it until I stand there in the hallway, listening, sensing within myself what lies behind the door but not yet able to allow the thought to surface. Then I turn the handle and push the door and it swings slowly into the kitchen and there, sitting at the table, just as I knew she would be, is Trixie. In front of her is one of the broken halves of the seashell. She's holding the other half in her hand, its creamy insides gleaming in the low light, and it's like she's doing some kind of puzzle, an expression of concentration on her face. And something else. I don't know whether it's anger, and if not, why not. She doesn't look up. I stand there for what seems like ages, and then I hear myself say, Ah didny mean it, Mum. It was—

When Trixie speaks, I barely recognise the voice or the huskiness of it, or the gentle sadness surrounding it. Everythin changes, Donald.

Ah'm sorry. Ah didny mean—

Everythin passes.

Could you not glue it back together?

Some things jist canny be mended. Ye huv tae accept they're finished. Know whit ah mean?

Something tells me it's best if I nod, though I don't have a clue what she's talking about. Trixie looks up for the first time.

Yer faither's gone, son. He's ran aff wi another wummin.

Sometimes things can get so bad that they just have to get better; you can only sink so low before you reach the bottom, but once you get there you can maybe get a purchase on it and push yourself up again, if you want to. That's how I think it was for Trixie then as winter was just beginning to dig its claws in and she contemplated a future without Carlo. I'm speculating, of course. Trixie never for one moment confided in me how she felt about what was happening to her or to those around her. What evidence do I have that she was somehow able to derive strength from all this chaos? Only this: it took Carlo's leaving for Trixie to start speaking again, and when she did, she took on a different voice—not the sad voice of that late night in her kitchen over the broken bits of shell, but a voice that came, quite soon, to be in command of itself, a voice that knew what it was about. And this, too: from that night on, she stopped taking her pills. She pulled herself together, gathering all the parts of herself that had lain scattered like old clothes around the house and constructing from them a credible person. And also this: she took control of her own destiny, determined at that point to make something real out of her gift for clairvoyance. She began to understand what she could and could not do, and to forge for herself a future out of her ragbag of beliefs and rituals. She began to believe in herself.

But the shattering of that shell around my feet was a beginning for me, too, because I did learn something from it. It forced me to face up to the fact that I was on my own now, that I had to find a future for myself. Which is what I did.

And yes, the Turtle helped me, I can't deny that.

Naw, ye canny.
Ye've been hingin aboot like a fart
in a trance,
sayin this and tellin the next bloody thing.
It's time tae get tae the point.
Tell them aboot the zoo.
Tell them aboot me, yer ain wee four-flippered friend.
And aw the bloody things ah did fur ye.
God help me, but, ah might as well
no huv bothered.
Haw, whit ur ye runnin away fur?

10

I *AM* RUNNING.

I've just remembered something, and now I'm racing through the wet, yellow-lit streets, feeling the weight of the meal I've eaten, heavy in my stomach. I push past the people queuing at the chip shop, skirt the pool of vomit outside a pub, ignore the looks from the local neds sharing their last can of lager under a bus shelter. I'm gasping for breath but I won't stop. Not until I get back to Trixie's house. I've got the key in my hand already and I've settled into a steady rhythm, thump-thump, thump-thump. Heart beating like Ginger Baker on speed. Can't get enough air with each rasp of breath. But I won't stop. Not yet, not now, no nay never.

The shell. I've remembered the damned shell. Suddenly I want to see it; the glowing orange against the deep sea black, the smooth creaminess of its inside, the jagged line of its jaws. I want to hold the broken halves together and step back into that long-ago moment when I stood, fearful, on the edge of something that came to be called hope.

That's why I'm running. Keep up with me if you can because I'm not going to stop talking, even though I'm already finding it hard to spare the breath.

Things changed a lot after Carlo left home. You might think he was there so seldom that it wouldn't make the slightest bit of difference, but you'd be dead wrong about that. The funny thing about an absence is that it can be felt just as strongly as any presence, and Carlo's desertion from the family home was felt by us not just as an abandonment, but as a kind of betrayal. He wasn't much, to be sure, but he was all that stood between us and Trixie and the full tapestry of her craziness. That's how it felt.

Who and what Carlo had left us for was not communicated to me, though by now you shouldn't be surprised by this, or by anything that went on in the bosom of our lovely family; communication with each other was not our strong point. No, we communicated with whatever else we could find that would give us what we needed, whether that was recognition, protection, escape, all three of these things or more. Luce communicated mainly with herself, and with Trixie just enough to elbow me off centre stage now and then. She needed to create a space of her own in Trixie's distracted mind, to show that she existed, to compete with me and my damned curse for our mother's limited attention. She had many ways of doing this: the temper, the slamming of doors, the sulking, the plotting and planning against yours truly. Never underestimate the power of sibling rivalry, even if the prize is as flawed and incapable a mother as ours.

Trixie, for her part, communicated feverishly with the nether world of sprites and spirits. She needed any number of things: a new life, certainly; her independence from Carlo; a transformation into something better than your average speywife reading tea-leaves from the bottom of a cup. Above all, she needed to find a way of either living with the fact that I was doomed to die, or of finding some way to break the curse. Just how preoccupied she was—obsessed even—in trying to do just that was not at all clear to me when I was growing up. But then a lot of things weren't clear then. I was too obsessed myself.

And denied now the possibility of escape into the orange-black mollusc of my dreams, I took what I could from that experience of water and webbed flippers, the impossible fluency of that diving body, the protection of that splendid carapace with its intricate design and pattern, which to me was a greater demonstration of the world's wonders than any spurious bit of superstitious nonsense that Trixie could serve up. I took what I could from it and I determined to learn more, the hard way if necessary. The normal way. I started reading books.

I wanted to know all about turtles. And about the power of the sea, how to live in it, how to adapt myself to its briny

ways, its depths and its shallows, its currents and its under-
tows, its gentle calms and its angry tempests. I wanted to be
able to hold my breath forever and to disappear far beneath all
this bloody surface tension.

I was desperate to keep this new obsession to myself, of
course, partly because I knew that Trixie would disapprove,
and partly because I liked this thing I'd found, this resistance
to my mother and her plan for my life—this parallel world
which I could build within the boundaries of hers, and which
I could inhabit without her knowing.

I started with the little library at school, spending every
playtime I could scouring the shelves for books on marine
creatures, amphibious reptiles, stories real or imagined about
turtles and tortoises. Kids' stuff, mostly. I learnt about the
seven species of sea turtle, along with the myriad of freshwater
varieties around the world—but it was the sea turtles that I
wanted to know about. The ones with names like hawksbill,
leatherback, loggerhead. They can live for well over a hundred
years, some of them, patrolling far out into the great oceans.
I learnt that they eat jellyfish, mussels, clams, squid, shrimp
and seaweed. That their only enemies are sharks and humans.
I also learnt that adult sea turtles come back to spawn at
the same beach where they themselves hatched many years
before. In the intervening years—about fifteen, though often
longer—many of the larger turtles simply disappear into the
deep ocean and into mystery. These are the 'lost years', and
little is known of their habits between hatching and spawning.
I liked this idea, and I would daydream about losing myself in
the vast and deep and empty oceans, of the journeys I'd make

and the adventures I'd have as master of my own destiny, lost and free and answerable to no one.

When I tired of the kids' books at school I joined the local library. This meant getting Trixie's signature, which I didn't do. I forged it, proving perhaps that I was my father's son as much as my mother's. I practised Trixie's spidery scrawl a few times in my school exercise book before committing it to the form for the library, savouring the delicious feeling of doing something illicit, of getting one over on Trixie.

And so I began my career in duplicity. Forging a signature was just the first thing. Telling lies was the next, and I took to this with all the ease of a natural fibber, as though the liar in me was always there, just waiting for the right conditions to occur before jumping up and talking shite like there was no tomorrow. I started going to the library after school, and I told Trixie that I was playing soccer or hanging around with Wee Malkie. Wee Malkie knew what I was doing, because he was my friend and I trusted him. But even though at first he was doubtful about the quality of fun that might be found in the local library as opposed to, say, kicking a ball about, or playing soldiers, or tending to the collection of dead mice mouldering behind his dad's garage, it wasn't long before he followed me. He, too, discovered the wonder of books, and I reckon that he owes his present sparkling success in the academic world to me, the ungrateful bastard. Not that anyone could see that coming, and you certainly wouldn't have picked it from his early choice of reading material, which tended to be along the lines of the *Famous Five* or some such nonsense. Or anything with pictures in it.

Anyway. On my very first visit to the local library I discovered *The Secret World of Turtles* and *Endangered Species of the Oceans*, both of which I devoured over several sessions in the reading room. (I have to admit that, after a couple of weeks, I also varied my diet, hoeing into the adventures of Biggles and various works of science fiction, and also Sherlock Holmes and stuff by Walter Scott. I discovered then how a good story can put up a fight against the real world, taking on time itself, making it stop, swallowing you up so that you disappear into the logic of its own wee world, leaving this one behind, at least for a while.) On a subsequent visit I found a thick volume bound in linen with the title *Sea Turtles in Myth and Magic*, by R. S. Jakowski, a book that I came to borrow again and again, so often that Mrs Semple the librarian one day looked over her spectacles at me and inquired if I knew it by heart yet, and if I did, perhaps it was time to let someone else borrow it? But no one else wanted it, and when the library next got around to clearing out its shelves she gave the book to me because, she said, it was an old and wise volume and she knew I would look after it. I took it home and hid it under the bottom drawer of the chest in my bedroom.

It wasn't that old, really—published in 1954—though it looked ancient enough to me. But then, at that age, most things did. The print was small and smudged, littered with drawings and sketches of turtle eggs and shells and turtles of various descriptions, from the beautiful hawksbill to the Kemp's ridley, whose only breeding site is on a small strip of beach in Mexico. The book had a curious smell—not the human smell of old library books, thumbed by all and sundry, but a faint smell of salt and wind, of seaweed drying on rocks. I knew this smell from our occasional trips to the coast and I would lie under my bedclothes at night, reading by torchlight, and hold the pages up to my face to breathe in their magic.

I read about how the turtle is a sacred creature to many societies, that much belief about the origins of the world and the capriciousness of fate is based on the idea that we're all really perched on the back of a giant hawksbill, floating through a universe of similarly flippered heavenly bodies, and that we have to watch what we do so as not to make the turtle we live on sick, because then we're truly fucked, so we are; living on the back of a dying turtle is nobody's idea of a good time. More, I learnt that some people like to use bits of the turtle for medicines. The flippers, properly prepared, can help cure boils and pustules and various other skin complaints that are the bane of existence in cultures that don't have ready access to a chemist's shop. And the shell can be ground into a powder that, when mixed with other rare ingredients and drunk in a secret ritual, supposedly gives you power over others.

There was lots like that. But don't think for a moment that I was taken in by any of it. What became clear for me, in this book more than any other, was that the turtle is pretty much a marked animal wherever you find it. Here's my thesis, Professor, which I submit with all due respect for academic process, though you can keep your constructive criticism to yourself for the moment. All this magical mythical rubbish that people confer on the turtle arises solely from one thing and one thing only, and that is that it's a damned tasty bit of eating—and in some places, just about all there is. Now, if you live in a society where the middens are sky high with old turtle shells and bones, you're probably going to find a use for them. Making fishhooks and combs and stuff like that is one thing, but eventually someone's going to start asking questions about why there are so many turtles and where do they all come from? It can't be just an accident that they're here and we're here, and it's so obvious that if they weren't here, we couldn't be. I mean, what would we eat? The whole thing's so perfectly balanced that it must be part of a divine plan. Ipso facto, the turtles on which we depend must be sacred, and if we don't start worshipping them with attendant ritual and hoo-ha, they'll get miffed and bugger off to some other tribe and then where will we be, eh?

The atheists in the community would sit around the campfire arguing that this is nonsense and that everything is because it just *is*—we're all accidents of the prevailing conditions of the universe, the products, as it were, of an existing set of circumstances. Change any one aspect of these circumstances and you end up with an entirely different universe, one in which we might be turtles ourselves or, indeed, not exist at all.

Needless to say this would be too much for the religiously inclined who would find it so hard to contemplate a universe without themselves that they'd spear all the atheists and fling their bodies into the sea. Afterwards they'd say that the gods told them to do it and in no time at all everyone would be following the new religion and that would be the rational world view out the window for the next few millennia and/ or until all the turtles had been eaten and the tribe was dead from starvation. The lesson here is that reason will always lose out to faith, because faith explains everything, and reason only explains what's reasonable. And if it all goes to pot it's not your fault because it's all ordained anyway. The other lesson, though perhaps not immediately obvious to the turtle-eaters, is that the turtle itself is just an innocent victim in all this, without a voice of its own. All it can do is enjoy its wee fishy morsels when it can find them, maybe engage in a bit of turtlish hanky-panky with whatever comely-looking bit of shell presents itself, and, apart from that, just swim like fuck, always in the direction of safety. The turtle is a good, fast swimmer.

But enough of this shite. Here we are at Trixie's front door.

I forgot to leave a light on, and I have to scrabble and scrape at the front door before I can fit the key in the lock. When it swings open I practically fall into the hallway. Stuff the evil spirits, I think, and I slam the door in their faces. They can do their worst, the pointy-eared wee bastards, why should I kowtow to them anyway? It's dark in the house and I'm sitting on the floor in the hallway, leaning against the door, needing to get my breath back, and feeling now like maybe I'm going mad, like maybe some of those evil spirits have actually invaded my body and any minute now my head's going to swivel three-sixty degrees and my voice will drop an octave or two and I'll start levitating all over the bloody place. That'll give them a shock at the funeral tomorrow. Though maybe not. It's probably just what they're expecting, and they'll make sure the minister comes armed with whatever paraphernalia he needs to deal with me before I embarrass everyone with my projectile vomiting. Funeral service with exorcism thrown in? Nae bother. We minsters are trained for all situations these days, the spiritual war on terror knows no bounds, fight the good fight and all that. A quick word to the holy rapid response squad and we'll have your mother cremated and those evil spirits locked up and blubbering for their mammies in no time at all.

I am going mad.

I've got to get up and turn some lights on, but I'm stuck here, sweating, fighting for breath, a pain in my chest. Maybe it's a heart attack. That'd be just bloody brilliant, that would. To be found dead here, in Trixie's house. Everybody would think I'd died of grief or some such shite. But grief is not my problem. Bitterness, rage, frustration, paranoia and a general inability to lead any kind of a normal life is my problem. Plus the fact that I'm not very fit and I'm totally out of puff.

Apart from that, everything's fine. I know exactly what I'm going to do. I just can't get up. Not yet. I have to sit here, breathe slowly, relax. Lean against this door which has seen enough dramatic exits to keep an afternoon soap opera running for decades.

As it turns out, leaving Trixie was the best thing Carlo ever did for her. It forced her to confront her own abilities, and to take on full responsibility for herself and her family. Carlo gave her some money on a weekly basis, but it wasn't enough, and it stopped every time they had an argument. Later on, Trixie took him to court, a preface to several court battles during the course of what became a long and bitter divorce.

But at first she was dependent on Carlo's meagre handout. Being Trixie, she didn't go out and find herself a job cleaning offices or behind a bar somewhere, fending off drunks. No, she took out an advert in the local paper. It read something like this: CLAIRVOYANT. *Anxious about your future? Madam Pinelli has the answers. Tarot and spiritual channelling. No tea-leaves.* That, and our phone number, which I for one came to regret, as the moment the ad appeared we were pestered at all hours by hordes of the weird and wondrous, the lonely and the desperate, the sad and the dispossessed.

It was surprising how many people out there needed the services of a good clairvoyant. All kinds of people. Wee grannies smelling of medicinal brandy; young mothers pushing prams and dragging screaming toddlers on the end of leashes; suave men in suits who parked their flash cars in the street outside, leading to all kinds of rumours and innuendo regarding Trixie and a supposed string of lovers; geezers in flat caps and mufflers, sometimes drunk, sometimes scrubbed and sober in their Sunday best and accompanied by their equally well-turned-out wives. There was a real need to be filled here; the whole city was seething with the unmet demands of the spiritually bereft. Legions of the buggers, all wanting to know what lay in store for them, whether they should marry now or wait for a better prospect, or whether dear old Aunty Mary was happy on the other side, and maybe you could find out what she did with the diamond ring she was supposed to have left us?

Trixie saw them all, as long as they paid upfront, cash only.

And not only did she do a roaring trade, she quickly developed her techniques as a clairvoyant and, more importantly, as a performer. Let me tell you, being a speywife dabbler is but simple arithmetic compared to the calculus of convincing paying customers that they're getting the most reliable, dependable, money-back-if-not-completely-satisfied top-of-the-range occult service available anywhere in Glasgow. And Trixie found she was good at that bit. None of this headscarf and crystal ball shite. She dressed carefully for her working day, looking every inch the professional counsellor, and she took time first to talk to her clients about their problems and to put them at ease before proceeding with the session, which would involve all kinds of things—tarot cards, certainly, but often also photographs of loved ones, locks of hair, and strange-smelling concoctions, herbs and suchlike. Oh, and tape recordings, but I'll tell you more about them in a moment.

She talked to her clients about their problems. *Their* problems? Christ on a bike, if any of them had anything near an inkling of the sad state of life that lurked beneath Trixie's professional demeanour, they would run a mile, so they would. But we've all got problems, haven't we? We've just got to get on with it. Keep the lid on, keep it all nice and zipped up.

She never once talked to me about *my* problems.

I'm on my feet. I've switched the lights on and I'm walking through the house towards the back door. The key to the garage is hanging on its hook, just like it always did, and that's where I'm headed now, across the wet lawn. The garage is dark and it takes me some time to get the side door open and when I do it releases a strong smell of damp and engine oil, and something else which is vaguely familiar, a mixture of old paint and newspaper. The tools are hanging above Carlo's bench, coated in rust and cobwebs, and I find a hammer and a chisel and a big screwdriver, and take them back with me to the house.

What do I think I'm doing exactly, with this claw hammer and a rusty old chisel? And at this time of night too? Nothing, officer. No disturbing of the peace intended, nor interruption of the sleep of honest neighbours, whoever they are. Just a little work around the house, a wee spot of renovating. God knows, the place needs it.

I walk up the stairway, the fourth and seventh steps creaking, and stand for a moment on the landing. The light from the overhead is harsh, like the bulb's too strong and it needs something softer. Everything has a sharpness about it, the paintwork on the doorway too reflective. It makes me squint, and for a moment a flickering spark in my head lights up the memory of a little boy, standing here on this landing, squinting at a closed door, waiting.

The door to Trixie's bedroom isn't closed now. It stands slightly ajar, but as I push it fully open it's like I'm pushing against an opposing force, the resistance of ages, Trixie's ghost with her shoulder up against it, heels dug firmly in.

I don't believe in ghosts. Nor ghouls, nor phantasms, nor poltergeists. Nor weird shadows that turn up in your photographs in the shape of people in Victorian dress. The only thing that goes bump in the night here is me and my trusty hammer, though I'll try and keep the noise down, because you never know what you might awaken in this place.

Door open, light on. Trixie's bed lies unmade, the sheets half pulled back and the pillow still crumpled where she'd laid her head for the last time. A faint smell of lavender. On the bedside cabinet there's a pair of reading glasses and a paper-back novel. And a box of pills of some kind—medication for her bad heart? I realise then that I have no idea how she died, my mother. A heart attack. But where and how and what happened? Maybe she died here in bed, maybe in hospital. It bothers me that I don't know, that no one wants me to know. It bothers me.

The bedroom is not like I remember it. I'd noticed some-thing different when I'd looked in earlier, in my first vague wanderings through the house, savouring all the strange-but-familiar sensations of a thirty-two-year absence, but not really taking much in. It isn't just that the wallpaper is different, or the furniture, or that there's a fitted carpet where once there had been lino and a rug. It's something else.

And then it clicks.

The cupboard has been rebuilt. It has been replaced with one of those built-in wardrobe things, with sliding mirrored doors in smoked glass. Trixie surely thought she was modernising, keeping up with the prevailing fashions in house design and interior decorating. That was always one of her things. She would pester Carlo to change things around the place—put in that ridiculous stone fireplace in the living room, for example, or replace the old sashes with the latest picture windows. And this. Where was I going to start now?

Empty the cupboard for a clearer look at what's what.

There's a light in there and I switch it on. The cupboard's full of her clothes, coats and dresses. Shoes and boxes of stuff. Most of the clothes look like they've hardly been worn.

It doesn't seem right to disturb them, but there's no point in stopping, not after all this time, with too many things connecting up between then and now. What would you do? I mean if you had the chance to pull the past into the present like this, to make it real and whole, could you resist it? I feel at this moment that it might all make sense, the mess and the fear and the anger and all the years of feeling on the edge of everything. I want to know that my childhood was real.

So I pull all the clothes off the rack and throw them on the bed. Then all the shoes and all the boxes. I don't look through the boxes, just heave them into the room where they spill out their bits of paper and old photographs. I want to clear everything off the floor, because I'm looking for the hatch cut into the floorboards, the space under the floor where I found the shell all those years ago. But it's not there; the cupboard is different from how it used to be. It's smaller, and the wall on the stairwell side doesn't angle back like it used to. It's been straightened out with some kind of partition—plasterboard by the look of it.

Without thinking too much about what I'm doing, I take the hammer to the plasterboard where it meets the floor and it falls away in a cloud of dust and fragments, revealing the ceiling space of the stairwell below. I need to get my arm in there, into the space that runs down below the level of the floor, but that means making the hole bigger. Can't make too much noise or the neighbours will have the police round and the game will be well and truly up.

More bits of plaster and splinters of wood and then I'm lying in the cupboard with my arm under the floorboards, fingers trawling through the dust that covers the lath and plaster of the ceiling.

It's not there. Not where I think I remember finding it before. That parcel, wrapped in cloth and string, nestling in the space between the floor and the stairwell ceiling. There's no reason why it would still be there; there are plenty of reasons why it wouldn't.

Let's just stop for a minute. Down tools, sit on the floor and lean back against the coolness of this wall. I'm tired. I've only just realised how exhausted I am—jet-lagged still and ragged as buggery. When was the last time I slept? Somewhere between Singapore and London, at thirty-five thousand feet, awash in white noise and the tinkle of a movie soundtrack in my earphones. I could sleep now, so I could, but there's this thing pressing on me, this idea that won't go away, like the crying of a wee baby, like that persistent grating sound of someone else's kid wailing its nut off and you just want to scream at it to shut up, can you not do something about that child, feed it or something, gag the wee bugger? But it won't stop, and nobody can stop it, and what I think is this: that it's me that's crying, and that there's no one in all the world who'll pick me up and soothe me. And that's really what I can't stand. It's me that's crying and nobody gives a fuck.

Okay.

Enough's enough. I'm tired and my ears are buzzing and I'm feeling sorry for myself. Pathetic. Don't think so much. Concentrate on the task at hand, which is to find the shell, believed to be stashed under the floor of the cupboard in Trixie's bedroom.

The floor is the problem, and I'm going to have to lift some of the boards. They're short, to fit the space in the cupboard, and they come up easily when I lever the hammer under them. I also have to break the frame of the cupboard door, which means taking off the doors and leaning them up against a wall in the bedroom. It's not difficult, just annoying that every little thing leads to something bigger, until the entire cupboard is all but demolished and there's a gaping hole in the floor. Fuck knows what time of the morning it is.

When I put my arm in the hole I can reach much further down, and almost immediately my fingers touch something soft and I reach in even further and I can feel dusty cloth and string, it must be string! I grasp it and it comes free in my hand, catching a little against the rough wood of the rafters. It's bigger than I expected, and heavier.

And then it's there, on the floor in front of me. Something wrapped in what looks now like an old pillow case, tied with string, and I'm tearing at the knots, pulling off the string until the whole thing unravels and spills its contents over my lap and over the floor, and I'm sitting there looking at it and it's like the world then is a maze so intricate and so cruelly tangled and tight, tight, tight, that I can barely breathe with the sheer lostness of it all.

What I don't find in the package hidden in the dusty recess of the cupboard floor: a seashell, orange and black, creamy inside, carefully restored to its former glory, its jagged jaws waiting to be pressed against my ear, the ecstasy of being drawn down into a watery heaven.

What I do find: a part of myself denied; a link restored in a tangled chain of love and hate and madness and malice; the sudden opening of a door long closed; the feeling of empty space and of a body falling through eternity.

That, and what now lies on the floor in front of me.

As I stare at the contents of the package it's becoming clear that my mother—my poor, mad, miserable mother—had seen this moment coming, and had planned accordingly, either to head me off or just to fuck me up even more completely than she had managed to in life. Or maybe to save me from myself. Who knows? She was capable of anything.

In the package hidden in the dusty recess of the cupboard floor there is a brown envelope, cardboard-backed and stiff, of the kind that holds documents; an audio cassette in an unmarked box; and a book, bound in linen, stained and browning at the edges.

Inside the envelope are two folded newspaper cuttings, undated, but their brittle yellowness suggests considerable age, as do their contents. They both concern the murder of Auld Smith the fishmonger.

The cassette is a cheap one, of the kind you might buy at the supermarket, and it's wound a little way in. It looks quite new. Written in ink on the label in a tiny scrawl are the words *For Donald*. Somehow, I'm not surprised, as if, deep down, I'd expected this. I feel myself smiling inside, a dull glow, as I contemplate the words and what they might mean.

And then I recognise the book. It's my old friend, *Sea Turtles in Myth and Magic* by R. S. Jakowski. As I look at the cover, I feel again the slipperiness of time, the uncomfortable feeling that past and present and future are all one and the same, that the linearity of our lives is nothing but a cruel illusion, designed to trick us into a belief in logic, order and certainty when no such things exist. There is only chaos, and a vast confusion of possibilities, intricate and inter-twined and beyond our comprehension.

When I open the book, there on the ruined floor of the cupboard in my mother's bedroom, its yellowing pages give off a faint smell of salt and wind, of seaweed drying on rocks, and I'm gone, spiralling away into infinity.

11

BOOK, NEWSPAPER CLIPPINGS, cassette tape. My inheri-
tance. It's all I'm going to get, but it's bigger and more valuable
to me than I can possibly take in at this moment. What does
it all mean? Apologies? Confessions? Amends? Perhaps none
of it means anything, perhaps it's all a product of Trixie's
peculiar mind, some kind of esoteric offering to whatever
spirits she might have offended, some magical protection
against . . . What? Against me? Against my coming back here?
Against the opening of old wounds? If that's the case, it isn't
going to work.

But it seems to me that maybe it's not the case. The newspaper clippings point to important moments in her life, to
pieces in the penny puzzle that was Madam Pinelli, speywife

turned professional clairvoyant. She wants me to understand something about her and why she was the way she was. And the tape? I would have to listen to that; there's bound to be a cassette player around somewhere. But not yet. Not just yet. There's a story to get through, and a turtle waiting—impatient, grumpy and well defended, full of advice and warnings, admonitions and insults, not to mention half-baked opinions.

That visit to Elderbank Zoo was on a cold, clear February morning in the second year of the 1970s, with frost underfoot and our ears red and nippy, breath billowing clouds as we chattered and carried on. We were dimly aware of a big wide world beyond us, where wars were fought and revolutions plotted; a world of music and clothes and symbols of refusal. We were on the edge of it then, waiting to be pulled into its vortex, from which, if we survived, we might emerge as adults, fully formed and ready to take our places in the bustle of life.

Look, here's Wee Malkie, his shirt hanging out over his short trousers and his tie still in shreds from the time we took a pair of scissors to it. There's a smudge of dirt on his forehead and his socks are at different heights, one down at the ankle and the other pulled up nearly to his knee. Can you see him? He's the one that's scratching at his elbows while he saunters along with a big grin on his face, like there's no place he'd rather be than here at the smelly old zoo, tormenting the exhibits and generally being a complete doolie. That was him alright, always trying too hard to show he could be as big a nutter as anyone else. Nobody liked Malkie very much, except me.

We were friends because we had no other friends, and because Malkie seemed happy to follow after me and that made me the leader. And because compared to him I seemed almost normal, intelligent even.

On the day the wee bugger stole my lunch we were, as I've said before, on a school excursion. The zoo was just outside the city, but not that far from where we lived and a short trip by bus from the school. As zoos go, let me tell you, this one didn't go very far. There were other zoos in other places at this time that were beginning to move away from the dim, dark ages of zoological garden practice, that were starting to understand that you have to re-create appropriate spaces and climates and ecosystems for the animals. That the tiger needs to be able to run around a bit and to have some long grass to hide in, or the monkeys need some proper trees to climb, or the polar bear something better than a concrete pit with a splash of water in the bottom stinking of old fish. Elderbank Zoo hadn't evolved to this point yet. It was a place of cramped cages and smelly bunkers, where the animals seemed always on the edge of hysteria, pacing fitfully back and forth or throwing themselves against the bars. Or lying prone at the back of their enclosures, licking and picking at their lank and dirty pelts, one wary eye keeping watch on the spectators bustling past.

And they had to keep watch, let me tell you. Because the spectators were quite capable of being animals too, especially the parties of schoolkids, often as grubby looking as the zoo's inhabitants, who delighted in tormenting the poor creatures who were at their mercy; throwing stones at the lions, startling the chimps with loud yelps, feeding doughnuts and greasy sausage rolls to anything that would eat them. If the keepers caught you at it they would throw you out, but there were always too many kids to pinpoint any one culprit.

So there we were, Wee Malkie and I, that nippy morning in February. I had been looking forward to this visit. Not that I was in the least bit interested in elephants or tigers or all the varied creatures that we were supposed to be fascinated by. I was there for one thing and one thing only, and the moment we were through the gates I began looking for my chance to sneak away from the noisy group and the teachers who were herding us. I had seen a sign for the reptile house, and was hanging at the back of the crowd of kids who had stopped in front of the chimpanzee enclosure. Wee Malkie pulled at my arm.

Haw, Donny, there's one over there looks like you.

Shut yer gob, or I'll shut it for ye.

I aimed a kick at his shins, and he danced away into the crowd, jumping up and down like a chimpanzee. Then he was back.

C'mon look, he said. It's playin wi its willy!

Sure enough, one of the poor animals was trying to induce some excitement into its humdrum existence, and the place was an uproar of giggling girls and shouting boys, the teachers already looking harassed as they tried to quiet them down.

You go an look, Malkie. Ah've seen enough wankers already.

Malkie couldn't help himself, he pushed into the crowd of kids and I took the opportunity then to slip away.

It took me a while to find the reptile house. I didn't have a map, and the signs were as haphazard as everything else in the zoo. The whole place had a strangely oppressive feel, something heavy hanging over it. The animals I passed were subdued, their listless forms half-glimpsed behind whatever shelter they could find in their enclosures. Even the keepers in their overalls and muddy boots seemed unhappy as they carted their buckets of fish or half-heartedly pushed a broom around, clearly unable to make a dent in the chaos around them. The whole place reeked of animal droppings and dilapidation.

Or maybe it was just me. Maybe I brought this gloom with me, carried it everywhere inside my head and trailed clouds of it wherever I went, tainting everything for miles around, draining all the colour and energy out of everything caught in my path. Where was the damned reptile house? I was completely lost now, at the bottom of a narrow pathway, surrounded by all kinds of strange birds in cages, raucous calls and melodic twittering. Birds held no interest for me at all, and I was getting impatient with myself, annoyed at the racket they made. I got to the bottom of the path and came to another, wider one that ran at right angles to it. There were no signs, and no one around, and the noise of the birds had receded, though I could hear water flowing from the burn that ran through the grounds. I turned to the left and, after a few minutes, the water sounds faded and I felt like I was no longer in the zoo, as if I'd accidentally wandered past the boundary and was now in some unearthly, alien place. The morning clouds had gone, and a mist was rising from the cold ground, catching the weak sunlight and making me squint against it. There were still patches of frost in the shadows, and I pulled my anorak tighter against the chill, my feet making a soft, scuffling sound against the broken tarmac as I plodded further along, fighting against a feeling of disorientation that bordered on dizziness.

And that's when I bumped into the reptile house. Literally bumped into it, because I'd been walking along with my head down, blindly following the tarmac path. When it turned to the right, I didn't, and then suddenly there was a brick wall and I was standing in front of it, rubbing my forehead. Looking up, I saw the sign that said REPTILE HOUSE, and further along, what looked like an entrance.

'House' was rather a grand title for what was really two rows of glass enclosures with a passage down the middle. The enclosures were heated to protect and invigorate their cold-blooded inhabitants, and the lights were kept dim as a further concession to various tropical and subtropical sensibilities. But even here there was a feeling of neglect. The snakes and lizards and other scaly creatures all lay perfectly still, wrapped around their bits of branches, or lying flat on their rocks and sandy beds, trying desperately to eke whatever energy they could out of the heat lamps glowing in their glass boxes.

When I found the turtle, it was lying still at the bottom of its enclosed tank, flippers pulled tightly against its shell, eyes closed. The tank was tiny, a cramped concrete box, painted blue, with an artificial sun picking out the cracks and chips in the walls, the motes floating in the dirty water. There was a rock ledge, and on the bottom of the tank, a bit of gravel

littered with sloughed patches of scaly skin. Nothing more—
apart from the turtle itself, that is.

A sign next to the tank said:

LOGGERHEAD TURTLE

*Distribution: Found in tropical and subtropical regions around
the world.*

*The loggerhead is named for its massive reddish-brown head and its
powerful jaws, which it uses to crush molluscs, crabs and encrusting
animals attached to reefs and rocks. The loggerhead travels widely
and has been found as far as 500 miles offshore. In many areas of
the world, this turtle is hunted for its meat and eggs.*

A photograph showed a magnificent animal swimming over a
coral reef, turbulence brimming behind its powerful flippers.
Its shell gleamed in rich seams of amber brown, its head
craned forward, seemingly pulling its body along behind it.
There was intelligence in its round eyes and it was clearly a
turtle that was going places and getting things done in its
busy turtle world.

The animal in the blue concrete tank bore so little relation
to this picture that I had to check I wasn't looking at the
wrong exhibit. Its shell was dull and had a greenish tinge to it
where algae had taken hold. Its flippers were loose and ragged,
with none of the sleekness of the turtle in the picture—more a
slightly flabby, kind of unused look. Its big head was stretched
out on the gravel, turned towards the glass divide. It was
looking up, straight at me, its beady eyes unblinking. As I
gazed back, my nose stuck firmly against the glass, I thought

I could see in its expression a reflection of myself, an echo of my own life, the familiarity of a kindred spirit. It looked sad. Sadder than even I could feel. But beyond its sadness, I sensed a mind at work, plotting and planning and calculating a way out of its prison. It was there, in its expression of weary cynicism, the tilt of its head, the way it lay so still.

And here was I. All those months of reading about turtles and turtle lore, studying their types, their habits, the way they lived and died. Envying them their freedom, and hanging on always to that vision of myself swimming through the singing water, turning and diving and spinning to the bottom of the ocean. What did I feel, face to face for the first time ever with a real, live amphibian? I felt the humid closeness of the reptile house, the cool of glass on skin, the feeling of being alone and unwatched. Important moments in life have a way of concealing themselves behind ordinary sensations. But as I gazed upon the motionless form at the bottom of the tank, I was thinking, *How do you do that?* How can you stay so long down there without coming up for air? Just lying there, small and still and quiet? And I found myself willing it to move. Just for me. To show me that it recognised something between us.

Thump!

I jumped as I felt the glass vibrate hard against my face, and with the sudden realisation that I was no longer alone, but was surrounded by boys. I hadn't heard them come in, I was so mesmerised by the creature in the tank. There were five of them. Joe Kelso and his mate Johnny McWhirter, and some other hangers on. Kelso had sneaked up behind me and banged the glass with the palm of his hand. At least it wasn't a brick—I wouldn't have put it past the bampot. All five of them were now laughing fit to burst.

Haw, Smelly Pinelli! Whit ur ye up tae, eh?

This was Kelso. He hated me. Not for any reason other than that I didn't hang about the streets at nights with him and his gang, telling him how wonderful he was. That, and being a Tally, of course, and an easy target for what little wit he possessed.

Thinkin aboot a wee bitta turtle soup, wop boy? Is that it? Tasty!

There was clutching of stomachs and cries of *boak!* from the other boys.

Tallies like that kinda stuff. Zat no right, Pinelli?

McWhirter hit the tank now, even harder than Kelso had, and I thought I saw the turtle flinch, though maybe it was just the distortion of the water. Then they were all banging on the glass, their shouts and yelps echoing off the brick walls of the reptile house as they tried to make the turtle move. I'd been pushed to one side, but as I saw Kelso raise his arm for another thump, and without thinking about what I was doing, I grabbed his wrist and pushed him away. He staggered backwards, lost his balance and fell over onto the concrete floor. The noise subsided raggedly into silence as everyone stood around trying to take in what had happened. Kelso was stronger than me, and known as a right headbanger, not to be messed with. There were rumours about him and what he'd done to other kids. Nasty rumours. The kind of rumours that some people wear like a halo, a ring of space around them, cool and unknowable. He moved slowly now, taking his time, still on one knee on the floor. No one tried to help him up; they were looking at me and smiling in anticipation of the massacre to come.

I realised then that I should do exactly what I never, ever do—go on the offensive, catch my opponent off-balance, stuff the Queensbury rules and all the nice-boy crap that goes with them. So I did. I lashed out with a right-footer that would have scored the decider at Hampden Park, aimed straight for Kelso's jaw as he raised himself up off the ground. And I would have followed through, too, with many more kicks to his head and his nether regions, hard kicks that would have taught the bastard a lesson he wouldn't forget in a hurry. Except that I missed. At the last vital millisecond, as my foot swung towards Kelso's face, the electric circuit in my head which tells me what a useless prick I am sparked into action and sent a message down my leg saying, what the fuck do you think you're doing exactly? I missed that first vital shot. Kelso dodged easily, caught me by the leg and pulled me onto the ground beside him, where suddenly I was trapped, straight in the path of his oncoming fist. He held it in the air for effect, just so that I had no doubt about what was coming. The other boys had formed a circle and were chanting *fight, fight, fight* in the moronic way that boys do. And then he hit me once, hard. Pause for effect, the chanting growing louder and more excited. Twice, harder. I could feel blood on my face, taste it in my mouth. His fist was raised again, the noise deafening, mixed with the roar in my own head. And then he was gone, his weight against me suddenly lifted. I was half aware of shouting and feet running away, and then someone cradling my head, and when I opened my eyes I saw a beard, blondish with streaks of grey, and I could smell fish.

Are you alright? The man had an accent that I couldn't place. Mudder of Got, look at that nose. Can you stand up?

Ah think so. My voice was a whisper.

He lifted me up slowly, then pulled out a handkerchief and told me to hold it over my nose. It was none too clean but at least it stopped me dripping blood over my shirt.

Come with me, he said, and we walked together out of the reptile house.

He led me up the road a bit, past various small mammals in their cages, and then down a side passage until we came to a hut that looked a bit like a garden shed, with one window and a door. He unlocked the padlock on the door and swung it open. Inside, it was bigger than I expected. And warm. There was a bench and a sink, and a couple of chairs, one of them quite comfortable looking, arranged around a paraffin heater. On the bench was a typewriter, and behind it some shelves with official-looking folders and a couple of thick books.

Sit down. Over there. The man pointed to the comfy chair. Lean your head back until the bleeding stops.

I heard him filling a kettle with water, and fiddling with the plug on the wall behind him. Then the kettle as it began to heat up.

Best ting for nosebleed is a good cup of tea, he said. What's your name?

Donald.

Donald? You can call me Jake. Not my real name, but will do.

What is yer real name?

Something you can't pronounce.

Are you a keeper?

He laughed, a little scornfully I thought, and then said, Sure, that's me. Keeper Jake.

Keeper Jake, he repeated to himself. He threw teabags into a couple of old mugs on the bench top and stood there, looking at the kettle.

Do you look after the turtle?

The turtle? He doesn't need much looking after.

It looks ill. Is it no well?

Jake turned and looked at me closely as if he was trying to work something out, though it may only have been that the light was dim and he was checking to see if my nose had stopped bleeding.

Oh, he is well enough, don't worry for that. How do you take your tea?

I asked for milk and three sugars, and he passed the mug to me. The hot, sweet liquid made me feel better immediately. For the first time, I noticed how tall Jake was; he almost had to stoop under the slanted roof of the hut. He was wearing green overalls, with the trousers tucked into welly boots, and a green cap on his head. The beard hid most of his face, but you could see he had one of those ruddy complexions that seemed common in men in those days, his nose bulbous, bordering on red. I watched him from the corner of my eye as he took a bottle from under the bench and splashed something into his mug. He'd half turned away from me and I understood by this that he was doing something wrong, something that others might disapprove of. I sipped my tea and pretended to be looking at the books on the shelf.

You are with the school trip today? Jake asked.

I nodded.

Why were those boys hitting you?

They were bangin on the glass, I said. Tryin to get the turtle to move.

And you wanted to stop them?

Ah suppose ah did. Ah'm not sure.

Jake sniffed. And the turtle, did he move?

No.

A smile played on his lips. Drink your tea and we go find your friends.

My nose throbbed and I could feel it swelling, and the last thing I wanted to do was leave the warmth of Jake's hut and go back into the harsh world outside. I imagined Joe Kelso and the rest out there waiting to finish the job they started. But Jake came with me, as he promised he would, and I felt safe with him, following his loping strides back up the path to the reptile house, where I'd left my schoolbag. It wasn't there.

We check in lost property, said Jake. Somebody may hand it in.

But I couldn't care less about the bag. I was already standing in front of the turtle's tank. He—Jake had called him 'he'— was still in the same position on the gravel at the bottom, hunched tight against his protective shell, small and sad.

Why does he never move?

Jake came over and looked into the tank with me.

He don't move much, that is true.

How can he hold his breath for so long?

Well, you know, he's had a lot of practice.

I thought maybe Jake was losing patience with my questions, but I kept going.

There must be some special way he does it, holds his breath like that?

Sure, he has many tricks. You like turtles, eh?

Ah've been studying them, I said, a little self-importantly.

It's good to study, said Jake. Come, let's go and—

Look! He moved!

I wasn't sure, but I thought I'd seen a flipper twitch. Jake gave a little laugh, as though the idea were too absurd to contemplate, and we were just about to walk away when the tank came alive. Without any more warning, the Turtle launched himself off and up, turning over as he passed in front of our noses, suddenly larger and more powerful as he raced to the surface. I realised then that the glass of the tank caused an optical distortion that made him look smaller than he really was, and that even though his shell was mottled with algae and his flippers seemed thin and weedy, the shape of his movement through the water had the grace and ease and strength of a dancer.

I watched as he settled on the rock ledge, half his body still in the water, his small round eyes reflecting the light from the heat lamps, one eye wider than the other, a bleariness there, a slightly hungover look. If this turtle had a head of hair, it would be tousled and sticking up in the middle. He turned and looked at me, and it was then I heard the singing. The same singing voices that I'd heard in Trixie's shell. Clear as day they were, though whether coming from inside the tank or inside my own head, I didn't know. What I did know at that moment, with more certainty than I've ever known anything since, was this: I was looking at my future. Although I had no idea what shape or form it might take, I knew that this turtle, imprisoned in his cramped, shabby tank in a run-down zoo, was the saviour I'd been looking for. I looked at him then and he looked at me and I wanted him to speak, to acknowledge that we were connected, our fates intertwined.

He spoke.

I swear it, the Turtle spoke to me.

I don't mean like speech with real language and sound that everyone else could hear. I mean he spoke just to me. We communicated, boy and Turtle. You can think what you like, but I heard him, and it's a moment I've hung onto all my life, as real as anything in this life can be. How can I explain it? Something passed between us. Feelings. Emotions, I suppose you'd call them. What the Turtle said to me that first time was just what I expected to hear, and what surprised me most was how real the connection between us was, how utterly I believed in it and in everything it promised. He spoke my language.

It all happened in a second or two. The singing, the Turtle moving, then the look, and the flash of communication. And then I was aware again of Jake the keeper standing next to me, his hands in his pockets. He was smiling his half-smile.

You see, he said. Good as rain, the old bugger.

We found my classmates at one of the outdoor picnic areas a little way off from the reptile house. It was lunchtime. Joe Kelso was nowhere to be seen, but I could see Wee Malkie sitting on his own at the edge of a pond full of ducks and other waterfowl. I could see, too, that he had my bag with him, as well as his own. He was throwing bits of sandwich into the water, and had attracted a gaggle of birds, screeching and pecking at each other as they raced to get the food into their beaks.

I pointed out Wee Malkie and my bag to Jake. He wanted to speak to one of the teachers about what had happened, but I told him he didn't have to bother, that I was alright now, and thanks for the cup of tea. He loped off back down the hill. Wee Malkie was watching.

Who's yer friend? he asked, when I sat down next to him.

No one you'd know.

Look at yer nose! Rudolph the Reindeer!

Shut yer gob, Malkie. How did ye get ma bag?

Joe Kelso had it.

Did he? Did he steal ma lunch, too?

Malkie looked away, studying the birds. Aye, he said. If it's no there.

There was nothing in the schoolbag, no books, no pencil case, no lunch. The books and the pencils could be anywhere, probably being chewed to shreds by some animal malcontents, but I knew exactly where my lunch was. Wee Malkie was feeding it to the birds. I could recognise one of my own sandwiches anywhere, even when it was being chased to blazes by assorted wildlife.

I didn't say anything, because it didn't matter. Wee Malkie knew that I knew he'd been fibbing. That he'd stolen the sandwiches out of my bag and threw everything away to make it look like Kelso had done it. That meant that Wee Malkie had also seen what happened in the reptile house, and he'd done nothing to help. It was enough for me then that he knew I knew, and that he felt bad about it. I could twist that to suit me at any time in the future.

I suppose you're wondering what it was the Turtle told me as he lay on his rock and our eyes met? What important and momentous message was communicated reptile to mammal? Well, nothing really. And everything. As I say, he spoke my language, and I knew what he meant, even if it wasn't what he said.

If it was a movie the script would've gone like this:

The Turtle looks up and establishes a connection with the boy. Their look together evokes the very mystery of life itself, the oneness of all living creatures in their shared origin deep in the primordial mud from which we all began, and from which we have each of us slithered in one shape or another in our long pursuit of evolutionary advantage. His lines are, 'Donald, your quest is over. Fear not, my boy, for I will save you from the curse.'

OK, got that, Turtle? Take a moment to fix character. And, action!

Haw, look at you, ya daft wee bastard. You're well fucked, int ye?

Cut!

That's what he said, the Turtle, my friend and mentor and the saviour of my miserable life. But he laughed as he said it, and I knew that he was on my side.

12

IT'S TWENTY PAST FOUR in the morning by Trixie's old
watch. Her bedroom's a mess. Dust, splinters of wood, old
shoe boxes full of useless bits of paper over the floor and the
bed. Clothes thrown anywhere. The two cupboard doors
leaning against a wall, where they've gouged holes in the wallpaper. They don't look out of place because the whole room
is a complete tip.

I take the cassette tape out of its box and stare at it, as if it
might start to speak on its own. It's a sixty-minute one, but
looking at the position of the tape I estimate that no more
than a few minutes have been recorded. I'm not sure I want
to hear what's on it, whether I'm ready to hear Trixie's voice.
Whatever she has to say is not likely to be along the lines of

Hello, long-lost son, I've missed you, here's what I've been doing the last thirty-odd years. That was never her style. More likely she just wants to spit on me from beyond the grave.

I get up anyway and start a half-hearted search through the house for a tape player, knowing there has to be one somewhere. Trixie was a pioneer, if nothing else, in the field of clairvoyance. She'd read somewhere once that people used tape recorders to pick up sounds from the beyond, spectral voices and that. It worked like this: the intrepid ghost hunter would take a tape recorder to a place that was known to be haunted and would plug in a microphone and let the thing run. Later, when they played it back, they'd hear the ghostie talking to them—or maybe just talking to itself, who knows? It was quite popular for a while, though most of the recordings were scratchy, slurred kinds of things that you'd have to listen to several times before you heard *MacDonald did it*, or *the evil one cometh*, or some such shite. Anyway, Trixie was quite taken with the idea, and one of the things she did when she turned herself into Madam Pinelli and started receiving paying clients was she bought herself one of those newfangled portable cassette recorders. She used it to record her sessions and then listen back later for any help or advice from the nether world. People liked it, she said, though I suspect it was really her that liked it because she thought she was being daring and modern, and she always tried to keep up with the times. She fair loved that cassette player, so she did.

There's nothing immediately obvious in the upstairs rooms, and I creep down the stairs, carefully, one step at a time, holding onto the banister for support, like the old man I'm coming to be. My head's pounding. I have that scratchy feeling that you get when you've been on the go for too long between a change of clothes. What I need first is a shave and a bit of a spruce-up, some coffee maybe. I find my way to the kitchen to put the kettle on, and then I think no, I'll shower, and then I can't remember where I dumped my suitcase and by the time I find it, in the living room, everything seems too hard. The thought of unpacking anything is beyond me, as though if I do that I'll have to admit to myself that I'm going to stay. Settle in. The idea grates on me like chalk on a blackboard. What am I doing here? How is it possible for this house to have continued to exist all these years without me, and for me to exist without it? There was a time when I thought it was a part of me, as real as an arm or a leg, but as I stumble around the place now, dithering about whether to make coffee or have a shower, I think something else. I think maybe I was merely a part of the house, a fragment of its history, like the architraves or the casement windows, and that the house is reaching out now to gather me back into itself. If I stay here long enough, I'll be absorbed into its brick like nothing more than a patch of rising damp. Maybe I should find a hotel. But at this time in the morning? What's the point? Trixie's funeral is at eleven-thirty, and I don't want to miss it. Anyway, sleep is dangerous. Find a tape player.

It takes me till after five am to find one, a relic from the 1970s, maybe the same one Trixie bought herself when she first got into her spectral voices kick. I eventually discover it where I should have looked all along, in the kitchen, at the bottom of a box of her stuff under the table. There's a power cord with it, so I plug it in. Amazingly, it works.

I'm not going to tell you yet what Trixie said to me on the tape. I could say it's none of your business anyway, that it's a private matter between mother and son. But that's not why I'm keeping stum. The real reason is that after listening to the voice of my mother I need more time to think, because my mother's voice—the voice of a stranger and yet at the same time so familiar that it hurts to hear her speak—that voice, and what it has to say, changes a lot of things, and it threatens to push me and my story aside. Trixie and her damned curse have controlled my life for much too long. Before you hear what she has to say about anything, you have to let me finish my version. It feels like it's starting to collapse around me anyway, but I need to press on. I can't let it go. Not yet.

I will tell you this though, just so you can understand how difficult everything in our life was and is. After I heard the tape I went back up to Trixie's ruined bedroom. I was troubled about how she managed to conceal things under the floor of the cupboard. Searching through the mess, I found the little trapdoor, which opened into the space I'd broken my way through to. In my haste and hurry I'd assumed it had been built over after all these years, but it was there all along, just not where I thought I remembered it. If I hadn't been so stupid I could have saved myself a lot of trouble.

It's five-thirty and I haven't made coffee and I haven't showered and to be honest I can't be bothered. Leave it for a bit. Sit down, pour myself a whisky, that's easy. Melt into this armchair. I won't go to sleep anyway, because I can't stop thinking. About Trixie and the stuff she left for me to find. About the Turtle. About Wee Malkie, Luce, Mr Disco, Carlo. And Anna McColl, God help me, who smiled at me the day she disappeared. But I smiled back at her all wrong, and my fly was open, and the conductor wouldn't let me on her bus because it was full. And by the time I got the next bus I was just too bloody late.

Too bloody late.

No, I won't sleep. Not yet. There's much more to tell you, more than enough to keep me going until it's time to leave for the funeral. Anna McColl smiled at me and her smile was like the second coming and the fireworks over Sydney Harbour all at once. She saved my life, so she did. Not that she ever knew this, because she disappeared on the very same after-noon—abducted we thought then, or something else. But I'm getting ahead of myself again. Before Anna disappeared, and before I took the plunge into my long exile from the family Pinelli, there were long, difficult years of growing up. Adoles-cent years, with all the usual complications—mood swings, acne, a nose that was growing faster than the rest of my face. Not to mention self-doubt and a shyness that bordered on the pathological. I wore an anorak with the hood up, even through the whole of one summer. During the first couple of years of high school I kept mostly to myself, making no new friends. Wee Malkie avoided me, too busy discovering himself, seem-ingly energised by the process of maturity, finding a confi-dence and purpose and blossoming into Mr One-of-the-boys while I sank further and further into my anorak.

Wee Malkie was, and still is, a complete wanker, but he never had Trixie to contend with. His adolescence wasn't presided over by a mother who sucked hope out of you like milkshake through a straw. A mother whose major contribution to family life was that everything is preordained, that you can't deny fate and that it's all written up there on the great whiteboard of eternity, clear as day for those ready to see it. If your name's down for a good and happy life, so be it. If not, you're buggered and that's all there is to it. I was buggered, well and truly, my fate scrawled out in red marker. *Confused*: tick. *Spotty and smelly*: tick. *Cursed to an early death*: tick.

Not a hope.

The girl at the undertaker's told me there would be a church service for Trixie's funeral. Why? The only religion she belonged to was her own tottering edifice of fears and superstitions. The Church of the Blessed Trixie, believer and unbeliever, heretic and martyr all rolled into one. But that's not right, because she was, of course, a staunch Protestant who distrusted Catholics, though she never really knew why. Maybe because they liked the colour green. More likely because she was just a bigot, and the world is a more comforting place if you can bleach the colours out and separate the black from the white.

Yet despite being a Protestant and a Presbyterian who would swear undying allegiance to the stodgy old Church of Scotland, she rarely set foot in the place. Weddings, funerals, that was it. If you asked her, she would say that she believed in God. But she believed in God the way she believed in everything else—as just another mystery in the great puzzle of life, and no different therefore from believing in the supernatural forces of good and evil which she dealt with daily: the few friendly spirit guides, revealers of the future, and the legions of malicious creatures waiting to take their revenge if you wore the wrong colour or sat at the corner of the table. That's to say, Trixie believed in God as a kind of insurance against the possibility that God existed and, worse, had her fingered as one of the more difficult of His creatures whose destiny in the hereafter was still under consideration.

The truth is that Trixie was her own religion. She was the centre of her own cult, and we were her unwitting followers. And that meant adhering to a set of beliefs that she, in her role as high priestess, would regulate and police. No alternative view was allowed, however much we clashed in the real world of school and play with other ways of looking at things. Trixie demanded that we follow only her, and that we reject all other gods.

But I was becoming a heretic, my resistance forged through an unholy alliance of spotty boy and curmudgeonly turtle, hammered out in secret and on pain of certain death at the hands of Trixie's inquisition. No matter how much Trixie drew me into her world of fate and fairies, clairvoyance and curses, a part of me was having none of it. It was a flaw in her logic, if you like, the inevitability of fate against a child's will to survive. As I got older I developed a habit of putting down Trixie's gift, belittling her abilities, laughing at her messing around with the supernatural and the 'world beyond'. It was a form of self-defence on my part, necessary to my survival, but it was just an act; deep down, I believed in her and, even though I would have denied it with my dying breath, I believed in the curse.

This is what I've only now come to understand, though none of it mattered to me then. I wasn't wandering around thinking all this shite about what I believed and didn't believe when I was twelve years old. I was too busy just trying to find ways to exist. But I do exist, as you've no doubt noticed. I survived the curse, didn't I?

I've often thought since that I survived entirely through my own wits, that I took control of my own destiny. But that's not how it felt then. How it felt then was like looking down from the sloping deck of the *Titanic* at a tiny wee lifebelt bobbing in the water far below. I had to jump, but before that I had to learn to swim. The simple fact is this: the Turtle taught me how to swim.

Aye.
An it wisny jist the swimmin.
Ah taught ye how
tae hold the sweet breath uv freedom in those
stupit mammal lungs uv yours.
How tae kerry the whole bastardin wurld on yer back.
Ah mean,
fuck's sake, pal,
that's whit bein a turtle's aw aboot.

13

THE NEXT TIME I visited the zoo, I was on my own.

It was a few weeks later, a Saturday. I told Trixie that I was going to Wee Malkie's. Not that she cared anyway, because it was one of her bad days, I remember, and she couldn't have given a toss what we did, so long as we kept well out of her way. At breakfast, Luce and I had fought over the last few Frosties in the box, and when it turned out there was no milk anyway, she'd thrown the bowl at me, giving me a bruise under the eye. The bowl had shattered on the floor, spilling bits of crockery and Frosties everywhere, and I remember the swelling pain in my face and the crunching underfoot as I stormed out of the kitchen, grabbed my anorak, and left the house, slamming the front door loudly. Luce could sort out the mess with Trixie, and I hoped she ended up spending the day in the coal shed.

I had brought nothing for lunch, I had no money for the bus, and I had no idea how I was going to get into the zoo once I got there. I started walking anyway, my hands deep in my pockets. I was seething, that's what I mostly remember about that morning. Angry, and walking as quickly as I could down through our suburb and along the main road, buffeted by the wake of the traffic tearing past, the rank smell of diesel fumes and the feeling of everything coated in a fine layer of grit.

It was nearly an hour's walk to the zoo, but the closer I got the more hopeless it all seemed to become, and the slower I walked. So I don't really know how long it took before I was standing outside the big gate with the turnstile to one side and the pay booth with its little window, wondering what to do next.

It was just on opening time, and there was no one waiting to go in. I hung around the entrance for a bit, watching the woman in the pay booth who was busy with some bits of paper. She didn't give me a glance. It was quiet, only the birds and the distant chattering of monkeys, the muted swoosh of traffic on the motorway. I sat down on a bench to one side of the entrance. After a while, a bus pulled up and a few people got off: a family with a pram and a couple of noisy kids; an old couple, the man walking with a stick; a man in a checked shirt with a camera slung around his neck. They all lined up at the ticket booth, where the ticket seller was still fiddling with her paperwork. Without really thinking about it, I joined the queue. I had some vague idea that I could sneak under the turnstile or something, or pretend to be part of the family that was waiting. I stood behind the old man with the walking stick, sandwiched between him and the geezer in the checked shirt. But then another bus arrived and suddenly there was a whole crowd of people forming a queue behind him, so that I found myself stuck there, in the narrow neck of the entrance. I suppose I could have squeezed back through them all, but for whatever reason, I didn't. The ticket seller had roused herself and the queue was moving forward and I moved forward with it, until eventually I was standing in front of the wee window.

The woman gave me a look. Twelve ur over? she asked.

Actually, ah'm here to see Jake. The words came out without thought, but I realised it was true, to a point. I was here to see Jake, because Jake looked after the Turtle.

The woman gave me a sour look. Ye can only come through here if yer payin, she said.

Jake said ah could come and see him this mornin.

Well, ye should've asked at the gatehouse.

The man behind me was becoming impatient. I could hear him tutting to himself.

Ah didny know, I said. Can ye no just let me through this way?

The ticket seller looked at the growing queue of people behind me. The look on her face said clearly that her day was not starting well and was only going to get worse. Mr Checked Shirt was complaining to the people behind him. The usual stuff. Inefficient service, it's a wonder they do any business at all.

Ye huv tae buy a ticket. She said it slowly, trying to sound firm, but I sensed her resolve was weakening against the impatience of the queue.

Ah've no got any money, but.

She sighed loudly and raised her eyes to heaven. Okay, ye kin go through. But wait on the other side, mind. Someone'll come fur ye. Don't you dare move!

As I pushed my way through the turnstile, I saw her pick up the phone next to her and dial. She eyed me suspiciously as she waited for an answer and then spoke briefly into the receiver and put it back down. I stood on the other side of the turnstile, on the edge of an open area where there were a few benches and tables. Off to one side there was the zoo shop and the information desk.

I waited for what seemed like ages, scuffing my shoes on the bitumen. The zoo was filling up with people and I remember thinking that I shouldn't have come on a Saturday, that there would be too many people around and I wouldn't be able to get close to the Turtle. Next time I would come on a weekday. I was already thinking about a next time, even though I wasn't at all sure they would let me in today.

Is that him, Marie?

The voice made me jump. A man in a blue uniform and a peaked cap was standing behind me. I thought at first it was the police, but he didn't have the chequered band on his cap, and he was the wrong shape, short and fat. Not like your regular Mr Plod.

Aye, that's him. Says he's looking fur Jake.

The man turned to me. Is that right, son?

I nodded.

Whit happened tae yer eye? He was looking at me suspiciously.

Ah walked into a lamp-post.

Oh aye? Ur you a friend a Jake's, then?

He's helping me with ma school project.

Och, school project, is it? Ur ye on the list?

Ah don't know.

Ye better come wi me, then.

I was led into an office around the corner from the entrance. There was a kind of waiting area, and I was told to sit down on one of the plastic chairs. The man in the uniform wanted to know what school I was from and who my teacher was and I knew that when I told him he would go and check up on his list and that would be that. They would chuck me out. I told him some nonsense anyway, and he said to wait there for a moment while he sorted it. Off he went, into another office.

The moment he was gone, so was I. No hesitation, I simply got up and walked outside and mingled with the growing crowd, and then I belted as fast as I could down the hill to the reptile house. There were zoo staff about, keepers finishing their morning duties, the clatter of buckets and cage doors slamming shut. A tractor with a trailer came crawling slowly up the hill towards me, belching fumes, and I slowed down to a fast walk, hoping no one would spot my anxiety. It was quieter at the bottom of the hill as I followed the path around the bend, just me and the echo of small animal noises, fed and contented presumably—though who knows, maybe those twitterings and scratchings and curious yelps were the sounds of despair, the murmurings of lost hope. That's what I was thinking as I ducked into the doorway of the reptile house and the noises faded out behind me. The swelling under my eye had started to throb again and I noticed for the first time that the eye had closed up a bit as I squinted through it towards the tank at the far end. But even from this distance, one eye blurred and neither eye adjusted to the darkness, I could see that the tank was empty. There was no Turtle.

Sometimes it seems like you know what's going to happen before it happens, as if you're walking several paces behind your own life. I realised, as I stood looking into the empty tank, that I knew all the time that the old bugger wouldn't be there. That he couldn't possibly be there, just waiting for me. That would be too easy, too much to expect. I knew all that, but it didn't stop the panic rising. Maybe he's dead? Maybe he's ill? Or they've taken him away to some other zoo? The next thing I knew I was banging on the door of Jake's hut.

At least *he* was there, all present and correct. And the kettle was on. Or was it? My memories play tricks on me, showing me now what I wanted to see then: Jake, in his cosy hut, with the kettle on and a welcoming smile. But maybe that's not how it was. Maybe Jake was round the back, or maybe he took a while to stash away his whisky bottle. And maybe I just barged right into the hut without knocking, calling his name frantically. And his look, when he finally appeared, might have been one of astonishment rather than welcome. In any case, I found myself inside his hut. It took a moment before he recognised me and then, finally, there was the smile, and a quizzical look.

Donald, isn't it?

The Turtle . . .

What have you done to your eye?

Where's the Turtle, Jake, where is it?

Be calm, Donald. What is the problem, now?

I think that's when I started crying. I remember thinking that it was all pointless, there was no way anyone was ever going to believe me about my mother, the curse, the Turtle. But when I looked up at Jake's concerned face, something about it gave me courage. What I said was this:

I'm gauny die, Jake. Ah need to find the Turtle.

At that very moment, however, there was a knock on the door and the gruff voice of Mr Security Guard, who had put two and two together and launched an investigation into my sudden disappearance from his office.

Ur ye there, Jake?

I swore under my breath and looked around desperately for somewhere to hide.

Jake looked at me and then at the door. He was quick on the uptake, I'll give him that. He kept his eyes on me as he replied in a calm voice, Just one minute, Bill.

Stay there, he whispered to me. Then he went out to meet the security guard, who was standing next to a green Land Rover. A walkie-talkie crackled occasionally from inside the cab and I could hear Jake and the guard talking but I couldn't make out what they were saying. After a while, Jake opened the door and called me outside.

Donald, this is Bill. You have met already, I think.

Why did ye no tell me ye were Jake's nephew?

Er . . . Ah jist panicked. Ah'm sorry.

Ah wisny gauny hurt ye, son. Uch well, it disny metter. As long as we've cleared this up. Come by later on for yer pass.

Pass?

Aye. As Jake's looking efter ye, ye're entitled tae a pass tae get intae the zoo. Seeing as ye're doin the school project an that, ye might find it useful. Okay? See ye later, then.

I didn't know what to say. One minute I'm expecting to be thrown out on my ear, the next I'm being given a pass to get in and see the Turtle any time I like. I mumbled my thanks, not daring to look Bill in the face in case he saw the lies and deceit in my eyes and changed his mind. But he turned and climbed back into his Land Rover, crunched the gears and drove slowly off up the hill.

I think you have some explaining to do, said Jake, as we walked back into his hut.

I think *you've* got some explaining to do, Jake.

And so, for the better part of the rest of that morning, Jake and I explained ourselves to each other. He'd told Bill that I was his orphaned nephew and that he was looking after me, and that he was helping me to learn about turtles. I told him . . . well, everything. The amazing thing is that I didn't feel stupid about it. Not with Jake. He listened to my story as if curses and mad mothers and criminal fathers were the kind of things every kid had to put up with. When he asked me what I planned to do about it all, I told him about the Turtle, and how it spoke to me, and how I was sure it was going to help me. This was pushing it a bit, I knew, but Jake never wavered. It was as if he were a child himself, effortlessly negotiating the impossibility of my child's world, not treating it as imaginary, but entering into it fully, as I did—a brutal world, dangerous and deadly and only too real.

The upshot was that Jake promised to help me. I could come as often as I liked to see the Turtle, and he would teach me how to look after it. He also mentioned that he helped out at a local youth club, and that along with a disco and the occasional Sunday hike in the country, he took the kids to the swimming baths once a week. He suggested I should join them.

It's good to exercise. Young boy like you, work off some energy.

My dreams of water so far had only really focused on the sea. It had never occurred to me before to go to the baths. No one in our family swam, and the only organised sport at school was soccer, which I hated. Even the thought of a swimming pool went against the grain of who we were and where we lived. It was usually too cold to contemplate the idea, usually too wet and dreary for it to make much sense. I knew that people did it, but I always thought of them as being a bit daft, like people who wear sandals all year round, or eat nothing but carrots.

But when Jake mentioned the idea, something clicked into place in my head and I saw myself cavorting effortlessly underwater like the turtles in the books I read, and like the Turtle himself when he'd surfaced that day in his tank and had spoken to me. I would learn to swim. It made perfect sense, didn't it, for a boy who was cursed to die by drowning?

Trixie was a problem, as usual. If I asked her if I could go to the swimming baths she was bound to say no. She'd be suspicious, trying to work out what I was up to. So if I was going to learn to swim, I would have to do it in secret. No one could know, not even Wee Malkie.

And that's what happened. From then on I was able to get into the zoo any time I wanted, and so began a routine where I'd spend most afternoons after school at the swimming baths or visiting the Turtle. And more often than not I'd be at the zoo on Saturday, as well. Trixie thought I was seeing Wee Malkie. At least that's what I told her, and she seemed to fall for it. She never checked with Malkie's folks, or even inquired if I'd had a good time, or what we'd done. And she never once asked why I came back with my hair sticking up, smelling of chlorine. I should have been more wary of how easy it all was, but I didn't know then what I know now. And even if I did, I'm not sure that it would have changed anything.

It was hard at first, the swimming. The baths were run-down and not very clean, the water tepid and uninviting. I hated the changing room, the putting on and taking off of clothes. I was self-conscious about my body—not just the weediness of it, but also the turtle-shaped birthmark on my neck, the mark of my doom. I was always slow getting ready, waiting till the other kids had finished. As for the water, it took me weeks before I could just jump in, rather than lower myself bit by bit, fretting about how cold it was and how much I hated getting wet. It took longer yet to learn to swim.

Jake was no help. He didn't swim anymore, he said; he was too old for swimming. He spent the weekly sessions at the baths sitting on one of the benches at the side of the pool, reading a newspaper, a pair of broken spectacles perched on the end of his nose. Every now and then he'd check to see that no one was drowning or getting into trouble with the authorities. There was lots of the usual clowning around; dive-bombing and splashing and sneaking up behind the more timid kids and pushing them in. They were having fun, as kids do in water, but I kept myself to myself, finding a quiet spot to practise my strokes. No one seemed to notice the lonely boy floundering about, ducking under the water and coming back up, choking and spluttering, time after time. They probably thought I was a wee bit daft in the head, which, let's be honest, wasn't far off the mark.

But I wasn't teaching myself. The Turtle helped me. Of course he wasn't physically there with me at the baths. But I heard his voice. As I floundered around in the dirty swimming pool, swallowing the chlorinated water and despairing of ever being able to hold my head above it, he'd be there inside me, haranguing and cajoling, laughing at my clumsy efforts, goading me on with his sarcasm. Even above the reverberating shrieks and cries and splashes, and the raucous, garbled messages through the tannoy, I'd hear him: Move the arms so, the legs like this, hold your head forward, breathe like this, tuck your limbs close to your sides and tumble.

No like that ya daft eejit. Christ, ah've seen a hawf-brick swim better than that. Listen. Pull wi yer front flippers, steer wi the back yins. Goat it? An ye don't huv tae swally the whole pool . . .

I also learnt from watching him at the zoo. I watched every graceful, if rare, movement of his flippers, the way he stretched his neck towards his goal, the way he gulped air and held it inside him, a bubble of hope and defiance against the world beyond the surface. In time, I grew stronger and bolder, until there came a point when I too could swoop and dive and propel myself along underwater at a decent speed. I never achieved his gracefulness, for I lacked his streamlined form and let's face it, there is nothing graceful about a human being trying to swim like a turtle. Other swimmers laughed when they saw my style—arms forward, bent at the elbows, pulling through the water while my legs trailed behind in a curious sideways kicking motion.

But the hardest trick of all to learn was how to hold my breath underwater, and how to stay there for as long as possible. The turtle insisted that this was vital, that I would get nowhere if all I ever did was flounder on the surface like all the other gormless specimens of humanity who thought they knew what swimming was about. He said he'd show me how to do it, and he did—though, as I say, it wasn't easy.

Time after time, I sat at the bottom of the pool, feeling like I was about to burst, and he'd laugh at my panic as I clawed my way desperately to the surface, gasping and retching when I broke through into the humid, chlorine-scented air. The secret, he said, was in the mind. To get the most out of that one last breath before your head goes under completely, you had, first and foremost, to relax, to let yourself become calm and focused. That meant getting over my fears, and there were lots of them, believe me; fear of Trixie, fear of failing in my quest, fear of drowning. The Turtle thought this last was hilarious. He couldn't understand how any creature—even one as ungainly as me—could be scared of something as benign as water. Didn't I understand that water was life itself, the element that spawned each and every creature on this earth, and that it was living on dry land that was unnatural?

We turtles've been aroon since the year dot, long before you bloody humans came oan the scene. So we know whit we're talkin aboot. Jist relax, wee yin. Let yersel come back tae the bosom uv creation. Find the turtle within. Or whitever it is you mammalian types huv within. It disny bear thinkin aboot.

Find the turtle within. I had found it before, the day Trixie forced me to listen to the shell. I knew it was there, and I knew what it felt like. But it wasn't until after many months of immersing myself in water at every opportunity—at the swimming pool certainly, but also by filling the basin in the bathroom with cold water and plunging my face into it, or by submerging myself in the bath, using a stopwatch to see how I was improving—that I gradually lost my fear of water and began to feel at home in it. And as that happened I found I was able to will myself into a particular attitude of mind which was more aquatic than terrestrial. It's hard to explain, but somewhere inside me *was* a place of calmness and ease, a gentle pool of relaxation; the singing voices that I'd heard, years before, in Trixie's seashell. At first I had to wait and concentrate, thinking of a particular image of a turtle soaring, full-flippered, over a coral reef. Then I would hear the voices, and I would feel myself change inside.

After a long time, it all became automatic. I found I could trigger this meditative state just through the touch of cold water on my forehead and temples. The instant this happened, I would feel my breathing slow and a warm glow suffuse my body. I could make it happen just by splashing water on my face at the bathroom sink, but if I was at the swimming baths, I would dive down to the bottom and stay under for as long as I could, sometimes swimming the length of the pool, sometimes just lying there in a deep corner. I was as close to bliss as I imagined any landlocked mammal could get, wrapped as I was in that sweet singing, and in the consoling water which ebbed and flowed around me. I wanted to stay down there forever.

The Turtle himself could stay submerged for hours, and sometimes it seemed, watching him, that he didn't need to breathe at all. I was never able to equal his turtlish capacity, of course, and he counselled me against trying, reminding me of my limitations, and warning me of the dangers facing human divers—namely that, if not careful, I might forget that I needed to breathe altogether, and would simply die without realising it. *Relax, breathe slowly, then wan last gulp*, he told me. *That's aw ye need before ye go under. Wan last big gulp.*

But all of this was in the future. Now I was in Jake's hut, basking in a new sensation of trust and sympathy. When I finally remembered that the Turtle hadn't been in his tank earlier that morning, I asked Jake where he was.

I'm cleaning his tank. Come, we rescue him.

We walked over to the reptile house, and I followed Jake through a gate at the side and around to the back. There, in a low building that looked like a large greenhouse, was a series of concrete baths, each full of water. The air inside was warm and humid. It reminded me of the glasshouses at the Botanic Gardens. Jake led me to one of the tanks and there was the Turtle himself, hunched in only a foot or so of water, barely enough to cover his shell. He looked small and vulnerable. Jake showed me where to hold him and we lifted him out together and carried him back to his newly scrubbed concrete tank, where the water now gleamed and sparkled under the rays of the UV lamp.

He immediately dived to the bottom and folded his flippers tightly against his shell, his back towards us. He was in a huff.

Uch yer arse
in parsley,
ah wis not in a huff!
How wid you like it onyway,
being manhandled by that reekin auld bastard
uv a keeper?
No tae mention yer good fuckin self,
touchin me up
like some sleazy pervert, yer paws
aw over me.
Ah wisny in a huff, but.

14

HE WAS ALWAYS in some mood or other. But I never let this put me off. While other kids were discovering drink, drugs and the delights of groping each other down the back of the dance hall, I was happily turning myself into a reptile, just like him. Not that I wasn't aware that I was missing something, or that I was looked on as some kind of sad weirdo by my peers. What they saw was a shy, spotty boy with a Tally surname who blended in with the background, and who had little interest in sport, music or fashion. Well, to some extent that was all true. I had no interest in being hip, that's for sure, and I was far too busy working on my survival strategy to be bothered with drugs or drink. But by the time I was sixteen I'd got over the anorak phase, and I'd started to care a little about what I looked like in public. I'd discovered Anna McColl. One moment she was part of the anonymous, monochrome mass of girls who kept to their own playground and their own curious games and rituals. Then she blossomed into focus and I found myself staring wistfully at the back of her head in class, watching her chew the ends of her hair, hoping that she'd somehow notice me. But she never looked. I think I told you that. She never gave me anything like hope. Not until the day she smiled.

As for the curse, I had come by now to think of it as something solid; a hard, jagged-edged kind of thing, though if truth be told, by this time it had melded more and more into the background of our everyday lives, part of the drab wallpaper and the dusty curtains, the weave of the rugs under our feet. But its impact on Luce and me was as baleful as ever, warping our growing personalities, feeding our sibling animosity. Luce only half believed in it, but that didn't stop her using it against me, taunting me with it.

You're gauny die.

Shut it!

Yer gauny die, yer gauny die, yer gauny die!

Shut yer gob!

Ye could save us aw the bother an just slit yer wrists now.

And she'd hold up one of Carlo's old razor blades, waving it under my nose. You might well ask at this point, what was Luce's problem exactly? And I might tell you lots of shite about sibling rivalry, the two of us forever squabbling over the few crumbs of affection that fell from Trixie's sparse emotional larder. I might tell you that she was jealous of me because I was the centre of our mother's attention, such as it was, and that, as far as Luce was concerned, I was the chosen one and she wasn't. Never mind that I was chosen to die. Anyway, I might tell you all that, and there might even be some truth to it, but all I know for sure is that she hated me, and I hated her.

It was inevitable that Luce would find out about the Turtle and about my secret aquatic life. Unlike Trixie, who seemed to notice nothing, Luce was alert to everything I did. She saw the telltale signs. Not just the smell of chlorine in my hair or the scent of zoo that I brought back on my shoes, or the fact that I was spending so much time away from the house. What Luce noticed more than anything—what she homed in on with the instinct of a hungry shark—was the fact that I was happy. Or as near happy as you could expect in the circumstances. Try as I might, I couldn't hide it, this strange idea growing inside me that there might yet be hope. I didn't have to say anything, but I was giving off signals anyway. A lighter step maybe, or a bit less attitude. Maybe I even smiled more.

Mr Disco noticed it too.

Haw, Donny boy, where's yer anorak?

It was the beginning of summer, before school broke up, and already unusually warm. Mr Disco had been coming round to our place a bit, sleeping over some nights in the spare room, and it was starting to feel like he'd moved in, with his stupid grin and his moustache like Frank Zappa's. He was upsetting Trixie, too. He wanted to borrow money. Not from her, she didn't have any, but from Carlo, through her. At least that's what I thought at first, that he was pestering Trixie to ask Carlo for money on his behalf, or to soften Carlo up before he made his own pitch. The chances of getting anything out of Carlo were minuscule, to say the least. But Mr Disco was an optimist. And ambitious. He'd try any angle, stoop to anything, to get what he needed. At that time he and his band were still a struggling bunch of long-haired heads who shared some damp flat in Byres Road. They needed money for equipment and for a van so they could travel to gigs. It cost a fortune to rent rehearsal spaces, he said, and to finance their own recording sessions. Anyway, the nett effect was that he was forever round at our place for a feed, and to try his luck on the money front, and he'd never fail to needle me while he was at it.

Careful ye don't smile, D-boy, ye'll crack yer face.

Pathetic? You bet. But Mr Disco hated me too.

Of course, you say, it wasn't his fault that he was a loud-mouthed prig with a superiority complex and a moustache that was too big for his face. He was, after all, the innocent victim of a broken home and a great family tragedy, having been not only abandoned by Trixie, but also by his own father, Drummond the Riveter, who went swimming with the fishes in the Firth of Clyde before his son was even born. I leave it to you to imagine what kind of crying in the wilderness went on in Mr Disco's young head as he coped with all that crap. But cope he did, by making so much noise that no one could ignore him; soccer wizard, dance hall king, rock star. And the only thing that would eventually shut him up was the drugs. The dope, cocaine, and God knows what else.

Mr Disco was about to become famous. You've probably heard of him, unless you've been hiding in a cave or something for the last thirty years. Kenny Drummond? That's right, the one with the drug problems and the three ex-wives. The one who was in trouble with the US authorities for allegedly having sex with a minor. And the assault of a hotel manager in Las Vegas. That Kenny Drummond. Not a major talent maybe, not up there with the Stones or David Bowie. But big enough to wallow in all the trappings of rock-and-roll success. The limos, the drugs, the girls, the expensive Californian clinics, and, eventually, the highly publicised crash and burn. In the early days, Mr Disco was the handsome rebel, cynical and charismatic, singing songs of love gone wrong and boys behaving badly. He toured the world with his band, Powerstrike, selling out the big venues, creating the kind of controversies that kept him in the news. He even survived the whole punk thing, reinventing himself in the nineties as a kind of rock crooner. You know: the open-necked shirt, the tan and the gold chain, singing risqué love songs to his knicker-throwing public. But the drugs got the better of him. He lives in Paris now, or somewhere, in semi-retirement, making the odd appearance on TV chat shows and in the 'Where are they now' articles in crappy magazines. Grainy pictures of a thin, middle-aged geezer with greying hair and dark glasses and a furtive, fugitive kind of look. Mr Disco is not a happy man, though still wealthy, if you can believe the shite that's written about him. Apparently he's discovered Scientology. And he's planning a comeback. But then they all say that, don't they?

Why am I telling you all this about Mr Disco? You might be one of his fans, for all I know, or even one of his team of lawyers, scanning this text for actionable offences against the reputation of your client. Well, I doubt you'll sue me over it, but I'm going to tell you something about Mr Disco that didn't make it into his authorised biography. Why not? Because it shows him up for the ruthless and ambitious arsehole that he was and probably still is. And not only him. Luce and I don't exactly come out of this smelling of roses either, but it can't be sidestepped, and it won't be.

So, here's how it goes.

It started the day I saw Luce at the zoo. She was standing at the entrance to the reptile house, the low sunlight at her back forming a halo around her. She was leaning against the doorjamb, watching me from behind her mane of black hair, a curl of cigarette smoke rising from a fist held up against her face.

I'm sure it was her, even though what I was actually looking at was her reflection in the glass of the Turtle's tank. She didn't see that I'd spotted her, and I pretended to be absorbed in watching the Turtle, who was himself, I thought, becoming a bit agitated, his flippers twitching a little, as though he was thinking about moving. I heard him cursing quietly to himself, and by the time I checked again for Luce's reflection, she was gone.

But that was it, wasn't it? The game was well and truly up. Luce would have seen me mooching around Jake's wee hut, carrying stuff for him, following him around, helping him look after the Turtle. She would have seen me standing for ages at the tank. She would have heard me talking to the damned reptile. She knew everything. And even though I realised she understood none of it, the fact that she knew was enough to send a jolt of fear through me. Because, like I said, what she'd witnessed was the very thing that made me happy, the one thing that kept me going. And that would be enough for her to want to spoil it, believe you me. That would be enough.

And then, one afternoon, I came home late from the swimming baths to find Luce and Mr Disco together in the living room. Trixie was God knows where. There was just the two of them, sitting together on the sofa. They were talking quietly to each other, or maybe it was just him talking because you could never get a word in edgeways when he was on the scene, and Luce would lap up anything he said, she was so enraptured by him. Anyway, they edged apart slightly when I came in, and I wasn't too slow to notice the wee bit of tension and the look that passed between them.

Mr Disco quickly recomposed his face into his trademark superior grin. Ye're late, Donny. Where've ye been?

None of your business.

Hud a bath lately?

The two of them cracked up laughing, and that's when I knew that all my secrets were out.

More than you've had, I said.

And it was true. Mr Disco's long hair was lank and dirty, his collarless shirt was grimy and his jeans looked like they should be condemned. He was all fashionable grubbiness, power to the people, bring on the revolution and all that shite.

He scratched his moustache for a moment, watching me, and I wondered what else he knew.

Ye ought tae be careful in the water, Donny boy. We widny want ye tae drown now, wid we?

That grin again. Loaded. I went up to my room and brooded over what they might tell Trixie and what she might say when they did. I avoided dinner that night. I went to bed early, but I didn't sleep, lying there in the dark, my stomach churning. The next few days were all like that—a nightmare of waiting for Trixie's summons.

But it didn't come. Not a word was said by Trixie, and presumably not a word to her. No running to Mummy and telling tales. Gradually the world settled down to its normal state of being. Why didn't they blab? Maybe they said nothing because they wanted to keep whatever power they thought they had over me, to keep torturing me with the fact that I knew they knew. But what did they know exactly? That I went to the swimming baths. That I visited the Turtle. They knew all that, but they didn't understand what it meant. And Luce didn't know that I'd spotted her spying on me.

So I refused to be tortured. I just carried on doing what I did, visiting the Turtle, and practising holding my breath and swimming underwater. That's what he told me to do, when I spoke to him again after Luce came to the zoo.

Keep up yer studies, wee man. Never mind those bampots. Work harder on yer back flippers, and fur Christ sake, get a haunle oan that breathin.

You want to know how low a family can get? How twisted and angry and all tangled up in itself it can become? Knots of jealousy, rage and dislocated love, all of it winding in and through itself and back again, unravelling here and there, but elsewhere tight and hard and beyond untying.

You see, Luce wasn't the only one who was being observant. I was watching her too. And that bastard, Mr Disco. The way they shifted apart on the sofa. I saw that, and though I didn't want to think what I was thinking, I thought it anyway, and I watched them closely after that. Nothing was beyond Kenny Drummond and his ego.

Trixie had no control over the situation. As always, she was too busy with her string of sad clients, her readings and prognostications. Mr Disco simply came and went as he pleased, playing loud music on the record player, dancing and showing off, giggling and carrying on with Luce. The two of them would sneak off to the garage to smoke dope. I'd discovered that much. There were probably other drugs too. There were always other drugs where Mr Disco was concerned.

And Luce hung around him like wet hair on a scabby dog. She seemed much older than her nearly fifteen years—make-up, short skirts, platform shoes, a fag in her hand whenever Trixie was out of the picture. If you ask me, she looked a right scrubber. But don't ask me, I'm just her brother, and though I knew she was probably beautiful, I would never admit it, and definitely not then. But there you are. Mr Disco was her brother too, wasn't he?

I remember this time as if somehow the scenery had acci-dentally shifted. As if, in the middle of the play, the backdrop had buckled and fallen open to reveal some unexpected bricks, a bit of gantry, someone up there doing things with ropes and wires. You're suddenly caught between two worlds, the imagi-nary and the real, and the play reverts to being the imitation of life that it always was, but which you'd agreed to believe was something more meaningful. What I mean is, it opens your eyes, you know? That's what I remember. My eyes being opened fully.

But not to what you might think, in the end. Or at least not to what I allowed myself to think, seeing them together, Mr Disco and Luce. Lover boy and femme fatale. Not some cheap incestuous business dredged up from the pages of the *News of the World* or some such. Not in the end. But the point is, you see, that's exactly what I suspected, and that's why I started watching them even more closely. And why we seemed now to be living in the pages of a spy novel, gathering our intelligence, manoeuvring covertly around each other, probing weak spots. I had yet to work out Mr Disco's part in all of this, why he was bothering to spend so much time with Luce, why he cared at all about what I was up to. But I watched him. I watched them both very carefully.

The first thing I saw was this: Mr Disco riffling through the bits of paper on the kitchen table. Bills, letters and that sort of thing. He stopped when I walked in on him, and pretended he was looking for something else. The second thing was a shifty Luce, trying to look like she wasn't copying something from the book that Trixie used to record payments from her clients. The third thing was an obviously botched attempt to steam open a letter addressed to Trixie, from her lawyer. I saw the letter, still damp, and the kettle, still steaming, evidence that I had disturbed one or other of them again. It wasn't hard to put two and two together. They were spying on Trixie. Mr Disco might have been good at lots of things, but he was a lousy spy. Or maybe he just didn't care. The question was, *why* were they spying on Trixie?

It took me nearly a week to find the answer to that. A few days of watching closely, peeking through doorways, and listening. It was the listening that did it, in the end. Our phone was in the hallway, and from the upstairs landing you could sit and eavesdrop on conversations. Mr Disco was always on the phone, usually because people rang him. He didn't often ring anyone himself, but I'd noticed him dialling out a couple of times lately, and so I made a point of concealing myself upstairs whenever I could—out of sight but not out of earshot. I noticed he tended to use the phone when he thought there was no one around. When Trixie was out, or when we were supposed to be in bed. But late one night, lying in my room practising my breathing, I heard the faint clicking of the dial being turned. I quietly opened my door and crept out onto the landing. For a moment there was no sound anywhere and then Mr Disco's voice, whispered and urgent.

Carlo? It's me . . . Aye, ah've goat what ye want . . .

What Carlo wanted—and what Mr Disco proceeded to give him—was a detailed account of Trixie's income: number of clients, how much they paid, what this added up to per week and per month. He then talked to Carlo about what seemed to be confidential matters concerning Trixie and a lawyer, when she'd been to see him, what he wanted to know from her about Carlo, how much she'd paid him. Then Mr Disco said, So, is that enough? When can ah get the money?

Carlo seemed agitated. Even from where I sat I could hear his voice hissing in the receiver.

Mr Disco kept calm. Naw, it wis a thousand . . . Whit! Can ye no get it sooner . . . Aw fuck off, Carlo, yer full a shite . . . Aye . . . Awright then . . . Friday week. Don't you forget.

Mr Disco hung up the phone and I heard him walking down the hall, muttering to himself, heading into the kitchen. I slunk back to my bedroom, climbed into bed and lay there in the darkness, thinking. Here's what I thought: Trixie and Carlo were in the middle of a divorce that had been dragging on for a couple of years. This was Scotland in the seventies, and there was no such thing then as a quick divorce, especially if one or other of the parties was being difficult. In this case, both of them were. Trixie wanted half of everything Carlo owned. That's what she deserved, she reckoned, for putting up with him and raising his children on her own. Nothing less. Carlo, for his part, wanted to give Trixie as little as possible, but even more than this, he wanted time. Time to hide the evidence of his nefarious activities, to brief his crooked accountants and to salt away as much of his wealth as he possibly could. He wanted to look poor on paper, and he wanted to look clean.

We knew all this about Carlo anyway. Trixie had complained to anyone who'd listen about his meanness and his slippery tactics. But now, Carlo was fishing for inside information on Trixie's financial position, presumably to undermine her claims against him, which were already costing him money. A previous court hearing had ordered him to pay Trixie fifty pounds a week for her upkeep and that of her children.

So, in the middle of all this bitterness, in walks Mr Disco. What was obvious to me now was that he was being paid by

Carlo to get the information he needed. What was also obvious was that Mr Disco had managed to get Luce onside—to spy on her own mother, to sell her down the river like a bargeload of green bananas. Was Luce also being promised something by Carlo, or was it simply her infatuation with Mr Disco that made it so easy for him to manipulate her? Whatever, Trixie was being well done over by the pair of them, and I now had the information I needed to get the bastards off my back.

So what should have happened next is this: in the morning, I should have found Trixie, sat her down at the kitchen table and told her everything. Well, not everything. Not about the Turtle and the swimming and all that. But everything about Mr Disco and Luce. I should have made her confront them and then sat back and watched while they got what was coming to them. That's what should have happened.

But it didn't happen, because if I did that Luce and Mr Disco would almost certainly tell Trixie about me, and that would be the end of my plans. Because plans I had, believe me. And they depended on being able to visit the Turtle, and on being able to keep taking his instruction in the fine art of reptile aquatics. I was going to become a damned turtle myself, even if it meant Trixie being done like a dinner by Carlo and his gang of fiscal thugs. All I cared about was getting the edge in the battle of the siblings. Shutting them up, and out. I'm not proud of it, but there it is.

So, what should have happened next is this: I should have called a conference. Mr Disco and Luce in one corner, me in the other. Maybe out the back in the garage. I can see the two of them there, Mr Disco rolling a joint as big as a cigar, Luce standing there with her suspicious, mascaraed eyes and her lipstick a shade too red, cigarette in hand. I'd outline briefly and concisely what I knew about them and I'd watch them turn pale as I spoke. Then I'd tell them that unless they laid off me, and kept what they knew strictly to themselves, Trixie would be informed of their indiscretions. Punishment was sure to follow, I would say, and you both know what Trixie's like once she's crossed. That would be enough. An agreement would be reached and life would carry on as normal.

But this didn't happen either. The scenario—you've no doubt noticed—was not in the least convincing. The two of them wouldn't roll over so easily. They would haggle and cajole and try to humiliate me. And they'd probably succeed, because I didn't have the courage to even imagine myself being so fearless, let alone competent enough to pull such a thing off. And besides, Mr Disco already had the information he needed. By Friday week he would also have his thousand pounds and we wouldn't see him for dust. Luce would be left in the lurch. Now, the truth is that Luce was always going to be left in the lurch by Mr Disco, only she couldn't see it coming. What she could see coming has puzzled me ever since. Did she think she and Mr Disco would disappear happily off into the sunset? If so, she was in for a long drop off a short plank. Not that I cared about that. What I did care about was her picking herself up and looking for someone to blame. I didn't want it to be me, because I was scared of what she might do in revenge. In the end it all boiled down to this: I couldn't afford to let them know what I knew about them, but I still had to find some way of getting them out of my hair.

So here's what did happen.

You'll have noticed by now what a devious bunch of bastards we all were, each of us out for ourselves, caring not a jot about the consequences. I'm not going to make any excuses for it. Not now, there's no point. We were a twisted lot of vicious wee shites who deserved nothing more than to have been drowned at birth. Tied into potato sacks and thrown off the Jamaica Street Bridge. But we weren't, and so here I was, hatching a plot to ensure the beans were well and truly spilt from a safe and blameless distance.

At first I thought I could maybe make Trixie think she'd divined what was going on through one of her various psychic channels. But how? The tarot cards I ruled out as too diffi-cult to engineer. I had little idea how they worked, but I reckoned it would be nigh-on impossible to get a complicated message across, even if I could find a way of manipulating the cards. Ditto the coloured beads or any one of a hundred smelly powders and ointments. What she did with those was completely beyond me, and probably beyond any other earthly being. I thought about some kind of psychic writing, something which appeared mysteriously in a place where only she looked. Then I thought maybe she could hear voices in the night, warning her about Luce and Mr Disco. But I couldn't work out how any of this could be done. Not in a way that would fool her.

In the end I decided it was too risky trying to get her psychic attention, and that she would either see right through the ploy or just miss it altogether. Easier, I thought, if I just sent her something in the post. A tip-off, if you like. So I spent a morning putting together a letter, a bit like one of those blackmail letters, made up of bits of type cut out of newsprint. Obvious, I admit, and by no means original, but the best I could come up with at the time. Here's what the letter said: *Luce and Kenny have sold your financial secrets to Carlo. Ask them. PS: the two of them take drugs.*

Okay, hardly prize-winning stuff, and difficult to read because it's harder than you think to paste up a ransom note, but I put it in an envelope and used our old Olivetti to type out the name and address. Then I stuck a stamp on it and posted it second class from a postbox near the zoo, just so it wouldn't look too local. That's what I did, and a couple of mornings later it appeared through the door and I saw Trixie pick it up off the floor with some other stuff and take it through to the kitchen. I was on my way out the door to school, and I thought there might be some interesting news when I got home.

But that evening there was only the usual. The dinner of frozen cod and chips, with French beans out of a tin. The sighs and the silences. Mr Disco was elsewhere, spending a rare night at his own pad, and I thought maybe Trixie was just waiting until he appeared before she started on them. She seemed very much her usual self, though, even with Luce. Her usual gruff, preoccupied self. And the following night was the same, even when Mr Disco did appear and showed all the signs of staying over, and he and Luce sat up late in the living room playing records. Trixie said nothing.

After three or four days I decided that the letter hadn't worked. Trixie wasn't taken in by it; she'd probably thought it was some prank by one of her more disturbed clients and thrown it in the bin. What could I do now? That night I overheard Mr Disco on the phone to Carlo again, teeing up an appointment to get paid for his services. I would have to think of something. Maybe the psychic communication ploy, naff as it was and as risky as playing tig in the traffic.

And then, the following afternoon, I came home from school, late as usual. It was glorious and sunny still, a light breeze brushing through trees in full leaf, the soft humming of bees in the clover. Completely contrary to my mood, in other words, steeped as I was in the abjection of failure. I'd gone to the zoo after school, and had found the Turtle as perplexing as the weather. In unprecedented good spirits he was, cavorting and carrying on in his tank, making tasteless jokes about the shortcomings of humankind. I couldn't get any sense out of him. I caught a bus home and as I walked up our street from the bus stop I heard voices raised in anger. Trixie's voice, definitely, carrying shrill through the summer air, but a deeper, more muted voice too. Then, as I rounded the slight bend in the road, I saw a beautiful sight. Mr Disco was being pushed out our front gate at the business end of Trixie's sweeping brush. She was pushing the bristles into his face, jabbing at him, screaming.

Never darken ma door again ya bloody wee so-and-so! If you so much as stick yer nose in this front gate ah swear ah'll cut it aff an choke ye wi it!

Ah didny do nothin! Ah'm tellin ye!

Away tae buggery!

With a final push from the sweeping brush, Mr Disco stumbled out onto the pavement and fell on his backside. He saw me coming just as he picked himself up, and he gave me a look that I swear would melt ball-bearings. As I drew close to him he kicked out viciously, but I dodged out of the way and made a face at him. He stalked off down the street.

In the house, Trixie was now laying into Luce and I could hear Luce screaming back at her in language every bit as choice. Then there was a thump and a scream, followed by Luce's bedroom door being slammed. Trixie came down the stairs and bustled past me as if I wasn't there. I was taller than her these days, but the darkness of her eyes and her lack of aware-ness of me made me feel small, and I inadvertently flinched as she passed, muttering to herself under her breath.

I have to admit to a pang of bitterness then that Luce wasn't being locked up in the coal shed, a fate she definitely deserved as far as I was concerned. But Trixie, it seemed, had other plans for her. The best thing I could do was to keep out of the way, so I went up to the bathroom and shut the door. I could hear Luce's muffled sobs in the next room as I filled the sink with cold water. There would be no dinner tonight, that much was certain. I took some slow breaths and stuck my face in the water and felt myself relax.

After that it seemed that Trixie was on the phone down-stairs for hours, ranting and raving tirelessly, presumably to Carlo amongst others, because at around eight-thirty or so Sandro arrived in his white van, and when he left Luce went with him. I watched her go from Trixie's bedroom window, dragging an overstuffed suitcase and a defiant expression. She looked up and saw me watching, and I ducked away from the promise of doom in her face.

But when she'd gone, I felt elated, overjoyed at the success of my wee letter. I had done for both of them good-style, Luce and that smirking bastard Mr Disco, and I could get on now with what I had to do, which was learn to survive.

Later that night, I crept down to the kitchen to get something to eat from the fridge. I was making myself a sandwich— cheese and pickle—when I noticed my letter to Trixie lying on the table. Or at least the envelope was lying there, addressed to her in Olivetti-print. I picked it up and stared at it, all thought of food forgotten.

It hadn't been opened.

15

YOU SEE, YOU COULD NEVER pin her down, my mother. You could never quite make out what it was she was really up to; what was dodgy, and what was something altogether more confusing.

The letter hadn't been opened.

It only meant that Trixie had found out about Luce and Mr Disco from someone else, or had been doing a bit of spying on her own. That's all it meant, didn't it? And in fact, it made things all the better for me. Perfect. They couldn't pin the blame on yours truly. Not only did I have the satisfaction of witnessing Mr Disco's undignified departure at the end of Trixie's broom, and of Luce's swift demise as a player in our family politics—I got away with it scot-free. I should have been breaking open the bubbly, stepping lightly up to the podium to accept my well-deserved prize. I'd like to thank my mum.

But.

There's always a but. Nagging and whining and usually Trixie-shaped. The letter hadn't been opened. As if she knew already what was in it. As if she merely held it against her brow until the letters lit up inside her head, typeface first, then a cloudy image, becoming clearer until she could see me and my wee tub of glue, laboriously cutting and pasting. She might as well just have read my mind—and who knows, maybe she did that too.

I have no idea how Trixie found out about Luce and Mr Disco, but find out she did, and now, having tired herself out dispatching them to their respective exiles, she sat in her old armchair, leaning forward, fag in hand, rocking slightly back and forth, hair wild from her exertions with the sweeping brush, strands over one eye. The lines on her face were like a drawing; lightly sketched-in crow's feet, heavier pencilling on her forehead, furrows running from the corners of her nose to the sides of her mouth. She bit her bottom lip between drags on her cigarette.

How old was she then, at that moment? Maybe in her mid-forties. Only those dark brown eyes said anything of the beautiful girl she'd once been, the young woman of her time, pulling herself up out of the post-war miasma of shortages and coupons. Throwing herself full-tilt into the jaws of the future, that beast that leads you on forever with its whispered promises until you stumble with the exhaustion of it. Then it turns and tears at your throat.

And here she was now, mauled and tattered and bitter as stewed tea. Everything about her was already old, her whole being slouched and tentative, picking its way through the rubble of her life like an old lady with a walking frame. Abandoned by her husband, betrayed by her children, and tormented by me, her cursed and cussed second son, doomed to die a gasping, heaving, kicking, watery death. And she could do nothing about it. Not now, and not when, or if, the fateful day finally came. So much for her gift.

It'll come as no surprise to learn that what happened next was this: Trixie took to her bed. She stayed there for what seemed like weeks, refusing to talk to me, or anyone else for that matter. At first I cooked her things—toast at breakfast, a cup of tea, whatever I could find in the evening, frozen this or that. I'd put it outside her door, but she'd hardly touch it. Then, after a week or two, she started to get up, but only late at night, after I'd gone to bed. I'd hear her footering about downstairs in the kitchen, and in the morning I'd clean up her empty teacups and old apple cores, bits of cheese and crusts of bread.

We spoke to no one, stopped answering phone or doorbell, abandoned a whole army of People Desperate For Answers. Mainly Trixie's clients, but also, after a couple of weeks, our neighbour, Mrs Wallace, sick of having her doorbell rung by bereft loonies wondering if she knew where Madam Pinelli was and when she might be back.

Mrs Wallace was a stout woman who lived next door with her son, Fergus, who was far too old to be living alone with his mother. Relations between us were what you might call strained, ever since she'd complained to the council about the state of our garden. None of us were gardeners, and in a middle-class suburb like ours that was almost a criminal offence. The houses weren't much, but they had two things going for them that supposedly made us better than the poor sods in the blighted Corporation schemes which encircled us: they were what we called *bought hooses*, which simply meant we were up to our white-collared necks in debt; and they had private gardens, in which you were meant to demonstrate your devotion to the work ethic by spending the weekends pruning and mulching and touching up the paintwork on your decorative gnomes.

Mrs Wallace complained to the council that our garden reflected badly on the neighbourhood. What she really meant was that it made her place look like shite too, and if they canny be bothered to look after things properly then why don't they just go back to the gutter where they so obviously belong. Really! She's from Maryhill, ye know, and her husband's Italian. Though he walked out on her, so he did.

I wouldn't say our garden looked like a tip exactly, it was just a bit wild. Like everything else in our place, the garden was neglected. But you wouldn't expect Mrs Wallace to understand why that might be. It was beyond her comprehension that everyone wasn't like her, a proud homeowner and a considerate, caring neighbour. Which may or may not explain why, one overcast afternoon, after trying the doors front and back, peering through the downstairs window and calling through the letterbox—all to no avail—she finally called the police.

When I peeped through the venetians and saw the police car parked on the street, I thought maybe this time I should answer the door. It was lucky I was in, because Trixie wouldn't have stirred for bloody *Dixon of Dock Green* himself, with a posse from *Z Cars* thrown in for good measure. I opened the door. Two constables, both tall, one of them adjusting his chequered cap.

Eh, hello, son. Does a Mrs, eh, Pinelli live here?

Aye.

Kin we speak tae her?

She's depressed.

PCs One and Two exchanged looks. A rustling behind the jungle of privet warned me that Mrs Wallace was listening too.

Aye. Well we need tae talk tae her, son.

She's no talkin to anybody.

Can we come in?

I shrugged my shoulders and they pushed past me into the hallway. They had a good look around the living room, then the kitchen. PC Two sniffed at Trixie's strange concoctions, and he poked at the stuff on the kitchen table, the beads and bones and bits of photographs, the notebook scribbled with strange characters and calculations. Then he picked up the pack of tarot cards and shuffled through them.

Whose ur these, son?

Ma mum's.

Mrs Pinelli?

Aye.

Whit dis she dae wi aw this stuff?

She's a psychic.

Is that right?

That look again between them. PC One bent towards me and spoke quietly but firmly. Is she, ye know, aw right? He tapped his head meaningfully.

Naw, I don't think so.

Where is she noo?

In her bed.

Upstairs? he whispered, and pointed upwards.

Aye.

And off they went, the two of them, to confront the dangerous lunatic above. I followed them, pointed out Trixie's room, and then retreated to my own, leaving them to their officious door knocking and calling of her name. Trixie eventually appeared on the landing in her dressing-gown, and the three of them trooped back downstairs. *Huv ye hud yer lunch? Wid ye like a wee sandwich?* This was followed shortly afterwards by the sound of Trixie in the kitchen. I could hear their voices murmuring, and the occasional chuckle. Maybe an hour passed, maybe more, before I heard the kitchen door open and the two policemen clump their way up the hall to the front door, Trixie's lighter step following. At the doorway, PC One said, Right well, look efter yersel, Mrs Pinelli. And thanks fur the tip aboot Tuesday's race.

The way he said it, you could almost hear him winking and tapping his nose with his finger. Ye know, ma Ethel wid love tae come fur a reading. When yer feelin a bit better, like.

Trixie said she would let him know. Then she closed the door and went back upstairs to her bed.

No one tried to speak to us after that, and the house turned quiet, responding only to the small echoes of our separate lives. I no longer had to go to Nonna and Pa's when Trixie took to her bed. I was old enough to fend for myself, making do with the tins in the cupboard and the remnants in the freezer. I made half-hearted attempts to keep the house tidy, but mess just seemed to accumulate—dirty clothes in the corners, dishes in the sink, newspapers and junk mail piling up in the hallway. I gave up trying. When I think about it now, I realise that someone must have been paying the bills and doing the shopping, and I suppose that someone was Trixie, so she couldn't have been in bed all the time. But that's where she was whenever I was home, as if maybe it was me she was really trying to avoid. It didn't bother me much then, because I wasn't home very much that summer. I had more important things to think about.

I kept up my training at the swimming baths and my visits to the Turtle. I practised holding my breath. School holidays came and I had nothing else to distract me. Over the long summer weeks I dived and swam and stayed under as long as possible. I would sit on the bottom in a corner of the deep end, looking up at the distorted world above. By the end of the session my skin was also distorted, wrinkled and soft like wet tissue paper, and I was usually desperate for a pish. But I didn't care. I felt like I was finally getting somewhere, that I was nearly as good as any amphibious reptile. I'd got over a plateau, as they say, and was ascending to the clear heights of knowledge and understanding. Or some such shite.

The Turtle was unimpressed.

Uch, ye've a heid on ye like a prize neep. Don't get kerried away wi yersel, yer no a turtle yet. No even close.

In contrast to my growing sense of confidence, the Turtle was becoming more and more grumpy. There were days when he refused to talk to me at all, and he would skulk in the far corner of his tank, unmoving, only reluctantly surfacing for air, though it seemed he needed it less and less. Despite Jake's care and attention—changes of water, copious scrubbing down, nutritious meals—he always managed to look dishevelled, like he just didn't care. His shell was mottled and stained with algae that burgeoned like weed as soon as you put him back in the water. He had some kind of skin condition, too, as if the scales on his face and his front flippers were about to rot and drop off.

And I swear he was shrinking. Or maybe he was just withdrawing into himself, making himself as small as possible. But I couldn't help thinking that I was responsible; that as I grew, he shrank, as if I was stealing his soul or something, filching away at his reptilian being, sucking the poor creature dry. No wonder he was grumpy. No wonder he wasn't talking.

But I needed him still. He hadn't yet told me what I was supposed to do with all this intensive training at the swimming baths, all this effort I was making to turn myself into him. Where was it leading? He knew, the wee bastard, but he wasn't telling. I just had to suck it out of him, along with everything else. And watch him waste away to nothing.

Jake, however, was unconcerned.

There's nothing wrong with him. Here, help me with this bucket.

I'd told Jake all about the eviction of Mr Disco and sister Luce. We were in his wee hut, drinking tea, sweet and hot. He listened to me, as he always did, with that half-smile, one hand absent-mindedly scratching his beard.

Your family, Donald.

What d'ye mean, my family?

So much hate between you.

Families are fucked, but.

Not everyone lives like you do.

Uch, it's normal.

Hating each other is not normal, I think.

He peered at me over the top of his glasses, that slight grin of his failing to mask his concern. Maybe you should try something else.

Like what?

Go home and tell your mother you love her.

Aye, right.

Jake shook his head, and then got up off his stool. Come on then, back to work.

But I sat there for a while, lost in my thoughts.

Jake talking about love. The word made me feel trapped, something inside me going *danger, danger*. I knew very little about Jake, but I knew he was lonely. A lonely man in a lonely world, and yet he could still be alright. Warm, sort of. I liked Jake a lot, and I liked the Turtle, too, and I found myself wondering if I loved them, if such a thing were possible. What did it mean, to love someone or something? What did it mean to say that I loved Jake, or that I loved the Turtle? Did it mean anything more than just saying I liked them?

And then I realised that what bothered me the most was that I didn't want to be without them. I liked them—loved them or whatever—because I'd be lost without them. I didn't like thinking that. I didn't like it one bit.

It occurred to me then that love is scary. It carries a lot of fear: fear of not being loved in return; fear of exposing yourself; fear of losing the things you love, or of having them taken away from you; fear of making a complete and utter fool of yourself. Where would we all be if we loved each other openly and expressively, if we didn't just bluff and head it all off with jokey insults and manly slaps on the back? If we acknowledged its existence. The world would grind to a halt, that's what. That's what I thought, anyway. You probably disagree, but it seems to me that this is one of the problems with life: it might well be love that makes us human, but you're still better off pretending otherwise.

What would happen if I told Trixie that I loved her? Nothing and everything. An uncomfortable silence, a tight smile, a tainting of the air between us. It would be unbearable, unbreathable, but the chemical balance would eventually reassert itself and we would shudder inwardly at the closeness of the call—nearly fell for it!—and carry on as before. But I would never do it. Because I knew that if I did, I would end up sore and sorry, hating her even more.

I've never understood love, anyway.

Here then was the circle of my life that summer of 1975. Working with Jake at the zoo, the long days filled with companionship, chatter and hard work; cleaning the tanks, feeding the animals, helping the vet during his regular inspections. Learning all I could about the care of turtles and amphibious reptiles. Thoughts about love and hate.

And, as I said, swimming like crazy.

I had started swimming in my dreams, too. I would wake up in the middle of the night with the bedclothes kicked half off the bed, my legs and arms still flailing. And always the same dream: grey seas under a grey sky, the water cold and gripping at my chest; sinking under the swell and kicking down, down towards endless black; and then the voices, sweet as air, calling me on forever.

But the end of that summer will forever be paired in my mind with the soundtrack of Mr Disco's first single, played endlessly on the radio, in cafes and pubs, blaring from the bedroom stereos of thousands of teenagers all over the country. You couldn't escape it, not even me. LOCAL LAD MAKES GOOD, screamed the headlines in papers and magazines, rising to fever pitch when Powerstrike appeared on *Top of the Pops*.

You'll never need me more than now, sang Mr Disco, power chords exploding behind him.

You'll never love me more than this.

Because tomorrow, I'll be gone.

It made me want to puke. Not just the sound and the sentiment, but the whole disgusting exhibition of it—the flying hair and the unbuttoned shirts, the arrogant presumption of dry ice and flashing lights. I hated it, but I think Trixie was secretly pleased.

Whether because of Mr Disco's success or not I don't know, but the hit single coincided with her emergence from her cocoon of absence, and with the same energy she'd used to withdraw from life, she began the process of coming back. She was on the phone now, ringing old clients with the news that she was once again open for business, talking to her lawyer, occasionally tracking down and haranguing Carlo in whatever lair he'd found for himself.

And Luce? I am dead-set one hundred per cent sure that she was bopping along like nobody's business to Mr Disco's musical debut. I'm surprised she wasn't singing backing vocals on the damned thing. But then she couldn't sing to save herself; she had the musical talent of a scratched china plate. Luce was still living with Carlo, and I supposed that she was happy there. I supposed we were all happy, though. I was soon to discover just how wrong that supposition was.

Uch, it wisny much uv a life
onyway, stuck
in thon stupit wee tank,
gawped at by aw and sundry.
Wi only some jeely-faced auld alchy tae
look efter me. An see you?
Ye've turned oot a right fuckin disappointment,
so ye huv.
Taught ye everythin ah know, an look at ye!
Yer whole life's mince.
Ye'll never get it sorted, not a chance.

16

THE SLOW DRIP of rain off the gutters. A breeze ruffling the leaves in the garden, rising to a small crescendo of waving branches in the wet light of dawn. The splash of car wheels on the road outside, the city waking up, winding up its siren song; the long, low rumble of a weekday morning.

The smell of damp, inside and out.

Give me a minute just to gather my thoughts, because I'm no longer sure what's real and what's not. I've been in Trixie's house too long already—I can feel it closing in around me, jamming me in from the outside world, reflecting my thoughts back at me in a gathering feedback loop.

I've been asleep, I think. For how long? My watch says 6.13, though it feels later. My back aches as I sit up and try to rub some life into my legs. Not sure if I can stand. Not sure if I want to.

I've been dreaming, haven't I? About Luce and Mr Disco and the Turtle. About love and hate and family. And about Trixie, the puzzle of her. The way she charmed those policemen, turned it on like a light and then just as quickly turned it off again when they'd left. She could do that. On and off, like flicking a switch. And then back to her bed without a word to me. That's what she was like, the switch was hers to flick, and she'd choose when to do it. You never knew where you were with Trixie, but she knew exactly where you were; she knew everything.

I have been dreaming.

Dreaming that the Turtle's still angry with me, even after all these years. Because while I was so busy improving myself, preparing for my future, gloating about getting one over on my siblings—thinking all that shite about love for Christ's sake—I failed to see the attack coming. He's angry about that, and about something else. What makes him really furious is that he saved my life and all I've done since is squander it. That's what he thinks, that I'm a miserable tosser, a complete waste of breathable air. A failure. Not only did I fail to protect him, I failed to be the person he wanted me to be. Failed, failed, failed.

That's what I've done, though, isn't it? Even when I've succeeded, I've failed. I've disappointed everyone, let everybody down, betrayed their belief in me. Like my own family, the woman I married and our two kids. I've told you about my boys, haven't I? Jake and Daniel. Jake'll be fifteen now, and Daniel twelve. They're great kids. We had it all, we did. The house in the suburbs and the cars and the dog and the cat. The whole family thing, except I had to go and fuck it up. Worked too much, drank too much, spent too much time leaving them all to it. I never figured out how to fit in with family life, how to be a father and a husband, what all that meant. It was as if I lacked some vital bit of the map. Eventually it all became too hard for everyone, the late-night arguments, the screaming and the crying. The slamming doors. The feeling like we were stuck in wet cement. One night I came home and she was gone. Her and the boys. She took them away. For their own protection, she said. I've been meaning to visit them, but it's a long way off, America.

Even when I've succeeded, I've failed. That's been my curse, and really, it's time the bloody thing was lifted.

I have no evidence that Luce was responsible for what happened at Elderbank Zoo in the same week we went back to school at the end of that summer. Neither does anyone else. No evidence whatsoever. No one saw her in the vicinity, no one connected her with what happened. Her name was on no files, her photograph appeared on no police incident board, nor did she loom large in the mind of some cocky young detective sergeant looking for a shortcut to promotion. The truth is, she was never a suspect, not even close. Except that I knew she did it. No one or nothing else could be that cruel, not even fate. But I suppose I'd better tell you the story. Of how I lost everything.

I got a phone call from Jake one night. He was drunk, and he started blabbering on about how sorry he was, and how could he have let this happen, and it was best now if I just stayed away from the zoo, because there was all kind of shite flying around, and really I wasn't meant to be there as much as I had been, doing what I was doing, helping and all that.

Jake, what are ye talkin about?

What do you mean, what am I talking about? The zoo!

Look, just take yer time and start at the start.

You mean you haven't heard?

Heard what, for Christ sake?

Ah shit.

What's happened, Jake? Tell me!

But he wouldn't tell me, not on the phone. He asked me to meet him in Shettleston, at the cafe near the swimming baths. We sometimes went there for a hot drink after a swim. I knew that Jake lived somewhere close by, and it was a short bus trip for me.

I rushed straight out the door and ran to the bus stop. I was wearing just jeans and a jumper and my slippers were still on my feet. I waited ages for a bus, pacing up and down the shelter, feeling like I was stuck in freeze-frame. My stomach was in what you call knots. More, I wanted to vomit, because I knew what Jake was going to tell me: that the Turtle was sick, or there had been an accident and he'd been hurt. I couldn't take the thought of him suffering, and me not being there to comfort him.

When I finally got to the cafe, it was getting dark. Jake wasn't there, just a couple of guys in the corner, the jukebox blaring. At least it wasn't bloody Powerstrike they were listening to. Luigi, the owner, told me Jake was in the pub up the road, and that he'd said to come up and get him. I knew well enough what that meant. Jake had already been drunk when he rang earlier, now he'd be well and truly sozzled, so he would.

I didn't even have to go into the pub. By the time I got there he was so steamboats they'd already kicked him out, and I found him in the gloom of a nearby shop doorway, sitting huddled in a pool of his own vomit. His eyes were glassy, reflecting the lamplight in the street. I don't think he recognised me, he was that far gone. I certainly wasn't going to get the story out of him tonight. I felt like kicking him. Not only had I come all this way for nothing, but now I was obliged to do something. I mean, I couldn't just leave him there, puking up in a shop doorway, could I?

So I tried to talk to him, and I tried to get him to stand up. He was still wearing his wellies and his green overalls under an old coat, and the smell of dung and rotten fish and vomit nearly made me throw up myself. When he didn't respond I slapped him across the face, like they do in the movies. I only did it lightly at first, and then a harder one when the first had no effect. That did the trick. His eyes opened, wide and frightened, and he struggled to get himself up, scared I was going to give him a doing and steal his wallet or something.

Jake, it's me. Donald.

Ngrrh mmf.

It's Donald, ya doolie. Hold onto me. We'll go to Luigi's.

Something got through to him, because he held onto me and the two of us staggered back down the road to the cafe. He wasn't that heavy, and I could easily handle his weight against my shoulder, but he kept veering off the pavement, drawn irresistibly towards the gutter, where he could lie down and sleep his nightmare away. I was having none of it. I got him to Luigi's and shoved him down on a seat near the door, where he slumped on the table and began to snore. Luigi came over.

E's pissed, like the newt, eh?

He is that, Luigi. Got anything to wake him up?

I make im strong espresso. Doppio.

Thanks.

Luigi shambled off to make the coffee. I tried to wake Jake up, but he hardly stirred until the hot black liquid was placed under his nose. I can't say he perked up or anything, but something of an improvement took place. At least, he sat up a bit and held the cup himself, though he swayed alarmingly and gibbered between sips. I thought maybe it was time to take him home, though where that was exactly I had not a clue.

Hey, Luigi, d'ye know where he lives?

He tell me once. Maybe Budhill? I forget the number.

I searched through the pockets of Jake's stinking coat, looking for his wallet. He giggled stupidly, but otherwise didn't try to stop me. The wallet turned out to be in the back pocket of his overalls, and in it there was a driver's licence. I had no idea he could drive.

Budhill Avenue. Twenty-four.

Luigi shrugged. Three streets up and to your left. It no far.

I went to pay for the coffee, but Luigi said it was on the house, so I thanked him and, after a bit of a struggle, managed to get Jake standing. The two of us staggered off up the road.

Jake's flat was a rented room on the third floor of an old tenement. The keys were in his trouser pocket and, as we approached the door, he got them out himself, though he couldn't get the key in the keyhole, so I had to let us in. I found the light switch and flicked it on. A bare bulb lit up the sad scene of Jake's domesticity. Or lack of it.

It was a toty wee room, mostly taken up by a single bed, on which Jake collapsed without another word, still in his coat and boots. I looked around: one sash window and a tiny kitchen in an alcove at the end. The room stank of mouldy rubbish and unwashed bedclothes. And something else; the smell of stale alcohol. Then I noticed that there were wine bottles, beer bottles, whisky bottles, everywhere. On the floor, on shelves, in the kitchen sink, under the bed. A sea of bottles. More than you could possibly imagine one man drinking.

I'd never thought of Jake having a problem. He seemed so reliable, in his own strange way. Dependable. He helped out at the youth club, had conversations, never seemed to be drunk at work. In fact, I'd never known him to miss a day, or not to work steadily when he was there. He sometimes had whisky on his breath, but I'd never seen him drunk. Not until tonight.

Which reminded me that tonight he had reason to be drunk, didn't he? I still had no idea what had happened at the zoo, what had made Jake go on such a bender. I tried to tell myself it was probably nothing serious, that Jake obviously went on benders all the time. But I couldn't quite believe it; my stomach was churning and my head had began to ache, a dull thud like the flat tolling of a bell. It was time to go.

Jake was snoring, huge nasally roars. I pulled his wellies off, the least I could do. Then I picked my way over to the sink to wash my hands under the tap. Tucked away in the dark recess was a small table and chair and the first thing I noticed was that there were no empty bottles on it. There was a lamp, and a stack of books, and a couple of photographs in frames. I switched the lamp on.

Both the photographs were of a much younger Jake. In one he was facing the camera, blond-bearded and smiling, his hair tousled. It was an outdoor shot, in a boat, bright sunlight with the sea behind, and Jake was wearing a wetsuit and scuba gear.

The other photograph had been taken underwater. There was a diver, presumably Jake—the colours of his wetsuit matched the other photo. He was swimming in clear water, a coral reef visible behind him, the lighter blue above suggesting the water wasn't very deep. I picked up the photo and stared at it for a long time. Because Jake wasn't on his own in this underwater scene. He had company, in the form of a magnificent loggerhead turtle, full-flippered and neck extended. Jake had one hand on its back and they appeared to be playing together, the creature pulling him through the water. Both looked to be entirely in their element.

I put the photo back on the table. The books were also about turtles. Studious books with long titles, some in a foreign language that I couldn't place. They were old-looking and well-thumbed, bits of paper sticking out here and there as markers. Next to them was a stack of handwritten notes, also foreign. And then, at the bottom of the pile, I found a book that seemed familiar, though it was a moment before I realised why. It was a copy of *Sea Turtles in Myth and Magic*, by R. S. Jakowski, though, unlike mine, this one had a dust-cover. On the flyleaf there was a picture of the author.

Dr Jakowski, the blurb said, *studied marine biology at the Polish Academy of Sciences before fleeing the Communist regime and settling in the UK. Today, he is a leading expert on the care and management of endangered sea turtles. In this book he explores the long history of our cultural interaction with these creatures, and argues that the health and wellbeing of turtles is vital to the future of our own species.*

I stared at the man in the picture, blond and confident, holding a pipe. Then I stared at Jake.

Dr Jakowski lay sprawled on his filthy bed, stinking of vomit.

There were a thousand questions I wanted to ask Jake at that moment—about him, about what happened at the zoo, about why everything in my life was such a tortuous puzzle. But it was clear from his snoring that there would be no answers that night. There was nothing else to do but go. I closed the door quietly behind me and made my way down the stairs to the dark street. I had no idea what time it was, but the pubs and the chip shops were closed, and most of the tenement windows dark. A sprinkle of rain had made the pavement shiny under the streetlamps, and there was the occasional whoosh of a car on the main road. I walked down the hill in that direction.

How was it possible for someone to fall into so much ruin? How much of it was his own choice, and how much of it was fate or accident? Jake never seemed to me to be unhappy, though he must have been in pain of some kind to drink so much. I never heard him complain. Not once.

The world makes people like Jake for a reason. There's always a reason, there's got to be. Or maybe not. We're all just blind organisms trying to cope with the bare truth of our own redundancy. Most of us aren't needed. We fill no necessary niche, we add nothing to the sum total of existence. We take without giving, destroy without building. We might as well not be here but, if we have no choice, then why not distract ourselves with drink and drugs and endless hours in front of the telly? Believe me, I know all about distraction and avoidance. Not to mention being unnecessary.

But Jake wasn't like that. We needed him. Not just me and the Turtle; he cared about all of us, *the future of our own species*. What had we done to destroy him like this?

The rain started up again, a steady drizzle, soaking through my thin jumper and making me hunch against myself as if it were a cold night. But it wasn't cold, just wet. The stupid slippers I had on my feet slapped and slipped against the greasy pavement, and that's how I walked, slip, slap, slop, not caring where I went.

At some godawful hour of the morning, I found myself outside the gates of the zoo. I've no memory of getting there, but I must have walked because there were no buses at that hour. The rain had eased off, but there was a chill in the early morning air, and I stood at the entrance, soaked through and shivering, listening to the water drip off the leaves and the distant running of the burn that ran through the zoo.

There was something else, too, that bothered me. A bitterness in the taste of the air, an irritation in the lining of my nose. A hint of fear, instinctive and primeval. It hung over the zoo like a shadow. I expected to hear some of the nocturnal creatures at least; the odd call or rustle in cage or enclosure. But there was nothing. Not even a night watchman. The gates were locked. I sat down on the wall opposite.

I don't know how long I sat there, sniffing the air. I was lost to a despair so deep I felt like I was sinking into the landscape around me, as if the solid wall, the pavement, the curve of the road, were nothing more than a visual quicksand, a cruel illusion. At some point I must have got up and got moving, because I next found myself at my own front door, a bit after dawn. The air had that hefty feel of a wet morning and the light was tentative, like a drunkard woken too early. I was damp and shivering, surprised to find myself there. The slippers on my feet were falling apart, sodden and broken at toe and heel. My feet hurt, and so did my head.

I had my key and I opened the door. The morning newspaper was on the doorstep and I picked it up and stuck it under my arm. I closed the door as quietly as I could behind me, thinking I would just sneak upstairs to bed. Not a chance. The living room door creaked opened and there was Trixie, standing in the hallway. She'd been waiting up for me. I'd rushed out of the house the night before with no explanation. I hadn't even thought about her, that she might wonder where her seventeen-year-old son could be going, and why he'd been out all night. It never occurred to me she might care.

Where've ye been?

Her eyes were red-rimmed as though she'd been crying, though I'd seen her look like that after an all-night session with her mumbo jumbo.

Something about her question annoyed me. You should know, shouldn't ye?

Her eyes flared. Ah know more than ye think, boy.

It sounded like a threat, the way she said it. And it hit right home to that soft wee bit inside that I'd been trying to keep safe, from her and everyone else. I swallowed, feeling like I wanted to run. But there was nowhere to run to.

Is that right? Well, you're the bloody psychic.

She looked up at me and her dark eyes narrowed. Aye, an ah don't like whit ah see, not one bit.

It was as though she was looking into my mind, playing back the film of where I'd been that night. I tried to think of something else. Then, as if she was satisfied with what she'd seen, she brushed past me and started up the stairs to her bedroom. Get oota they wet clothes, she said, before ye catch a cauld.

Sensible advice, but I didn't heed it. Because as Trixie went up to her bedroom, I threw the newspaper I'd been carrying onto the hall table and the headline on the front page jumped up and punched me straight in the jaw. I picked it up and read it again and then I went and sat on the couch in the living room in my wet clothes and I stared and stared at it.

FIRE GUTS ZOO: REPTILE HOUSE DESTROYED.

Fire raged through the Reptile House of Elderbank Zoo yesterday, gutting the building, despite the efforts of three fire crews called to the scene.

No one was hurt in the blaze, believed to have been started acci-
dentally by one of the zoo keepers. The man has not been named by
Elderbank management, but is reported to have been stood down,
pending an inquiry.

Several valuable animals were destroyed, including a rare
Australian lizard and the zoo's popular loggerhead turtle.

And that was that.

From the moment the newspaper slipped to the floor and
I tumbled after it, spinning and spinning through an endless
void, I realised that I'd known everything all along. That I had
carried it around inside me since the day I was born. And now
everything was suddenly blindingly clear, as if understanding
had leapt out from the jumble of bits and pieces that made
up my life, like those letters in cartoons that scrabble about
and then form themselves into words. Everything was just
as it should be. Fucked up and pulled apart, saturated in the
drench of loss. Situation completely bloody normal. I know
what you're thinking, that I'm too ready with the self-pity and
the world's got it in for me and all that poor bloody Donald
shite. But I'm telling you, this was only the start. The newspaper slipped to the floor and I tumbled after it, into a place
so vast and dark and empty that I've never really been able to
find my way out, though the tears have long dried and the
memory is now just a memory of a memory of a memory.

That was that.

Well not quite. Because prodding at me through the melee
of stabbing and lancing that made me wince and cry out
and roll myself up into a tight ball on the couch, was one

particular pain, almost exquisite in its pointedness. Luce. Luce had taken her revenge. My victory early in the summer now stood there shivering, exposed for what it was: an illusion, cruel and cold. She did it, and I hadn't even seen it coming.

She did it with fire. She took a creature of water, air and earth and she killed it with fire. That's Luce's element, the tormenting flames of hell, dressed in the colours of vengeance, reducing matter to a formless, grey dust. She'd like that, so she would. Complete annihilation with only a smouldering shell to remind you of what was once a living, breathing animal, and the finger pointed squarely at poor, drunken Jake, lighting up his pipe or something, a sly smoke when no one's watching. But I couldn't believe that and I wouldn't. Not Jake, he would never do something so stupid, no matter how pissed he was. No, Luce did it alright. That's what I thought then, and that's what I clung to for a long time afterwards. It was easier to blame my sister than to admit that Jake had fucked it up.

When, finally, sleep came (was it that morning, or the next night, or even later?) I dreamt again of being in the sea, not drowning, but calm and untroubled. Sunlight plied the blue water, filtering through its motes and specks, making the fish sparkle in sudden bursts of fire as they twisted and turned in and out of the rocks below.

I was swimming down towards a sandy bottom between two ledges. As I glided under the rock, brushing through fronds of swaying green weed, I saw that the Turtle was already there, waiting for me, and I settled on the sand next to him. He was in a terrible state. His shell was blackened and the skin on his head and flippers was raw and blistering, here and there peeling off in strips. He didn't seem too fussed about it, mind you. He muttered something about being kept waiting, and then he told me that I was on my own now, ready or not, and that I would find out soon enough if I was ready. He told me I hadn't a chance in hell of doing what I had to do, but that I had to do it anyway. That, or drown on my eighteenth birthday, and only a bloody nyaff would do that. Only an eejit with mince for brains would let water get the better of them. That's what he said, the miserable bugger, sitting there looking like an overcooked Sunday roast.

And then he told me what I had to do to save myself.

I suppose you're thinking that when I woke the next day, I had the whole picture in my head. That the world suddenly made perfect sense. That the fog had cleared and all the details now stood out, stark and solid. How to defeat the curse and survive Trixie and Luce and Mr Disco and Carlo and all the bloody madness and mayhem that we call family. Well, let me tell you, the fact is I did not have a bloody clue. Not beyond what I already thought I knew, that the sea might be my saviour, and that becoming as turtle-like as possible was my only hope. I'd known all this for a long time, ever since Trixie made me listen to the seashell, but what I needed now was details: where and when and how? And that's what I didn't get from the flippery old fart. He left me high and bloody dry, so he did.

Oh, he told me lots of things as we sat together under the seaweed-fringed rock. Like his pearls of wisdom on the nature of humankind. Like how much he'd loathed being treated as if he was some stupid wee hatchling in the zoo, having his shell cleaned and his water changed, eating bloody fish flakes day in and day out. Like how he wanted to pish on the gawping faces of the people on the other side of his tank—*especially they weans*—with their tap-tap-tapping on the glass, and all he could ever do was turn his back on them. Like his loathing of Jake and his whisky-sodden breath.

But you, son. Ah thought ye were different.

Then he told me that he'd recognised in me a kindred spirit. And that's why he was going to set me free.

That's what he said: set me free.

As I listened to him talk nineteen to the dozen, I realised with a jolt of panic that he was fading away beside me. At first I thought it was a trick of the light, the refraction of the water. But no, he was fading away, starting to look like some bloody ghost or something. I could see his ruined skin turning translucent, and his shell too. The rocks and the seaweed and the wee fishes were showing through him, dimly at first and then more defined. It was such a slow and gradual thing that I hadn't noticed until now. He was leaving me. I wanted to grab him and shake him.

Tell me, ya bastard. Tell me what ah'm meant to do!

He shimmered in and out of view, his body distorting with the ocean current.

S'easy, son. You're me and ah'm you, eh? Zat no right? Jist haud yer breath an swim like fuck. Nae bother.

Where? When? What d'ye mean?

But it was too late. With a final ripple he melted into the waters around us.

Bysie-bye then, son. If ah don't see ye through the week, ah'll see ye through a windy. Heh-heh-heh . . .

And he was gone forever.

***

So, great dream, eh? A real stoater, that one. To say I was flat was an understatement. I was flatter than a week-old pint of lager.

Here were my options, presented to me as I lay in bed that morning, with the covers pulled over my head to ward off the daylight seeping through the curtains. It was late, but there was no point getting out of bed.

Option one was to do nothing and to let the curse unfold. Death by drowning.

Option two was to follow the Turtle's advice. From what I understood of it, same difference. Death by drowning.

Option three was to kill myself, by any means quicker and less awful than death by drowning—and that, in the end, seemed the best way to deal with the situation. Lying there under the bedclothes, trying to ward off the world encroaching with its disappointments and its cruelties, I thought this: the situation is shite. Take control of it while you still can. Best to just do away with yourself now. That's what I thought, and I even thought that I could find the courage to do it.

But I wondered just exactly how best to commit suicide, and over the next few weeks, I entertained myself with thoughts of all the terrible things I might do, ticking off the possibilities and putting a wee mental cross against the things that seemed just too unpleasant. I decided against cutting my wrists—too much mess; I decided against pills—too unreliable; I decided against hanging—too gruesome. I thought maybe the gas oven was a possibility, but then discarded the idea because

Trixie would smell the gas. I thought about jumping off the top of a high-rise, but I had no head for heights.

I just couldn't decide.

I got up in the mornings and dressed and brushed my teeth and went to school and I sat in classes, oblivious to what was being said, my mind obsessed with the best way to top myself. And then, on Tuesday, October the ninth, 1975, after discarding the idea twice, I reached a decision: I found The Way. It wasn't the ideal way by any means, but it would be quick and easy and pretty damned final, I thought. Except I hadn't reckoned on one last twist of fate, sugar-sweet and sour as bitter lemon.

A smile and a missing girl.

17

THE NINTH OF OCTOBER 1975. At 4.18 in the afternoon, Anna McColl smiled at me. We were standing at the bus stop, kids milling about, cries and yelps as someone's schoolbag sailed onto the road and into the traffic. I turned to see who the victim was and Anna was standing there, just behind me. She looked at me and she smiled and the sun came out and sparks went off in my head—then I started to worry that my fly was undone and I wanted to check but I couldn't because I wanted those eyes to drink me in forever. So instead I stood there, like an eejit, thinking up opening lines which remained unsaid until the bus came and she got on it but I didn't because it was full.

And now, Anna McColl was dead.

No one had seen her since she got off the bus the day she smiled at me. She was alone. She had to walk ten minutes from the bus stop to her house, on a route that took her through a wooded park. Three weeks later, she still hadn't been found, and I knew by then that she was dead, and that her killer had hid the traces and was long gone, getting ready for his next victim.

The police were everywhere, knocking on doors, asking questions, cruising the streets in their white cars. What could I say to them? Yes I knew her, she was in my class. No, she wasn't a friend. No, I noticed nothing unusual about her that day. Should I have told the truth? That she smiled, that it was unusual for her to smile, that it was especially unusual for her to smile at me? Maybe. But I couldn't say it. Hugged to myself, the moment was a secret source of comfort and promise; spoken aloud it was merely a fact to be noted in evidence—embarrassing, tawdry, mean and measly in its revelation about my empty life. I told them nothing.

The McColls lived in a semi-detached house with a grey slate roof. It was an ordinary kind of place, a neat garden in front, privet hedge carefully trimmed. Anna's dad was an accountant and her mother stayed home and looked after Anna and her sisters. An ordinary, everyday family, their lives punctuated, I imagined, by Saturday shopping, Sunday drives, weekly bridge parties and summers on the beach at Saltcoats. But now Mrs McColl was under sedation, and the gossip was that Mr McColl wasn't coping too well either. Anna's two sisters had been packed off to stay with relatives.

People in the neighbourhood would take a walk past the house, just to see what was going on. When they met they'd pretend it was coincidence, but they'd stop to chat and someone else would happen along so there was always a bit of a crowd hanging about outside the McColl house, talking quietly to each other and casting anxious glances at the curtained windows. That went on for a while, but slowly, day by day and week by week, the McColls were left to them-selves and their misery. Sometimes a raised voice might be heard from inside the house, sometimes muffled screams, and once a series of crashes that sounded like an entire dinner service being smashed on the kitchen floor.

The police were said to be 'hopeful' that Anna was alive, but I knew she was dead. One night, three weeks after she disappeared, there was a knock on our door. A soft kind of knock, tentative. It was about ten o'clock. We were sitting watching telly—Alfred Hitchcock, I think it was—and drinking mugs of tea. Trixie had made cheese and pickle sandwiches. When she heard the door she made a face and tutted and said with a mouth full of sandwich, Who could that be at this time of night? But she knew exactly who it was. She got up and switched off the telly, telling me to go to my room because she had a visitor and needed to talk in private. I snuck into the kitchen. From there I could see the hallway and the front door as Trixie unlatched the security chain and opened it.

Jeanette, she said.

There was silence for a moment, broken by a sob. It was Anna's mum. She stood on the doorstep and looked around her like she was afraid she was being followed. Trixie took her arm and led her into the hallway.

Come on now, come ben the livin room. It's warm in there.

Mrs McColl was a small, stooped figure, her eyes blood-shot and sunken and her face grey. She seemed startled by the light of the hallway, as if she might run back out the still-open door. Trixie settled the matter by closing it firmly. Mrs McColl gathered her strength. When she spoke, her voice was flat and throaty.

Ye know what ah've come for, Trixie.

Trixie led Mrs McColl into the living room. I crept up the hall to the doorway, taking care to avoid the creaking floor-board. They were sitting in front of the fire, talking quietly.

Jeanette McColl wanted my mother to use her powers to tell her where her daughter was, and whether she was alive or dead. I could tell that Trixie didn't want to do it, but Mrs McColl was sobbing quietly now and Trixie finally agreed to try. She asked her to bring something of Anna's—a comb with some of her hair in it, or something special and close to her, like a stuffed toy. Mrs McColl wanted to go home and get it right away but Trixie said No, gie me a day, ah need tae get ready. Come back the morra efternoon and ah'll see whit ah kin dae. Are ye sure ye won't huv a cuppa tea?

I crept back into the kitchen as Trixie showed Mrs McColl out. I tried to be quiet but the squeaky floorboard gave me away.

Trixie came bustling down the hallway. Whit ur you up to? Huv you been listenin?

Ah was getting somethin to eat.

Ah telt ye tae go tae yer room.

She's dead, isn't she?

Trixie stopped and threw me a look. I could feel the pressure of tears behind my eyelids, and for a moment I imagined her giving me a hug, and how I might bury myself forever in the folds of her cardigan.

Go tae bed Donald, an don't be so stupit.

She sat down at the kitchen table and she seemed suddenly distant, lost in a world where I was no longer visible to her. I brushed past and headed for the stairs. I knew that she would be up half the night now with her cards and her powders and her bits of coloured beads, and in the morning she would be bleary-eyed and distracted.

Every now and then in the months following Anna's disappearance there were sightings. Anna in Edinburgh wearing a short skirt and lipstick, being bundled into a white limousine in Princess Street. Anna in Glasgow saving souls with the born-again Christians in George Square. Anna on a train to London, in a smoking compartment, her feet up on the seat. But even though the police followed every lead, and her picture was in the papers, and her frantic parents appealed on the television news for her to come home, no trace of her was ever found. Nothing. She simply vanished from our lives and in a short time was just a memory, more or less painful, depending on how close you were to her. No one was close to her, as far as I knew. Except her family and, unknown to them or to anybody else, me.

Before she smiled at me that afternoon I had worked out how best to do away with myself. I had it all planned. Get off the bus at my usual stop, walk around the corner, but then double back through a wooded path which took me to a quiet part of the railway embankment. I'd lay my head on the tracks, I thought. Face up or face down? I wasn't sure. These were details to be worked out when I got there. I thought maybe face down, though. So there I'd be, the cold metal of the railway track pressing up into my Adam's apple, waiting to feel the first, faint shudders as the train approached, then hearing its noise, distant to begin with but gradually getting louder and suddenly then a roar as it thundered round the bend and bore down upon my exposed neck. I'd close my eyes and that would be me. Finito. A mess to be cleaned up but that's all.

That's what I thought, until Anna smiled at me and I realised I was in love, and that I wasn't going to the embankment after all.

Which was pretty fucked, because if I had I would have walked down the very same lane that Anna disappeared from, and I might have seen what happened, maybe even stopped it.

Life's shite, isn't it? But now, for the first time ever, I was worried about someone else more than myself. A real person, frail and human. I decided against killing myself, at least until I knew for sure what had happened to her.

18

IT'S A BIT LIKE THAT; life, fate, luck, whatever you want
to call it. As if there really is someone up there pulling the
strings. Some malicious old bastard, sitting there in his cloud,
thinking up traps and twists and wee surprises just to keep
you off-balance, and having a right old laugh about it too.
He's got me fingered, that's for sure.

Everything was gone. The Turtle, Anna, hope. Even Jake
had disappeared. I walked down to the zoo one evening
after school, drawn there despite myself, wanting to see
what it looked like after the fire, horrified by what I might
find. Hoping maybe to see Jake or some friendly face.
Or something. Truth is, I didn't want to believe the Turtle
was dead.

But they'd stopped my pass. The woman at the turnstile told me it was no longer valid, and to go and see the man at security. No chance! I turned and ran and kept on running until I couldn't run anymore, then I walked the rest of the way to Jake's place in Shettleston. The door was answered by a stranger who said he didn't know anyone called Jake and suggested I talk to the landlord. Through the doorway I saw that the bed was made and the bottles cleared away. Everything neat and tidy. Not a trace of Dr Jakowski anywhere. He hadn't wasted any time in making himself scarce, that's for sure. I assumed there was going to be an inquiry of some sort and he'd done a runner, rather than face whatever music he thought was in store for him. Down at the cafe, Luigi hadn't seen hide nor hair of him either, not since the night he was drunk.

A day or two later I went to the youth club to see if they knew anything, but the guys there had no idea where he was. Someone else was already helping out with the swimming. Then I went to the baths for the first time since the Turtle died. I sat there at the edge of the water for ages, unable to go in. It didn't feel right. The pool was teeming with noisy kids but it seemed empty, the water and its promise of buoyancy nothing more than a trick of the light.

I stopped going to school, too. I had been doing alright, despite all the distractions at the zoo and with the swimming and everything. I'd managed in the previous year to get myself a couple of Highers with not too bad grades, and I'd been intending to get some more in my final year. Why bother, you ask? Lots of reasons—because it was a way of claiming a future for myself, a way of saying to Trixie, stuff your curse; it was a place to be that wasn't home, and it was a way of proving to myself, and anyone else that needed proof, that I wasn't just some dumb bampot, even if it seemed like it. And it was a way of being near Anna McColl.But when Anna disappeared, all the other reasons for dragging myself to school disappeared with her, and I stopped going.

No one noticed for weeks, not even Trixie. When she eventually asked me about it, I just told her I wanted to leave, that there really was no point in going. She gave me a strange look when I said that, as if she didn't quite believe me. Then she simply nodded and told me that it was up to me. When the school eventually sent someone round she got them to organise the paperwork and that was that. Nobody tried to talk me out of it. No concerned teachers worried about my academic future, no careers master anxious about what I was going to do with myself, no disappointed mother nagging me about lost opportunities.

I wasn't idle, though. I was busy thinking. I was busy thinking about being miserable. And I was busy distracting myself from thinking about being miserable. I watched the afternoon soaps on TV. I watched the kiddies' programs, *Blue Peter* and *The Magic Roundabout*. I watched *Starsky and Hutch* and *Kojak*, and I'd even sit there right up until the Reverend bloody Sourface came on to deliver *The Epilogue*. It's amazing how the shite they put on telly can numb your mind. That and the Valium I stole from Trixie. The days fair flew by, so they did.

And then one day I got jack of it.

It was a cold morning I remember. I got up and dressed and packed my duffel bag with a towel and trunks and I walked out and caught the bus to the swimming baths. I did it without thinking; if I had thought about it I would have pulled the covers up and stayed in bed. But I'd done enough thinking, and enough avoiding—it was time now to be doing. I went to the baths and I put on my togs, shivering in the cold air of the changing room. I stood at the edge of the pool, watching the steam rise off the chlorinated water. I had to force myself to get in. Jump, you silly bugger! Jump! And eventually I did. The moment I hit the water and felt the cold shock of it against my skin, my whole body seemed to unfurl in a long wave of relaxation and I realised how much I had been missing this, the comfort and the beautiful pressure of its embrace. I stayed there nearly the whole day. I think it was the best day of my entire life.

You see, I discovered several things that morning. I discovered that it's bad for you to think too much, and it's bad for you to try not to think at all. I discovered that I needed water as much as I needed air to breathe, that it was my true element. And I discovered this: that the Turtle wasn't dead. At least, not when I was swimming. Then, I could feel him with me, the weight of him, his pressure on the water around me, the eddies from his flippers brushing my face. And I could hear him, too, cajoling, jeering, making rude remarks about my progress. It made me want to laugh out loud, there under the water, big bubbles of laughter rippling to the surface. I swam like I'd never swum before, full of a new energy. His voice was in my head, the way it had been when he was alive, and I understood this; that the Turtle was in the water and the air around me, that he inhabited my body just as surely as I lived inside him—*You're me and ah'm you.* That's what he'd said, and I knew now what he meant: that we lived on in each other, and that as long as I lived, he lived. Ipso facto, Professor, I had to live, because if I died, he would die too.

Something like that. Don't expect any of this to make sense—what does, after all? But it was this, too, that kept me from heading back to the railway embankment to put my head under a train. This, and the stubborn hope that Anna was alive, somewhere, and that she was calling for me.

And now, winter was coming. Frost in the mornings and dusk in the afternoons, heavy and unwelcome as it settled in for an early night, the streetlights on at four, their meagre glow lost in the gloom. Sundays were always the worst, so they were, the church bells tolling dismally through freezing air, calling us to God. Fuck off, why don't you? Give us all a bit of peace.

But peace was never part of the deal. Especially in our family.

Luce was still living with Carlo, though we'd heard she was being difficult, argumentative and rude towards Carlo's women friends, causing fights and ructions between them. She was also refusing to go to school, hanging around with a bunch of no-good spongers who were helping her spend Carlo's money. She was too young to leave school yet and the authorities were not happy. A different set of authorities were equally unhappy with Carlo. Something to do with the colour of that very money and the dodginess of his overseas accounts.

Mr Disco, for his part, was long gone, chasing rock stardom in London and New York, now sporting glitter make-up and a glam-boy pout. His reputation was growing, expanding in direct proportion to the size of his head, his drug habit, and the distance he put between himself and the rest of the family.

As for old Pa and Nonna, they no longer spoke to us. The situation between Trixie and Carlo had deteriorated beyond repair after the spying incident, and Pa and Nonna took Carlo's side, I suppose because it had reached the point where sides had to be taken, though I expect Carlo had put some pressure on them.

Granny Mac died that winter. Of a heart attack, they said, but it was just as likely she died of loneliness and neglect; she never got used to not having Mr Disco around. Trixie buried her at Lambhill Cemetery, no service to speak of, no mourners. Just a cheap coffin and a death certificate.

It got colder.

By Christmas there was still no sign of Anna. Her mum had come round with Anna's hairbrush and a photograph, and Mrs McColl and Trixie spent a long time together in the kitchen communicating with the nether world. Mrs McColl left late that night, grey-faced and teary, and Trixie spent the whole night at her table, presumably doing what she did, tingling all over, feeling that dull ache in her fingers, listening for the spectral voices on the tapes she'd recorded. But she was having trouble with the signs. I could tell by the weary look on her face, and the way she snapped at me for no reason.

The police believed that Anna had been abducted. They had evidence, they said. But now, weeks later, their investigations had come to nothing. In desperation—and it must have been desperation, what else could it have been?—they too turned to Trixie for help.

It was PC One who put them up to it, he who had been so impressed by Trixie and her patter the day he'd turned up to investigate our absence from life. He and his wife had subsequently visited Trixie on a professional basis, seeking guidance from the spirit world. PC One probably thought he'd be in for promotion by suggesting that the police employ a psychic to help them see the things they couldn't see for themselves. He somehow convinced his superiors to take the chance.

Despite the trouble Trixie was already having trying to find Anna, when the police approached her for help she agreed readily enough. They said they would give her access to the little evidence they had. They even offered to set her up in a room down at the station. But Trixie declined the offer. Her kitchen was her nerve centre, she said, and she had everything she needed there. She told them to bring whatever evidence they had round to her, and that's what they did. Special investigator Trixie got right on the case, new cassettes for her tape machine and a brand new pack of tarot cards. I left her to it. I knew she had not a chance. Desperate they were, the lot of them.

I, on the other hand, was a little less desperate. I may have lost the Turtle and Jake—and Anna, who I'd never really found—but I was swimming regularly, and that helped me feel better. Also, Wee Malkie and I were friends again. He came to see me one evening, just after the New Year, wondering why I hadn't been at school for so long.

He'd changed, had Wee Malkie. He seemed to have grown into himself, to have shrugged off the gormless wee boy who was bullied by all and sundry, including me. The new Wee Malkie was different altogether. He had that same restless energy but was now more self-assured, cockier, cooler even. And he was funny, with a wicked sense of humour, making jokes about people we knew at school. I liked him like this, more of an equal, with a delicious superiority now about our misfit status. We'd been friends since we were seven, for God's sake. Friendships that old can survive just about anything. Just about.

We got into the habit of sitting in my room a couple of nights a week, talking about all sorts of nonsense. Malkie was into music and he'd bring some records and I'd drag the old portable up from downstairs and we'd sit in there like two normal kids.

But one night, he said, So what're ye gauny do?

About what?

Well, are ye still cursed? He smiled when he asked this.

What do you think?

I think yer mother's an auld witch.

She likes you well enough.

Aye, well, ah hope that means she's not gauny drown me, too.

Naw. That's for people she disny like. She'll turn *you* inty a budgie.

We were talking about it like it was some kind of joke, like we didn't really want to admit that there was anything serious going on. How could we? A curse, a madwoman, some super-stitious nonsense? So we broached the subject and avoided it at the same time. But gradually I took Wee Malkie into my confidence, and I told him things that I probably shouldn't have told him, looking back now. At that time I just needed to talk, to sort out all the nonsense with someone who wasn't involved. And he listened to me, Wee Malkie did, he listened like a good friend, with concern and sympathy, and without making me feel stupid.

There was a lot to listen to. Things were beginning to happen now. Indefinable things; a slow boiling, a feeling of urgency and a growing anxiety. Something in Trixie. Some-thing in me. Something in the air of the house.

I was seventeen and a half years old, and I had six months left to live.

19

I'M FLOATING THROUGH space, turning slowly over and over, one moment lit by the giving life of a burning sun, the next pitched into perfect darkness. On my back I'm carrying the world, the whole infested edifice of life abundant, scurrying here and scurrying there, everyone absorbed in their own self-importance. No one knows what lies beneath their feet. They clamour and clang, hammering on my back, unaware that I'm sleeping, unafraid that I might waken. Clack, clack! Clack, clack!

I sit up with a start, and for a moment I don't know where I am, the chill in the air and the strangeness of the room around me in the half-light; the looming furniture, the outline of wall hangings, the frame of a doorway. It all comes back to me quickly enough, though—Trixie's house of ghosts. I've dozed off again here in the old armchair, though surely not for more than a few minutes. I'm so tired I can barely keep my eyes from closing, but it really is time to think about a shave and a shower. Soon. I'll just sit here for a bit longer, collect myself a bit.

My eyes drop closed and when I open them again a moment later there's a woman standing in the living room doorway, watching me, and it's a second or two before I understand that she's actually there and I'm not dreaming. I let out a yelp and just about jump out of the chair with fright, but my legs give way from under me and I fall back into the cushions, wide awake now, my heart going thump. There's nothing like a good fright to get you going.

Oh god, ah'm sorry! Ah thought . . .

When she speaks, it takes me only a second or two to realise she's not some kind of spectral bouncer come to send me on my merry way. I would have gone, believe me. Got up there and then and straight on the first plane back to Sydney. You don't mess with ghosts, especially not those you find in Trixie's house. But the tone of her voice says that she's really mortified for scaring me like that, and ghosts are not generally known to apologise after they turn your hair white and send you off trembling to the funny farm. I collect what few shreds of dignity I can find around me. No bother, I hear myself mumble, I was just getting up anyway.

Ah knocked at the front door, she says. Ah thought maybe ye'd gone out, so I let myself in.

I'm sitting there blinking at her.

Ah've got a key, she says.

A key?

She holds her hand up and waves a key at me. At least I think it's a key—I can barely see straight between the sleep in my eyes and the dimness of the room. Then she says, D'ye mind if ah open the curtains?

Sure. Make yourself at home. Let the sunshine in and all that.

I'm trying to be nonchalant, though I feel anything but. The woman walks over to the windows and pulls the heavy curtains back and when she does so the watery light streams in exactly as I remember it used to do when I was a kid, bringing with it a faint optimism for the day ahead, a muted feeling of excitement in the pit of the stomach. It's later than I thought, I see now; the curtains have been masking the daylight too well. I glance at my watch: five past nine.

The woman turns in the light and something about her seems familiar, the chestnut eyes, maybe, or the glint of playfulness in them, as if she knows something I don't. She's about my age, I think, or a bit younger. Medium height, a hint of middle-aged solidity. She's wearing black like she's dressed for a funeral, a black coat over a dress and knee-length boots. Her hair is dark and straight, falling to her shoulders. She's carefully made up, and the hair and the look in her eyes lend her a certain girlishness. I find myself thinking that there are worse ways to be woken suddenly.

Sorry to disturb ye, she says.

Just as long as you're not the axe murderer. Are you?

What? She shakes her head slowly, confused by my eejit

mumbling. There's an awkward pause as I struggle to sit up in the chair. Then she says, D'ye not remember me, Donald?

Christ, she knows my name. That means I'm supposed to know who she is. A friend of Luce's maybe? An old girlfriend of Wee Malkie's? I haven't a clue.

Do I owe you money?

No. She shakes her head, a hint of a smile. Nothing like that.

That's a relief. Go on then, surprise me.

Anna, she says.

Anna?

Anna McColl. We were at school together.

And she smiles. All I can do is stare at her, wondering if I have actually woken up or if I'm still asleep, or maybe even dead and off to some kind of stupid hell to be tormented by all the things I missed out on in life. And then I realise that she's waiting for me to say something, and that the niceties of polite society still apply, even when you've been startled out of your undershirt twice in quick succession.

Are you having me on?

No, she says, it's true. And she laughs then at the idea of playing a joke on me, as if it's perfectly normal for someone who disappeared over thirty years ago to suddenly just waltz in and say hello, do you mind if I open the curtains? Her laugh is warm, a rich chuckle, laugh lines around her eyes, her face lighting up. I can feel myself starting to smile now, too. I stand up and we do what two people do who've never met each other; we shake hands, awkwardly.

I'm a wee bit shocked, I say.

Ye look terrible.

She laughs again when she says this, so I know her direct-
ness is intended as a token of concern. But I can feel the
dry roughness of the skin under my eyes, and I'm only too
conscious of my rumpled clothes and the grit under my shirt
collar. I've been up all night, I tell her. And travelling before
that. If I'd known you were coming . . .

Ah'll make a cup of tea, she says, and she's already on her
way to the kitchen, trailing a faint scent of something, jasmine
maybe. Don't worry, ah know where everythin is.

I'm not worried, just tired. Too many surprises, too much
thinking about the past, too many puzzles with no solu-
tions. This woman, she can't be Anna McColl, because Anna
McColl disappeared. Anna McColl was abducted, murdered,
sold into slavery. Anna McColl was never seen again. And
anyway, even if she is Anna, what the hell is she doing here in
Trixie's house?

It doesn't make any sense, and yet there *is* something I
recognise about her. Something in that smile, the way her
eyes crinkle up, the tilt of her head. And for a moment, I'm
standing once again at that long-ago bus stop, with the sun
coming out and a stupid grin on my face, and I wonder if I've
maybe conjured up Anna out of thin air, through thinking of
her so much these last few hours.

I go upstairs to the bathroom and quickly splash my face
with water to try and rub away the tiredness. In the mirror,
a middle-aged man looks back at me. His hair's sticking up,
and he needs a shave and the attentions of an entire depart-
ment store of skin-care specialists, if not the full-quid plastic

surgeon, preferably one who likes a challenge. Anna's not wrong; he looks terrible.

And now, Anna McColl sits at the kitchen table drinking tea and talking. She's put the heater on and the little room is warming up nicely. I'm standing by the sink, lost in wonder at the situation I find myself in, hanging on to her every word and feeling like I'm regressing to the love-sick teenager I once was, silently admiring her from afar. As I listen to her talk it comes to me with a sudden lump in my throat that we've never really spoken before today, and that the sound of her voice is exactly as I'd imagined it would be: warm and assured, her words measured like a woman who knows herself and the world around her. She's taken her coat off and hung it carefully in the hallway, and in the light of the kitchen I can see more clearly how she wears her years. No one would mistake her as anything but a woman over forty, but she's still good-looking, I think, and she carries herself well, a straightness in her back and shoulders, a lightness in her step, the calm way she deals with our awkward meeting. But what I really find myself noticing is her warmth as she talks to me now and the relaxed way she laughs, that chuckle, putting me at ease. It's stupid, but within a short time I feel like I've known her forever.

And it is a short time. Anna is dressed like she's going to a funeral because that's exactly what she's doing. In fact, she's going to Trixie's funeral, which doesn't surprise me when she tells me, even though it should. Nothing surprises me anymore. Not only is Anna McColl going to Trixie's funeral, but she's been organising the flowers, and she's here dressed and early because she's on her way to the undertaker's to take care of some last-minute details before the funeral starts at eleven-thirty. She just dropped in to see if I needed anything, and to say hello.

How did you know I was here?

Uch, everyone knows yer here, Donald.

I'm just looking at her then, my jaw hanging open.

It was me that phoned ye, she says. Ah left the message telling ye yer mum had died.

But you didn't leave your name.

Ah was nervous. And you, ye sounded so crabbit, so ye did. Ah got a wee bit flustered. Ah didn't think ye'd remember me, anyway.

The last time I saw you, Anna, you'd disappeared.

Uch aye, ah was such a stupit wee girl.

So what happened, then? Did you just come back?

Yer mum found me, Donald. Ah'd be dead now if it wasn't for her.

I think you'd better start at the beginning.

She looks at her watch. It'll need to be the short version, she says. Ah have to go soon.

Okay, I say. The short version will do fine.

And she puts her cup down on the table and tells me then what happened to her after her disappearance. She wasn't abducted at all, or murdered, or sold into slavery. She'd simply run away, like so many kids do, frustrated with her mother and father and the constraints of the neat, middle-class life that wouldn't let her be the young woman she was growing into. Just another mixed-up teenager who thought her parents were old fuddy-duddies who knew nothing, and who were just there to spoil her fun. So she walked out on them. She'd planned it for weeks, and when the day came she'd simply got off the school bus at her usual stop, picked up a bag that she'd hidden in the woods and then hitchhiked south, heading for London.

She never got there. Only as far as Birmingham, where she fell in with a crowd of assorted musicians and dope-heads, spending her nights in pubs and clubs, off her face mostly, sleeping around with different boys. It was a wild time, until it started to go wrong. She took up with a bloke who was a heroin addict. He abused her. Anna wanted to leave him, but he threatened her whenever she tried. She was in fear of her life, trapped, lonely and miserable. And then Trixie tracked her down.

Wait a minute, I say. What d'you mean, tracked you down?

She used her gift. She had a wonderful gift, yer mum.

That mumbo-jumbo stuff?

Anna looks shocked, and I realise I've overstepped the mark. I backtrack quickly. Well, she was a great one for the clairvoyance, right enough. I remember she was helping the police to look for you.

That's right, and she found me in the end. A couple of burly Glasgow detectives turned up at our squat one day and they took me home. Ah was happy to go, let me tell you.

I bet you were.

Ah became quite good friends with yer mum after that. Ah used to come over here and talk to her. You know, troubled youngster and that. She was easy to talk to, not like my own parents. She didn't judge me, but she helped me sort things out. And later, with my daughters, she was good to them. They loved her, so they did.

I'm nodding my head at this, trying to take all this stuff in; the fact that Anna has a life, with children, and I want to tell her about my kids too, but maybe this isn't the time for it. And then there's this person she's talking about that I'm finding it hard to recognise. Not Trixie, surely? Who would let Trixie anywhere near their kids? But I feel something opening up under my feet then, a kind of dislocation, a sense that there's a whole world that I've been missing, and it's just there, beyond my reach, revealed in tantalising glimpses as Anna talks. A bit like I felt when I listened to Trixie's tape. And then I find myself wondering if Anna knows about the tape and whether I should mention it or not, but she's still talking about Trixie.

. . . and she knew things, you know? She predicted my marriage, and my daughters, and when my husband was going to die, though she never let on to me at the time.

I'm sorry to hear about your husband.

Och, it's ten years now. All in the past.

Would've been hard for you, though.

Ah've been through better times. But Trixie was a great help to me then, too.

She must have liked you.

We were good friends. Ah saw a lot of her when she was ill and she needed help with this and that. Do you know she asked me to find you, Donald, when she knew that she was dying?

The sound of rainwater dripping off the window ledge outside. I shift uncomfortably on my feet.

No, I say. I didn't know that.

Well, she did. She wanted to see you again before she died, so ah promised her ah'd find you. It was the least ah could do for her. But it was too late. Ah was on my way over to give her yer phone number but when ah got here she was gone. Massive heart attack. The doctor said she wouldn't have suffered much.

Was she alone?

There's a tear welling in Anna's eye as she nods slowly. No one was expecting it so suddenly. No one but her, anyway. Ah found her in her bed upstairs. Ah'm so sorry, Donald.

I should have been here, I say. It's my fault.

I want to reach out and hug her tears away, but I don't know if that's the right thing to do, and I'm not sure I can move from the support of the kitchen bench. You did what you could, I say.

It took me weeks to find ye. Searching all the old records and everything. Ah was determined to do it, for Trixie's sake. She said she couldn't see ye anywhere, the signs were all mixed up, there was a shadow over them or something, so ah thought this was one thing ah could do to repay her. For her kindness.

And you did find me, Anna. You kept your promise.

Aye, ah found ye, right enough. Too late, but.

She rummages in her handbag for a tissue and dabs at her eyes gently, trying not to upset her make-up. Then she looks up, remembering something. Ye know, Trixie said she was going to leave ye a message. A cassette. Did ye get it?

Yes, I found it.

What did she say?

Oh, this and that. I'm smiling, but I'm a bit taken aback by Anna's question and it obviously shows.

Ah'm sorry, she says, and she's looking at her watch. I've no right to pry. Oh, look at the time! Ye'd better get yerself spruced up. And ah'd better be going or there'll be no flowers for the funeral.

She's all businesslike suddenly, as she gets up from the table. I follow her through to the hallway and help her on with her coat.

Right, ah'll see ye there then, Donald.

But I'm not ready yet to say goodbye. As she buttons up her coat, I hear myself say, Anna, you know the family's disowned me, don't you?

So they say. But ah don't believe them. Not a word of it.

They tried to stop me going to the funeral.

They can't stop ye. Not if ye want to go.

They think I'm going to make trouble.

Maybe ye should. Anna smiles when she says this, but I'm not sure she's joking.

Why do they still hate me, Anna? We're not stupid kids anymore.

Maybe they don't hate ye as much as they think they do. People get stuck in the past, ye know?

I nod at this, and she gives a sigh, choosing her words carefully. When ye left, she says, it upset people. All that weird stuff about a curse and whatever. Ah know yer mum was so superstitious and everything, but, well, she was upset.

She had quite a bit to do with it, you know.

Aye. And she blamed herself. She went through some terrible times, Donald. It was hard for all of us. Yer brother and sister . . .

They were glad enough to see the back of me.

It was never that simple.

No, I say. Maybe not.

And it's time now to move on.

I'm starting to see that. But the others . . .

Look, things might be different when they see ye at the funeral. Trixie wanted ye to be there. Just remember that.

I'll be there, I promise.

Good. Don't you be late then.

She kisses me on the cheek, her hair brushing against my face, the warm hint of jasmine, and something deeper. Ah'm glad ye're home, she says.

I watch from the doorway as she gets into her car and drives off. The outside air smells of damp leaves and the distant traffic on the main road. I close the door against it and it latches to with its familiar rattle.

I should start getting myself ready for the funeral, but it's like time's slowed down for the moment, or that it's somehow not important any longer. I won't be late, don't you worry about that. But before I make myself presentable, I've got a bit more of this story to tell, even if it's not the story I started with. Even if the story I thought I had is being overwhelmed by something else—those glimpses into another world beyond the limits of my imagination.

See, *ah warned ye. Everythin's*
mixed up, the good an
the bad,
the right an the wrang,
the maw,
the son,
an the flippery fuckin turtle.
Yer poor ol mammie wis a good wummin
efter aw, get yer heid roon that.
Cos when she wis good, she wis very, very good.
But when she wis bad she wis
mental.
C'mon, wee man, get tae the bit where ah save yer
miserable skin.

20

WHAT HAPPENED ON my eighteenth birthday? I wish I knew, I really do. I wish I knew beyond the bare facts that I'm going to tell you about now. It's all true, all of it. It all really happened. It's just that I don't understand. I can't get under the surface of it.

It was a long time ago.

Those last six months with Trixie were sheer murder, so they were. It felt like being inside the mechanism of one of Carlo's fruit machines with someone pulling the handle slowly, the ratchet clacking and the whole thing building up power as the spring coiled tighter and tighter. At any moment the catch would be released and everything would start spinning and who knew where it would all stop. That's how it felt.

Trixie would fob me off whenever I asked her about Anna, and eventually I gave up trying. She didn't want to talk about it, her psychic investigations were not going well. And there was something else she never spoke about, though it was looming like a spoilt child, angry at being ignored: the curse, and my birthday, the two intertwined. Trixie never mentioned the curse now, as if the closer we came to the fated day, the less there was to say about it. That's how it was. There was no emotional resolution between doomed son and soon-to-be-bereaved mother. No heart-rending moment of connection, no tearful scenes or tender goodbyes. In typical Pinelli fashion, there was nothing. *Niente*. We went on doing our usual things, Trixie busy with her clients, me swimming, seeing Wee Malkie, eating, drinking, sleeping. It seems incredible now that normal things could just continue like that, but they did. For a while.

And then, Trixie went completely mad. Okay, she was always mad, but what I mean is, she went even madder. The closer it got to my birthday, the worse she became. That spring, she once again stopped seeing her clients and gave up any pretence of looking after herself, washing or changing her clothes. In no time at all she looked haggard and grey, like a pantomime witch, her hair uncombed, her dressing-gown stained and fraying at the edges. She smoked constantly, sitting in her old armchair, gazing into the distance. Or if I was in the room with her she'd stare at me, follow me around with her eyes, a pleading kind of look, though I didn't think it was me she was pleading with. She was looking for answers from a different world. I took to avoiding her as much as I could.

A few weeks before my birthday, she locked herself in her room. But it wasn't like the other times she'd done it. This was different. This time, I knew for a fact she wasn't just dozing or whatever else she did there. This time I heard her, day and night, pacing the floor, burning her weird-smelling stuff, playing back her cassettes, chanting to herself, occasionally letting out a scream, sometimes stifled, sometimes not, as if she was waking up from a nightmare or something. Sometimes she would sob for hours on end. For a whole week, she stayed in her room and didn't come out, except to visit the bathroom. She didn't speak to me once in all that time. I was terrified; I didn't know what to do. I thought she was in pain and I wanted to get near her. I did, that's the honest truth, I wanted to help her, I wanted to stop her suffering. But she refused to answer my anxious knocks on her bedroom door, my cajoling and my threats. And in the end I had to call on Carlo. At least he would know what to do, even if he never actually did anything himself. What other course of action was there? I didn't have a clue who to talk to, where to begin to deal with a crisis like this. So, like any normal teenager in trouble, I turned to my dad. I tracked Carlo down and finally got him on the end of the phone. He sent round a doctor, and the doctor had Trixie admitted to the hospital.

I was left alone in the house, fending for myself as I had done many times before. But this time I liked having the place to myself, the solitude of it, no one to think about, or worry about. You're maybe asking, was I not worried about Trixie? My own mother, in hospital? Well, as usual, I was glad to see the back of her. It was a relief to have her gone, and anyway, I was a bit preoccupied.

I was troubled by what the Turtle hadn't told me. How exactly was I supposed to *jist swim like fuck*, as he had said? I thought he probably didn't mean I should just jump in the River Clyde somewhere, but that I should find my way to the sea. But where? We weren't a family that spent much time at the seaside—maybe once or twice when I was very young and there was still some pretence of a marriage between Trixie and Carlo. But holidays in the sun were never really our thing. And then I remembered that one particular time at the beach, not long after I'd listened to the seashell and realised that my salvation lay with water and with swimming like a turtle. Trixie had been shaken. She'd taken Luce and I to the beach to cast a healing spell upon the water. Near Fairlie—the place where William Drummond's rented boat had been found washed up. It seemed fitting somehow, the connection with family history. I decided then that I would go to Fairlie to make my escape—and the sooner the better. My birthday was coming up soon. It wasn't a birthday I wanted to celebrate with anyone, and especially not with my family. The more I thought about it—and I thought about it a lot—the more certain I became about what I had to do. I had to be out of here before the 7th of July.

That night I rang Wee Malkie, and he came over with some fish and chips, hot and salty with lots of vinegar. I made some tea and we sat eating in the living room, the TV on in the corner, *Upstairs, Downstairs* or some such, though neither of us were watching it. I asked him if he knew how to get to Fairlie.

Train frae Central, ah think. Or there's maybe a bus.

Know how much it costs?

No idea. Ye plannin a holiday?

Somethin like that.

Why Fairlie, for God's sake?

It's the place to be, Malkie. Didn't ye know that? Highly fashionable.

Aye, fashionable my arse. He wiped the grease off his lips and lit up a fag. Then he smiled. Ye're plannin somethin, aren't ye? Ah can tell.

But when I told him what I wanted to do, he looked at me and shook his head.

Yer fuckin mad, Donny.

Ah need ye to help me, Malkie. Ah canny do it alone.

Jesus. Yer serious, aren't you?

Well?

Naw. He was agitated, his lips pursed. Naw, Donny, ah canny help ye.

All ye've got to do is keep them off my trail. Ah'm not asking ye to come with me.

Ah don't get it. Where will ye go?

Anywhere, it disny matter.

Look, it was like this. The Turtle was dead—he existed now only inside of me; Anna was still missing, despite the police and despite Trixie's divinatory powers; Trixie herself was madder than ever, and due to come home in a week or so. What I wanted more than anything else at this point was to get away as far as I possibly could, to disappear completely, to take my chances on my todd somewhere, live off of my wits or something. That's what my plan was about. It was quite simple. I was going to get on the train to Fairlie. Once there, I thought, I'd know what to do next.

God knows why I thought I needed Malkie's help. I had some stupid idea that he might be able to cover for me, to give me time to escape. I think I'd been watching too much telly. In the end, things worked out differently, and I would have been better off keeping stum about it, telling nobody.

But I didn't. And in the end, Wee Malkie caved in. I think now he was quite seriously concerned for my welfare, that he went along with me because he was worried, and that he thought maybe he could help me by keeping close. So he was enlisted in Donald's bampot army, and the two of us got down to working on my escape plan. Malkie was going to point everyone in the wrong direction when the time came, spinning some great fib or other. He also agreed, after a lot of hoo-ing and ha-ing, to help with the train fare to Fairlie. He worked in the newsagent's on Saturdays, and he promised to give me something from his next wages. That would be Saturday night. I planned to get an early train on Sunday morning.

Alright, there was more to it than just running away. I was desperate, and I was mad myself, thinking back on it now. Madder than I've ever been since. But mad then was kind of normal, and I was convinced that this was the right thing to do. I was infused with the certainty of it, crazy as it was. So, Sunday morning, train to Fairlie. Exit Donald.

Except that two things happened: Trixie came home unexpectedly from the hospital, and Wee Malkie betrayed me.

Sandro brought Trixie home late one afternoon, this time in Carlo's Mercedes. I tried to be pleasant to her, even though I was seething because her return made carrying out my plan more difficult. Sunday was only a few days away. But I settled her in and made a cup of tea, and later I cooked for us, though there was nothing much in the house so it wasn't a very special meal. Trixie was quiet, but she seemed to me to be better in herself. She wanted to do some of her work, so I washed up the dishes and left her sitting in the kitchen with her psychic stuff.

I rang Wee Malkie and told him the situation. He thought I should abandon the plan, but I was determined to go ahead. He said he'd come over the next day. We rang off, and I went to bed. Some time later, I was dimly aware of the doorbell going, and Trixie answering the door. One of her late-night clients probably, a sure sign she was feeling better. But I think now that it was Malkie at the door and that he told Trixie everything.

The next day, he didn't show up, and when I rang his house I was told he was out and wouldn't be back until late. Trixie seemed somehow lighter, more animated than the day before. She bustled about doing things, getting the house in order, hoovering the carpets, cleaning up the kitchen. She went out to the shops and came back with fruit and vegetables, and some fresh fish, which she fried up with chips and salad for our tea. It was the best meal I'd had in ages. The two of us sat together in the kitchen, not talking much, but I caught her looking at me sometimes, and I thought there was something about the softness in her look that was different. I felt like she noticed me, in a way that she hadn't for a long time. It made an impression, maybe because of the change in Trixie, but more likely because it's the last thing I remember clearly until the day of my birthday.

In between, there are only ghosts; fractured images and scattered words, echoing and hollow, my head feeling like it was going to burst. Trixie by my bedside, urging me to swallow something. She holds up a glass with liquid in it and says something about not being well. Me? Or her? Then, nothing. A damp pillow, too hot under the blankets. Dreaming of turtles . . .

Trixie leading me to the toilet, holding me steady, her small frame surprisingly strong. I can smell her perfume. I sit on the lavvy with the tiles cold beneath my feet. Afterwards, she watches me fill the basin with cold water but she stops me dipping my head in. She takes me back to bed. I hear the door lock when she leaves . . .

Shouting, thrashing around under the covers, trying to get out of bed. Someone's holding me, talking gently, pushing me back. I hear my own voice. The Turtle's waitin for me, ah've got to go, ah'm late . . . Poor Donald, there's nae turtle, there never wis. Here, take a sippy this. Yer favourite soup, there's a good boy . . .

Stumbling around the room, trying to open the door, trying to open the window, feeling suffocated, crying out for water. I'm burning up, shrivelling, dry and crackling like old leaves . . .

Waking in the middle of the night, the room lit by the moon. I open my eyes and the darkness swims into blue shadows. Trixie is sitting on a chair beside my bed. She's muttering something, talking to herself or to someone I can't see. Her words float into meaning through the fog of blue light and then recede.

Ma son, ma ain wee boy . . .

It seemed that now, in the final days before the curse was due to fulfil itself, Trixie had decided—what? That she didn't want to lose me after all? That by locking me away and keeping me drugged with God knows what—maybe something the hospital had given her—she could stop me going anywhere near water? That if she did that until after my birthday, then the curse would be beaten? Who knows. She always said you can't deny fate—*It's aw written doon, son, there's nothin ye kin dae*—but when it came to the crunch, she was a mother, and mothers can't let go of their children that easily. Not even mothers like mine.

Sisters, though, are a different matter.

Of the few fragmented memories of those strange days, the most vivid and complete is the final one.

I was half-aware of the conscious world beyond my torpor, the birdsong outside the window, a meaningless jangle of noise like the ringing of small bells and the sound of spoons on a tin plate. And something else: voices, angry voices, distant, as if they were deep inside my own head, my own angry self. Behind the curtains, impossibly high above me, a dim light. I know now that I was lying on the floor of my bedroom, wrapped in a stained blanket, looking up at the window, at the underside of the sill where the paint was patchy and flaking. But I didn't understand that I was on the floor until I heard the door being unlocked, opened, and then light footsteps and the sound of drawers being pulled, a hurried rustling and riffling, the noises prodding at me, trying to wake me up. A hand shook my shoulder and I turned my head towards it. A face loomed just out of reach.

I sat up, shook my head to clear it, and groaned at the pain behind my eyes. There was a figure standing by the open door. It approached and knelt down beside me and put a bowl in my hands and I could practically smell the water in it, I craved it so much. I poured it over my head, gasping as it dripped off my hair and down my neck and through my pyjamas. The figure stepped back, and I was trying to focus on it through the fog and the dripping wetness when it spoke, the sound of its voice dragging me violently into consciousness. It was Luce, framed by the doorway in the dim light of dawn, her black hair haloed by the glow from the landing window. Her face was in shadow, but I sensed she was smiling.

Get dressed, Donald, she said. It's yer birthday.

Then she disappeared down the stairs, leaving the bedroom door wide open.

My head felt like someone had put it through the wringer, but I was more conscious at that moment than I had been for days, which admittedly wasn't saying much. Birthday, she'd said. It was my birthday? How could it be? On the floor were the clean clothes that Luce had found: jeans, a T-shirt, underwear, socks and shoes. Tucked inside the laces of one shoe was a rolled-up ten-pound note. Everything was damp from the water I'd splashed around, but I didn't care about that. Somehow I made enough sense of things to struggle into the clothes and the shoes, frantic, trying not to cry out with the frustration of it. I didn't bother tying the laces. I stuffed the money into a pocket and I stood there, swaying, weak and wobbly, a great rushing and singing in my ears. I thought for a moment that I should just lie down again, but then I looked out through the open door of the bedroom, into the freedom of the landing and the stairs beyond.

It was my eighteenth birthday. Trixie had thwarted my plan to escape with Wee Malkie's help, but now I was being helped by Luce. Why? Did she want to be sure I'd go off and fulfil the curse, was that it—she wanted me dead? Maybe Malkie had told her—as well as Trixie—about my plan to escape. Or maybe Luce put two and two together on her own; she was a smart girl. I could hear her downstairs arguing with Mum, the same angry voices from earlier. I dimly understood that I had to get out of there fast, while Trixie was distracted.

I threw myself down the stairs to where the front door was standing wide open, the shadow of the garden beyond it and the glorious singing of the birds. Then I was out in the world, through the gate to the street, and running. At least, running as well as I could, because my legs weren't working too well and I didn't have a lot of puff. But I had to get as far away from the house as possible before Trixie discovered I was gone. I was heading for Fairlie. It was still my plan. I didn't have the wits to think of another. Fairlie. I'd know what to do when I got there.

I won't bore you with the details of the journey I made that morning, breathless and sick to the stomach, my ears ringing. The world seemed to float behind a net curtain, billowing in and out of focus. Somehow I managed to catch a train into town, and drag myself through the city streets from Queen Street to Central Station, dodging the traffic and the early morning commuters. I felt the weight of the grimy sandstone buildings around me, their purposeful shape, immovable, comforting in their solid reality. The morning sun was already hot on the back of my neck.

In the echoing concourse of Central Station, smelling of diesel and stale chips, I sat down on a bench to wait for the world to stop spinning. The station clock said seven thirty-five, and I watched the second hand slowly circling the clock face, then the big minute hand clunking into place, over and over, but slower and slower, as if time itself was dragging to a halt. I think I dozed off, right there on the bench, until I came to with a jump, groggily remembering where I was and why I was there. When I stood up, I started retching, and had to hold onto the back of the bench until I calmed down enough to walk over to the ticket office. I bought a one-way ticket to Fairlie, but there was nearly an hour before the train left. I found a quiet spot from where I could watch the entrances to the station without, I hoped, being too easily seen myself. I paced around, trying to keep awake and alert, expecting all the time for Trixie to appear on the concourse, willing me with her witch's tricks to come back to her. At least I had plenty of time to find the right platform, and I was in there as soon as the barriers opened. Hurry up train please hurry up God help me don't let her come. Relief when the old diesel engine finally backed in, belching fumes and clanking and shuddering to a halt. I climbed straight up and found a discreet spot at one end of the carriage where I flung myself down in the padded seat, thanking God and British Rail and anyone else who was listening. But it was fifteen minutes yet before the whistle blew and we crossed the Clyde and were weaving through the south side, the sun now well and truly up and the day begun in earnest. It was going to be a gorgeous summer day. A perfect day for the beach.

By the time we pulled into the station at Fairlie, I felt much less queasy, though my head was wrapped in cotton wool still, and it was as though I wasn't part of the world, but somehow beyond it, or it beyond me. I'd been scared I'd fall asleep and miss the station, so I forced myself to notice everything on the journey, the backs of houses and factory yards, the farm labourers at work in the fields, the stations with their swept platforms and neat wee flower gardens. I read the names, Glengarnock, Dalry, Kilwinning and all the rest, so I would know exactly when to get off. I took heart from the wideness of the countryside, the rolling hills and the green of it all, and eventually, when the train swung north to Saltcoats, the grey ribbon of the Firth of Clyde, sparkling and twinkling in the sunlight. Across the water was the distant shadow of the Isle of Arran, and as we got closer to Fairlie, the two hummocks of the Isles of Cumbrae came into view, with the craggy tip of Bute beyond.

Once off the train, I walked down to the main road, crossed over and turned north. The sea was to my left, still some way off behind houses and trees, but I could smell its tang in the air and I could hear the seabirds squabbling beyond the rooftops. I was heading for a spot just outside Fairlie itself, a triangle of sand and shingle beyond the north jetty that I remembered from being here with Trixie, the place where Bill Drummond's rented dinghy was washed up all those years ago.

The heat of the sun grew more intense as I trudged on, though it didn't bother me. I had found a new energy, bolstered by the salt air and the feeling of freedom. I followed the dual carriageway until I was able to turn off to the left, on a road that crossed the railway line and led to the north jetty and, finally, to the sea itself. Here the water lapped with little slaps against the shoreline, but further out it was dark and spiky, choppy waves scudding along with the breeze, which I could feel now, cool against my cheeks. The beach itself was broader here than I remembered, with rocky outcrops covered in barnacles. The railway line ran close alongside it, but I had only to jump a wall and descend onto dry shingle and sand which became wetter and stickier as I neared the water's edge. I took my shoes and socks off, leaving them on a rock, and picked my way onwards up the beach.

What was I thinking at that moment, barefoot and bedraggled, on a mission whose end was by no means clear? Not about Trixie and the nightmare of the last days. Not about my birthday, or Anna McColl, or the curse, or Luce. Not even, just then, about the Turtle. What I was thinking about was the sea. I was mesmerised by the expanse of water, seemingly alive, full of mystery and promise, and calling to me, beckoning me to its nameless depths, pulling me irresistibly towards it. I walked closer and closer to the edge and then my bare feet were in the shallows and the cold was like an electric shock through my whole body and I stopped like that, facing out to sea with the hot sun on my back, the water lapping around my ankles and calves. And I knelt down then, not caring about my clothes getting wet, and leant forward on my hands and dipped my head in the briny foam. As the cold hit my temples a ripple ran through me and I felt the life flowing back into my body. I held my breath for as long as I could, with the salt stinging my eyes, and the taste of it, sharp and potent.

That's why I didn't notice the white Mercedes pull up at the foot of the jetty behind me, nor hear the squeal of brakes as it stopped, nor the opening and slamming of car doors. But when I raised my head from the blissful water, I heard a cry, curiously muffled by the wind. I turned at that point, the water lapping at my thighs, my hair dripping and my shirt clinging to my chest, and I saw Trixie, standing unsteadily near the car, a look of such shock and horror on her face you'd think I was the ghost of old Drummond himself come back to get his hat. I took a step or two back, further into the water.

Then the other car doors were opening to reveal my sister Luce, and who else but Wee Malkie, his perplexed expression hiding the treachery within. Finally, out of the driver's door climbed Sandro, Carlo's proxy. He looked sad, I thought, probably regretting getting caught up in the madness of our family once again.

I gazed smiling upon my rescue committee as they milled around ineffectually on the shore, Trixie picking her way down the beach, slipping on the pebbles, calling me to come back. Her voice was nearly lost in the breeze, but it didn't matter, I wasn't listening. Standing there in the water, I could feel my breathing slowing down, my heart rate falling and my body sliding into that state of relaxation and readiness that the Turtle had so painstakingly taught me to reach. *Gaun yersel, wee man. That's the way tae dae it.*

I moved slowly backwards, further into the slapping sea, the rocks slippery underfoot, the cool water now up to my chest. The mid-morning sun dazzled me, reflecting sharp points of light off the surface of the water, so that I had to squeeze my eyes half-closed. And as I squinted into that halo of brightness, the whole beach undulated and shimmered, and it seemed to me then that I had been mistaken about who had arrived in the white Mercedes. Trixie and Luce for sure, but was that not also Carlo and Mr Disco, taking their places in the family group? Look, can you see them now? There's Trixie, wiping away a motherly tear. And next to her Carlo, with his arm around her shoulder, a proud smile on his face. And beside them Luce and Mr Disco, both grinning broadly, giving me the thumbs-up.

The water was up to my neck. It lapped and licked against my ears, the choppy surface distorting and magnifying every sound, the splashes, the seabirds, the voices from the shore. I looked one last time at my family, already so far away.

And then I took one last, big gulp of air, my mother's cries flat and distant and then lost forever in the gurgling darkness. Over and over, down and down, no turning back.

But ye huv turned back, huven't ye?
Ye've turned back, an now
ye've goat tae face whit's comin,
whitever that is,
however much it dis yer heid in.
You mammals ur beyond me,
but it's time ye fun yer way back there
an stopped actin
the feart
wee turtle.
Poke yer heid oot an see whit happens.
Ur ye up tae it, pal?

21

NO TURNING BACK.

I could tell you all about it, the underworld below the surface of the ocean. The silvers and browns of wee fishy things prying into cavities, fat lips pecking on strips of weed, shadows heaving and swelling around dark rocks prickly with molluscs, and everywhere the slow, grinding momentum of the sea. Behind the next rock some poor bugger's being dismembered, someone else is being squeezed down something's gullet. And all around, crabs claw and lobsters lumber, fins flap and gills gulp, every living thing trying to get the edge on the next guy, trying to put the boot in before someone gives it to them.

I could tell you that, and more. About the creatures not so easily classified, sorted, caught or eaten. The ghosts of drowned sailors and hapless fishermen, the souls of the cursed and the damned, trapped and tormented in ancient sea-chests or within the folds of twisted shipwrecks. The singing voices of the Turtle God, leading those who can hear them through dangers real or imagined, towards sanctuary. Real or imagined. But I'll leave you to picture for yourself what battles took place there in the cold, murky waters of the Firth of Clyde, where no turtle worth the name would wish to find itself. Don't think for a minute it was easy.

When I dived under the water, I didn't come up again for an awful long time, and when I did finally surface, I was far away from the shore. Trixie and the rest were stick figures on the distant beach, the car behind them a white blur. They couldn't see me at all with just my head showing, not from that distance. And even if they did, with another breath I was gone for good. As far as they were concerned, Auld Smith's Curse had delivered as promised, on the dot.

But had it? The truth is sleek and jagged-mouthed, turning and squirming and ripping at your fingers as you try to grasp it. The curse was not fulfilled, and yet it was.

That bright and blustery day, deep beneath the choppy waters of the Firth of Clyde, I died and I was reborn. This newborn me was more like the old than I or anyone else might have expected, given the nature of my leaving. That was my first disappointment, though it didn't become clear for quite some time; I had more pressing things to think about to begin with. I won't bother you now with all the details of how I got from drowned boy to some semblance of normal life. Getting there involved a journey south, weeks of homelessness and hunger, shelters and soup kitchens, the bureaucracy of welfare and, eventually, menial jobs, dreary bedsits, the emptiness of London.

And after I got settled, if that's what you could call it, many months later on a darkening winter's afternoon I wrote to Trixie. I needed to tell her she was wrong, that she'd always been wrong. About me, about the curse, about how life works. I told her I never wanted to hear from her again, and I told her not to look for me; no police, no missing-persons hunt, no psychic nonsense. I was done with her forever. That's what I said. I'm done with you, leave me alone. I posted the letter from Southampton, where I'd gone to see about a job as a deckhand on a cargo ship.

But though I took care to hide myself and not give Trixie any clues as to my whereabouts, I was always me. I didn't take on a new identity, a false passport or any of that rigma-role. I was determined to be me and not some fugitive, always looking over my shoulder for fear of being caught out. In time I obtained a copy of my birth certificate from the Glasgow authorities, I got myself a passport, I paid my taxes. My exis-tence was recorded in records of employment, tax files and, eventually, immigration papers. I could always be found, with a bit of effort, and in the end I was.

I worked on the boats off and on for a while, and my home became the sea, restless and forever shifting. It suited me. Somewhere along the way I learnt to scuba dive and I started working then as a commercial diver, mainly with salvage companies and various port authorities, sometimes with scientific research projects. I swam and dived in all the oceans of the earth, a migratory turtle, until eventually I landed up in Sydney, where there was plenty of work. I don't do so much these days, but I'm a good diver, efficient, careful, at ease in the water.

On dry land, though, it was always a different story. I made friends, cooperated with colleagues, socialised, but it forever felt to me as though there was a barrier that no one could penetrate, a barrier of my own making, as if I was cowering under a thick carapace that let no one and nothing near me. It was my defence against a world I thought I'd left behind, but which I carried with me unwittingly upon my back like a parasite, the old world infecting and poisoning the new.

And that's not all. There were the nightmares, the moments of dread, the days and nights of not being able to stand myself anymore, when I just wanted to lie down with the bedcovers pulled over my head. That, and the shouting, and the throwing of things around the room, the slamming of doors and the long days of angry silence. And too often, the taking of drink. It's what I came to think of as the true curse, the real legacy of my upbringing. Not the curse of Auld Smith the Fishmonger, but the curse of Trixie. This was the curse that was fulfilled.

And yet, despite all this, I got married and had two children. My two boys. It's been years since I've seen them, not even a letter or a Christmas card. They live in California with their mother. She doesn't want them to have anything to do with me. These days I live on my own, and I can cope with that most of the time, though even now the dawn sometimes finds me sleepless and glassy-eyed, and I wonder what it might be like to have a real family around me, a normal family where people look after each other. But it doesn't seem possible. You can't live a normal life, locked away in a shell.

But I expect you're wondering about the Turtle and whatever became of him? Well, the truth is that he pulled a disappearing act at the same time I did. For thirty-two years the Turtle was absent in every way—no dreams, no ghostly presence, no spiritual melding of reptile and mammal. No more voices, not until now. It's as though he was there only for my childhood, as if the situation I found myself in called him into being. And he came then, as he's come now, to stand between my mother and me; first to hold us apart and now to bring us together. My last chance.

And here I am in Trixie's house, slumped in her armchair, contemplating her funeral and all the ghosts of the past dredged up with it. I'm aching from lack of sleep, and holding in my hand a cassette tape addressed to me, the final words of my dying mother.

The funeral is in an hour and a half. I pick myself up and riffle through my luggage for a suit and a change of clothes. Everything's crumpled, but I find Trixie's old iron and give it all a good press, shirt and suit, careful to use a damp dish-cloth so as not to ruin the fabric. Then I shave, shower and dress, and all the while there's something running through my head, something Wee Malkie said about no one wanting me to make trouble, and something Anna said: maybe I should.

Maybe I should. I stick Trixie's tape in the pocket of my jacket and ring for a taxi. When it arrives ten minutes later, I take a quick glance in the mirror, straighten my tie, close the front door and lock it behind me.

The rain is still falling.

The girl at McMurtrie's told me yesterday (was it only yesterday?) that we would all assemble there for a moment of reflection before getting into our cars and following the hearse to a nearby crematorium. There would be a service in the chapel, the full Presbyterian thing, with a eulogy delivered by the minister, after which we could choose to inter Trixie's ashes in the Garden of Remembrance, or dispose of them in any other way we thought fit. That was the plan, anyway. Apparently it had been worked out in full consultation with the family. I suppose that meant Luce, or maybe even Anna. I couldn't imagine Mr Disco getting involved, nor for that matter Carlo, though one of the two of them might be paying for the whole shebang, who knows?

Anyway, I have no intention of assembling at McMurtrie's or of joining the procession, and I've told the taxi driver to take me straight to the crematorium. I want to get there early.

Fifteen minutes later, he drops me off outside a large brick building, set in the middle of carefully tended gardens. This building turns out to be the chapel, though it doesn't look like one from the outside, except that the entrance is large and ornate, with big wooden doors, swung open. Inside, it's just like any church, with the dim, rainy light filtering in through stained-glass windows set high in the walls, rows of pews and an organ in front of a raised pulpit. At the far end is the stage with a dais where the coffin will sit while we sing hymns and listen to the minister try to sound like he knows something about someone he's never met.

The place is empty, as I hoped it would be, so I wander up the aisle and have a wee poke around. Behind the stage and the pulpit, curtained off from the rest of the space, I find what I'm looking for. There's a rack of technical equipment, including a cassette deck and CD player and such. I expect this is where they play the chosen funeral music. I'm wondering if I can hijack it.

Behind the technical area there's a back entrance. The door's open, and there's a noise of machinery coming from beyond it. Outside, in a fair-sized yard, a young guy on a miniature bulldozer is pushing tons of flowers into a tidy heap and dumping them into a large metal bin. There are wreaths and posies of all sorts, some brown and wilting, others obviously new. Some of them are the remains of elaborate arrangements with messages on them from loved ones—*Goodbye Mum* and *You're always in our hearts*, that sort of thing. I suppose something's got to happen with the flowers once the dead are disposed of, but it's a shock to see it. The sad leftovers of grief, dumped and forgotten, sent on their way to God knows where. I think about Anna, and the effort she's gone to over Trixie's flowers.

I watch the boy work for a minute, and then I walk around the building back to the front entrance. That's my wee reconnaissance. Too easy. Back in the chapel, I settle down in a seat up the back, and wait. I feel quite calm about all this. Resolved.

It's not long before cars are pulling up outside and people start milling into the chapel, choosing their seats. I don't recognise anyone. Strange men in black suits and ties, the women dressed a bit more brightly but looking like they're up for an audience with the Queen. And there's so many of them. Where did they all come from? They're mostly elderly, with a few around my age. Friends of Trixie's? Clients, more likely, maybe people she's helped. I remember all the strangers who used to call at our house, anxious and awkward, some of them a bit mad, I thought. But here they are now, the legions of the saved, come to say their goodbyes. Trixie must have done something right.

As I think about this, the seats around me are gradually filling, the chapel echoing now with rustling and quiet whispers. I see Anna come in, accompanied by two young women, presumably her daughters. They walk behind her in their dark funeral clothes, looking a bit self-conscious, maybe intimidated by the number of people here. They sit down in the second row. The organist has arrived, and the minister has now taken up position near the pulpit, where he shuffles through his notes. I see Sheena, the girl from McMurtrie's, sitting near him. Only the front row of seats is empty, left for the grieving family. But either they're all late, or they've decided to make a dramatic entrance.

Entrance is right. Suddenly the buzz in the chapel changes slightly and I turn around to see the last person I expect. It's Carlo, and he's not alone. People are turning to look, because Carlo is handcuffed to two uniformed men who must be prison officers or something. I have to stop myself laughing at the sight. Carlo. The man who was never around when you needed him, the original absent father, turning up for his ex-wife's funeral. He must have really wanted the change of scenery. Look at him. He's lost most of his hair, and he walks with a bit of a stoop, but his suit is sharp, his white moustache neatly trimmed. And even though he's handcuffed, he manages to look like he's the one in command. He says something to one of the warders, who laughs as they take their seats down the front.

Luce and Wee Malkie follow Carlo a few moments later. Luce looks brittle, thin, the same anxious bite of her lower lip that Trixie always had. Her hair's as black as ever, tied tightly back, her make-up too thick, her lipstick a shade too red. She looks like an Italian widow, black from head to foot. And Malkie, he looks like the corpse, pale and pasty, like it was his funeral or something. They sit on the far side of the front row, away from Carlo, without even so much as a hello. Ashamed? More likely they're just not talking. Luce cranes around, maybe trying to find me, but I'm well hidden down the back. I see her nod and say something briefly to Anna, who's sitting behind her.

The biggest entrance, though, is reserved for none other than Mr Disco, who has obviously waited until everyone else is seated before he saunters in, dressed in ripped jeans and a purple velvet jacket, a pair of sunglasses hiding his eyes. His hair is long and grey. People turn to look at him, and the whispering and rustling rises audibly around the chapel. A smile passes across Mr Disco's lips before he sets them into something more appropriately grim. He walks slowly down to the front, chats to Carlo for a moment, nods at Luce and Malkie and sits down in the middle of the row.

As if that's a signal—and knowing the egotistical excesses of my half-brother, it very likely is—I watch Sheena disappear behind the curtain, and then return to her seat as music starts up over the loudspeakers. Something churchy and slow. Bach, maybe. Did Trixie like Bach? I don't think she knew who Bach was, but it doesn't matter, it fits the mood as the minister stands, followed by the congregation, who turn around to look once again as the final entrance of the morning is made. Trixie's coffin is carried slowly into the chapel, all polished wood and shiny brass handles, and bedecked with flowers. I've no idea who the pallbearers are. Three oldish men and three younger. One of the older men might be PC One, but I'm not sure. The young guys are probably McMurtrie's people making up the numbers, and just as well, because none of we Pinellis were ever up to carrying our mother. Not in life, and not in death.

But I haven't got time to ponder on that now. Trixie's arrival is my cue to get up and quietly leave the chapel. Once out the big doors, I rush round to the back of the building, to the yard of old flowers where the rear entrance is. The door's closed but not locked, so I let myself gently in, and as I do the music swells, but this time with a hollow, discon-nected sound, boomy and harsh. It's the sound of reality. All the world's a stage but the real business takes place behind the scenes. That's what I'm thinking.

There's no one else here. I risk a peek from behind the curtain, and I can see them settling Trixie's coffin on the dais,

ready to be taken down into the underworld at the appropriate moment. The family sit facing me, closer than we've been
to each other in years. Luce bolt upright, shoulders squared;
Carlo with his legs crossed, looking uncomfortably close to his
warders, as if they're actually holding hands rather than just
chained together. Mr Disco is slumped down, legs akimbo,
managing an air of sufferance. Or maybe he's just being cool.
After all, he still has his sunglasses on. The pallbearers take
their places, the music comes to a stop, everyone sits and
the minister ascends into the pulpit and waits there for the
rustling to die down. Someone at the back coughs.

The minister gives a signal and then the organ pipes up and
he leads us all in song, some hymn or other. I reckon he'll
follow up with a prayer before he starts his spiel about Trixie.
It'll be safe now, I think, to do what I'm here for; change the
mood, alter the ambience, give it the old switcheroo. So I
change the tape in the cassette deck for the one in my pocket.
Then I wait for my cue.

I don't have to wait long. They're nothing if not predictable,
these men of the cloth. After the prayer, the minister taps the
microphone and clears his throat.

Dearly Beloved.

We are here today to remember the life of Patricia Jean
Pinelli, nee McDuff, and to commend her soul to our Lord
who art in heaven. My text this morning is from One Corin-
thians, chapter fifteen. Behold, I tell you a mystery: We will
not all sleep, but we will all be changed in a flash, in the
twinkling of an eye, at the last trumpet. For the trumpet will
sound, the dead will be raised imperishable, and we will be

changed. For the perishable must clothe itself with the imperishable, and the mortal with immortality.

He pauses for effect, and that's when I press the button.

If ye can hear this, says Trixie, her voice echoing around the
chapel like some great biblical miracle, *it means ah've already
passed over. But ah've left this message fur ye, in a place where ah
know ye'll find it. Ah want ye tae listen carefully tae whit ah huv
tae say . . .*

Everyone's listening carefully alright. I wish you could see
their mouths hanging open as Trixie starts to speak from
beyond the grave. Luce gasps and stands up suddenly, looking
wildly about her, as if she expects to see the ghost of our
mother as well as hear it. Mr Disco, too, is bolt upright in his
chair, all semblance of cool lost for the moment, while Carlo
puts on his trademark smile, one corner of his mouth up, the
other down, a mix of amusement and exasperation, as if he
alone might have expected something like this. Wee Malkie
is hiding his head in his hands, and Anna just looks shocked.
Meanwhile a hubbub of whispering and shushing has erupted
from the faithful up the back, confronted with this sudden
confirmation of the existence of the world beyond. Someone
lets out a wail. Others are muttering prayers to themselves. At
this point I walk out onto the stage and stand there next to
Trixie's coffin. I'm hoping I look kind of defiant, but the truth
is I probably just look a real doolie, appearing like that. So
dramatic. We're all so bloody dramatic, my family, we should
be in the films. Luce is trying to say something to me, but
I ignore her. I ignore them all. The minister looks around,
panicky like. He catches Mr Disco's eye, and to my great

surprise, my half-brother motions him to come and sit down, and does the same to Sheena, who's on the point of going backstage. She hesitates, but moves back into her seat. When the minister sits down, not looking all that happy about it, everyone else does too. Trixie's voice now fills the chapel, commanding and irresistible.

. . . an it's no been easy, believe you me. Many's the night ah've sat wonderin where ye ur and how yer gettin on. Ye might as well huv been deed aw these years, even though ah knew ye wurny. This last wee while ah've hud Anna lookin fur ye, through aw the records an that, but she's no huvin ony luck. Ah jist wanted tae see ye before ah passed away. Uch well, it's too late fur that. This tape'll huv tae dae insteed.

Ah know ye want me tae say sorry fur everythin that happened, but sayin sorry won't change anythin. Too much time's passed fur that, too many mistakes, an too few chances tae set things tae rights. Ye can blame me fur summy it, maybe the mosty it, but the truth is, Donald, we made oor ain fate. We made it the gether, that's how it wis. We wur both uv us cursed, an ye kin think whitever ye like aboot that.

Ye want tae know somethin aboot that curse? Ah'll tell ye somethin. Ye aye said it wis nonsense, aw that stuff, but ye believed in it as much as ah did. Ye believed in it enough tae want tae save yersel. Uch, ah knew aw aboot the Turtle, Donald. Ah knew aboot the zoo an the swimmin an everythin. Ye wanted tae keep it secret cos ye were feart ah'd stop ye, but why wid ah deny ye hope? Even if ah did think ye were wasting yer time. Ah spent years trying tae lift that curse, trying tae save ye frae it. Ah wis determined ye wur gauny live, whitever the cost, however unhappy it made me and everywan else. An you well know, Donald, we were none uv us happy. It cost an awfy lot, so it did. Ah never gave up on ye, but. Even at the end, ah only wanted tae save ye ony way ah could.

Ye thought ah hated ye, didn't ye? Ah know ah wis hard on ye, son, ah didny huv ony choice, but ah never hated ye. Ah jist couldny love ye like a real mither. It's hard tae love whit ye know yer gauny lose. Ah don't expect ye tae understand that and it's no an excuse. Ah wis a bad mither. Ah'm no proud uv it, not wan bit.

But if ah maybe did wan thing right, son, it wis tae let ye keep yer secret. Tae let ye keep yer hopes goin. An ye did, didn't ye, through everythin that happened tae ye? Ye never lost hope. That's how it wis, an maybe that's how it wis meant tae be. Ah jist don't know.

Ah don't huv much longer tae live, Donald. They aw tell me ah'm fine but ah know better than them. Ah huvny goat much longer. Ah'll no ask ye tae forgive me fur whit happened between us. It's too late fur that. But there's wan thing ah will ask ye, Donald, an it's this: make up wi yer faimly, yer sister an brother, an yer da. It's no too late. It's never too late tae fix things up. Tell them that's ma dyin wish.

That's it, well, son. Ah've said whit ah was gauny say. Ah'm lettin ye go, now. D'ye hear me? Ah'm lettin ye go, an you huv tae let me go, too. Goodbye, Donald. Ah'll see ye in the wurld beyond.

A long silence, just the faint hiss of empty tape, and the rain dripping steadily off the eaves of the chapel. All those sombre people sitting there, stunned by Trixie's spectral voice, staring at me, waiting for me to do or say something that will explain the words they've just heard. I'm feeling just a wee bit awkward, I can tell you, exposed and on show—the long-lost son who abandoned his poor mother all those years ago and has come back now to make trouble. My shirt collar feels too tight, and I don't know what to do with my hands. For a moment, I'm worried that my fly might be open. What in hell's name have I done?

As nonchalantly as I can, I cross the stage to where the minister is sitting. He watches me with a look of fear, as if I'm the spawn of Satan come to carry him off. I bend down and gently suggest that we pick up proceedings from here. He nods, swallowing, his face as white as his dog collar. Sheena gets up and goes backstage and the Bach or whatever it is starts up again.

Then, with a sudden mechanical whirring, audible beneath the music, my mother's coffin slowly begins to descend on the dais, taking her off on her final journey to oblivion. Or maybe to a world beyond, much like the one she herself believed in, and where she might, if she's lucky, find peace. For a split second there's an image in my mind of a loggerhead turtle, vivid as real life, curling down in a long dive to the sea floor, its shell gleaming amber and gold, its flippers back and its neck extended. It skims along the bottom and swoops upwards with all the grace and strength of a dancer, trailing behind it the turbulence of its passing. I look down, past my family shifting restlessly in their places, to where Anna McColl is sitting, no longer the awkward girl of my dreams chewing on the ends of her hair, but every bit as beautiful. Our eyes meet.

She smiles.

acknowledgments

This book began life as an MA thesis undertaken at the University of Technology, Sydney. My supervisor was Jean Bedford, and it is due to her expertise, guidance and encouragement that, first, the thesis was completed, and second, was able to take on a life beyond academia. Thanks are also due to Debra Adelaide, Rose Moxham and Mandy Sayer in the Writing and Cultural Studies program who read and commented on the work as it developed. Mandy Sayer also very kindly read the completed manuscript and provided invaluable advice.

A number of other people took the time and trouble to look at the manuscript at various stages of its gestation. Philip Adams read some early chapters and provided helpful comments, as did Julie Browning and Deborah Rice. Completed drafts were read and commented on by Stephen Adams, Jen Craig, Stephen Hodge, Meredith Hopes, Peter Kingston, Chris Maher, Tony Slowiacek and Victoria Wearne. Special thanks are due here to Giles Clark, Gretchen Miller, and to my good friend David Riddell for encouragement, support and feedback above and beyond all reasonable expectations.

Thanks also to the wonderful people at Allen & Unwin: to Patrick Gallagher, and to Annette Barlow, Catherine Milne, Siobhán Cantrill and Ali Lavau, whose enthusiasm, care, and gentle but thorough editing made completing the manuscript a joy.

And grateful thanks finally to my family for putting up with it all, and in particular to my wife, Jenny Berg, who not only put up with it, but who read every draft of every chapter and whose insights helped me to see the fact in fiction and the fiction in fact.